World of Myth XI

Battle for Redemption

Travis Bughi

DEDICATION

To Ralph,
For the origins of self-confidence

ACKNOWLEDGEMENTS

Patricia Hamill for the editing

ISBN: 9781657817180

World of Myth Series

Emily's Saga

Beyond the Plains
The Forest of Angor
The Fall of Lucifan
Journey to Savara
Juatwa
A Legend Ascends

Takeo's Chronicles

Fated for War
An Enchanted Sword
Fortress of Ruin
A Dagger in the Light
Battle for Redemption
A Legend Falls

Prologue

Sir Gavin Shaw of the Knight's Order hadn't been called so in a long time. He had many other names now in this foreign land, surrounded by foreign people, fighting a foreign war. They called him sellsword, outlander, goldy, or simply knight. The worst nickname he'd earned, though, was traitor.

But earned it he had. Gavin had knowingly turned his back on the very man who'd brought him to Juatwa. Gavin could argue it was Takeo who'd turned his back first, yet no one seemed to see it that way. Takeo, despite all his terrible qualities and horrid reputation, was at least given the benefit of the doubt because he was a Juatwa native. Gavin, though? He was a foreigner. Always was, always would be, and so no one ever called him Sir Gavin Shaw of the Knight's Order.

Except for Lord Botan Katsu.

"Sir Gavin," the lord said now as they rode along, motioning with his hand. "Won't you please join me?"

There were a good two dozen of them riding through the Juatwa flower fields, all Lord Botan's personal guard minus Gavin. Like any trip outside his room, Lord Botan was dressed for war in his regal blue Katsu colors, hair and mustache cut to sharp corners, and his mount and all his guard were so adorned that no one would mistake their importance. Not that Botan would be mistaken anyway, for the man had about him a confident and commanding aura, yet not unkind. His smile was warm, fatherly almost, and Gavin saw in him the type of commander he'd always wanted to be.

Perhaps, Gavin thought, *that was why I took the deal at all.*

Gavin did as he was told and spurred his mount, trotting ahead of the throng to join Botan in the front. They were traveling at a meandering pace, in no hurry as far as anyone could tell, though Botan had yet to tell Gavin where they were headed or why. None of his guards would say, either; in fact, none had mentioned it for the entire day's ride.

"Yes, my lord?" Gavin said, pulling alongside the shogun.

1

"I want to apologize for my aloofness of late. We spoke much when you first came to me, but I've since been a rare figure, haven't I?"

"No apology is needed, my lord," Gavin replied. "I understand the urgency of battle. The Hanu army approaches, and you needed to gather your forces. I have to ask, though, wouldn't it be better to let them come to our walls? Why meet them on the battlefield so far from the city?"

Gavin did his best to sound like a Juatwa native. He'd dropped much of his conversational tone that was so well received in Lucifan and instead adopted the more cowed words of a lowly peasant speaking to a lord or lady whose existence was worth so much more than his. He wasn't happy about this, but he had a daughter to think about now, and a wife, and two friends, and he couldn't afford to offend anyone. Sir Gavin Shaw of the Knight's Order, who once served the Angels of Lucifan, was now just Gavin of the Shaw family, and he served a mortal lord.

Better than a dirty ronin, right?

There was no conviction behind the thought. Gavin called Takeo many things, but dirty wasn't one of them. He'd only thought those words because that's what everyone else said, often.

"We are out here for a purpose, I assure you," Botan said. "Although Takeo has outsmarted a rakshasa, that doesn't mean I need be afraid. Last time we fought, he had a thick wall to hide behind and an enchanted sword to swing. He has neither now."

Gavin's eyes cast down to Botan's hip, where Takeo's family blade, the Karaoshi sword, bounced along with the sway of the komainu. Just the look of it was enough to unsettle Gavin, for one glance brought to mind the history of that weapon. Forged in an unknown land, it had slayed so many souls, and would slay countless more. Gavin wondered at the number of dead it had made, the sheer volume of blood that had stained its metal. Some weapons were just tools, no more responsible for the harm they caused than the blacksmith that forged them. The Karaoshi sword, however? Gavin wasn't so sure.

"Do you ever regret leaving him?" Botan asked.

There was no mention of who *him* was, and there was no need.

2

"Sometimes," Gavin admitted, hanging his head. He wouldn't admit so to anyone else, but Botan had a disarming aura. "He was like a brother to me, in some ways, before the war. We saved each other's lives more than once, and also almost killed each other more than once. That's how we met, actually. On our first encounter, he nearly killed me. Only an angel's touch saved my life."

Botan nodded but did not drop his gaze from the forest ahead. They left the flowers behind and entered the woods where the noise from their clanking armor echoed off the trees. The komainu were silent, though, ever the hunters seeking prey.

"Yes, I remember," the shogun said. "You've told me much about Takeo, and how he thinks, and I appreciate that. I want you to know this, Sir Gavin, that I really do appreciate you. I know that can be hard to see in this land, surrounded by people you don't know or understand."

"Oh, I understand them just fine," Gavin replied. "They'd understand me, too, if they'd just stop thinking about where I was born. It's not like I had a choice in the matter."

"A komainu can't change its nature any more than a man," Botan answered. "It's simply who we are. One's upbringing commands much in a person's life, and we people of Juatwa understand that."

Yes, Gavin thought with a sigh, *I know. Hence why you have royalty, and you think status has anything to do with blood. You think men and women are given the right to rule at birth, and peasants must stay peasants because they were born that way. You have no idea I was once a lowly peasant, too, but raised a knight on my own merit. Such a concept is unthinkable to you. I see now what Takeo means when he says this land looks beautiful but hides so much ugliness.*

"Can I ask again, my lord," Gavin pressed, "why we've left the army and ventured out here? Isn't it dangerous, with the Hanu forces approaching? And such a slow pace, Takeo is sure to find us. He'll have word that I am with you, too. You know he's sure to come?"

"I'm counting on it."

Gavin didn't ask for more. Botan's tone made it clear none would be given.

3

They made some distance through the forest, ever still at a meandering pace, until they came upon the outskirts of a small village.

There were a few dozen huts scattered about the place, hidden among the woods, littered with villagers. Upon seeing Lord Botan and his entourage, they understandably went into a panic. Parents looked for their children, farmers and workers dropped their tools, two or three children even screamed or gasped. Upon realizing these warriors were dressed in the regal colors of the Katsu, though, they stopped fleeing and flung themselves to their knees to bow before their lord.

Botan flicked his head to the side, and his warriors rode out before him to inspect the village. Botan stayed, and so did Gavin because the knight was smart enough to know that he didn't move until told to do so.

"Tell me again, Sir Gavin, how Takeo enchanted his sword," he said.

"As I explained, I didn't hear the deal," Gavin replied. "The jinni spoke to Takeo through his mind while the rest of us were fighting Qadir. Afterwards, though, Takeo said he'd asked for the power to defeat his enemies, all of them, and that he'd traded his soul for it."

"Doesn't that strike you as odd? Soul, soul, what did the jinni mean, you think? It clearly didn't mean soul as in life, for Takeo still lives. He didn't trade his consciousness, or attitude, apparently. In fact, you say that Takeo was very much unchanged after the ordeal. It's as if the jinni took nothing at all."

Gavin looked from the lord to the sword, to that black sheath, so simple and efficient, yet unmistakable and not to be underestimated. His eyes rose to Botan's right hand, his sword hand, which wore a single glove, and the arm that was covered in a long sleeve. The left arm had no such glove or covering.

"You've been asking a lot of questions about Takeo's sword, lately," Gavin said.

Botan was fixated on something ahead, devoid of emotion. This was telling, as Gavin had known the lord long enough to see Botan smile easily and often, or at least he used to. Nowadays, with Takeo and his army approaching, smiles grew rarer by the day.

4

"Things have grown tense in my home, Sir Gavin," Botan said. "My wife, you see, never wanted me to try for the throne. She said it would only endanger our family. My counterpoint was that we were already in danger and that it was my destiny to help the good people of Juatwa. She'd quieted down when things looked to be well secured, but now, with the infamous ronin at our doorstep, she is scared. No, that's not the right word: terrified. We argue frequently."

"Nothing to be ashamed of there," Gavin ventured. "My wife and I argue plenty, too. That's the mark of a strong woman, I'd say."

The knight forced a chuckle. Botan did not share in it.

"Out last argument grew heated," he said, voice dropping to a whisper, and he flexed his gloved hand. "I . . . I struck her, for the first time in our marriage. I was so stunned that I fled our chambers. I haven't spoken to her since. The memory haunts me.

"When Takeo asked for the power to defeat his enemies, I don't think it was strength and speed the jinni had in mind. I think this sword gives less than it takes, petty abilities in exchange for something far more human. I tell my subjects all the time to be grateful they are not in my position because they will never be forced to choose between what is right and what will win. They will never have their families threatened for power. They will never decide the fate of an entire countryside with only a moment's notice. They'll never issue an order to slaughter innocent people. Those are decisions that I must make, and they weigh heavy upon me, or at least, they did."

He flexed his gloved hand again. Gavin swallowed.

"Destroy it, my lord," the knight said. "That sword is a plague."

"I can't," he replied. "Not yet."

"Why?"

"There is one more life to take."

Botan sighed and nudged his mount forward. Gavin followed. They strode into the village, where so many people lay bowed on their knees with faces to the dirt. Many more looked out from the shelter of their homes. Arrayed about the place was Botan's guard, with expressions Gavin could only describe as eager.

"You see, Gavin," Botan continued. "It's not this sword that's a plague; it's the creator. Takeo Karaoshi has slayed a shogun in her own throne room, held a crumbling fortress against overwhelming odds, and outsmarted a rakshasa. He's done all of this in such a short time that more than a few have begun to wonder if he's made of more than flesh and bone. They say he's called a lord in some Hanu circles. They say there are many under his command who would die for him. Do you understand what I'm saying? Do you understand what I'm up against?"

"I'd argue I understand more than most," Gavin answered.

"If I fail, Juatwa will be ruled by either a ronin or a rakshasa, and I can't decide which is worse. Not to mention I will die, along with all my family."

Gavin wanted to say Takeo wouldn't do that. He wouldn't kill a man's wife and children simply because the man had been an enemy. Then Gavin remembered the ninja clan and stayed silent.

"In this battle, Sir Gavin, I must show no mercy," Botan said. "For the good of humanity, I must win, or there will be no one left to stop him."

They came to halt outside a small, aged hut that looked like it hadn't been repaired in decades. In fact, before they stopped, Gavin had assumed it was abandoned, for there were no windows and the door hung crooked in the opening. The village took a collective breath.

"My lord, what is inside this hut?" Gavin asked, his nervousness showing in his tone.

"Redemption," Botan replied.

"What? I don't understand."

"You will," he said. "I have spent nearly all my wealth finding this hut. Rumors abound that it didn't even exist, but I had faith. I persevered where others gave up, and all my efforts have been rewarded. In this tent lies the power to defeat a monster."

He paused, and Gavin was about to say something when a multitude of hands grabbed hold of him. The knight shouted as he was hauled off his mount and flung to the ground by Botan's guards. His sword and shield were torn away as they surrounded and held him down, faces grim and determined. Gavin fought until a fist slammed into his stomach and a foot cracked against his jaw. He tasted blood and the world spun.

"Please, don't fight," Botan asked. "I promise, no harm will come to your family."

6

Gavin spat blood. His vision came back to him slowly, enough for him to hear the crackle of a fire. He glanced around, seeing only a handful of guards still holding him. The rest stood at the ready, forming a shield between him, Botan, and the villagers. Several of the peasants had screamed and tried to run when Gavin had been assaulted, but the guards had stopped them with a word. The villagers drifted back to their spots.

He wants an audience.

It was then that Gavin noticed the guard by the fire. The woman had taken a large flat blade from one of the villagers, a tool to cut trees and brush, and had thrust it into the flames. The broad span of metal grew red in the embers.

"What are you doing?" the knight shouted. "I swore to help you!"

"And you will," Botan answered, still sitting comfortably atop his mount. "In fact, you've already helped me immensely. Wasn't it you who told me that Takeo only has two rules: to remain calm and never let go of his weapon? He's already broken one of those rules. I must make him break the other, and I have you to thank for that."

Gavin pushed against the guards, but they were many, and he was but one. A palm slapped onto his forehead and forced him down, head twisted to one side. The dirt ground into his beard, his teeth, and fear rose within him. He thought of Yeira, and Pleaides, and Krunk, and Emy. He thought of Takeo and regret welled in his stomach. Tears that he'd held back for months flowed free.

"Please, my lord, I'm begging you. I don't know what you're thinking, but don't play his game," Gavin begged. "You're better than him. Please, be better than him."

Botan frowned, his brows sitting heavy at the bottom of his wrinkled forehead. He seemed to have aged ten years in a flash. His face wasn't so warm and welcoming anymore.

"Thank you for saying that," Botan whispered.

The shogun nodded to the woman with the red-hot farmer's tool. She stepped forward, close enough that Gavin could feel the heat. Another guard came over and drew his sword. It shined bright in the daylight, as if it'd been sharpened just that morning.

"Wait, wait, please!" Gavin begged.

But they weren't listening. They tightened their grip until it hurt so bad he could scream. He watched helplessly as they took his left arm and stretched it out. The guard stood over him and raised his sword.

"No," the knight yelled. "NO!"

Chapter 1

Nicholas took a deep breath in through his nostrils, dragging along a load of phlegm in that loud, annoying fashion of his that made his throat sound like it was sawing a log. Once he'd done this for a few solid seconds, the viking held his breath, arched his back, and spit a disgusting combination of mucus and saliva onto the nearest tree. Afterwards, he smiled and admired his handiwork until the komainu he rode passed it by. Then he turned to Takeo.

"Okay, you're turn," he said.

"Nicholas, I already told you I'm not playing this game."

"Oh, come on! By Valhalla are you a poor stand in for Krunk. You're as boring as you are thin, and I can assure you neither is a complement. I've seen babies born heavier than you. I'm surprised you've traveled by sea because, I swear, you'd blow away in the wind. One storm, that's all it would take and off you'd go, like a wimpy flag cut loose for the good of the crew. You know, in your current state, you stand a good chance of playing dead on any battlefield. If you ever find yourself on the losing side, just throw yourself down and stay still. I can hear the enemy approaching already, saying something like, hey, you think that poor fellow is dead? Course he is! Just look at him. Half-starved corpse is what he is, probably collapsed before the fight even started. They'd just sweep you to the side, wouldn't even pick you up. I mean, why bother? You're already dead. Just be careful a light breeze doesn't kick up and roll you over or—"

"Nicholas."

"Hm?"

"That's enough."

Nicholas sighed. "Boring. Just plain old boring."

Takeo glanced over his shoulder and then to either side. He and Nicholas rode as a pair, but spread out across the forest was a small army. He'd brought the full gambit out for this trip, including Kuniko, Ping, Qing, and more than a handful of his followers. Kuniko took his right flank, while Ping took his left, and each of them had a strong number of warriors in tow. He'd have brought more, but there were only so many komainu the main army had on hand with such short notice, and he dared not do this on foot. Mobility was their best bet against what might lie in wait.

"So, is this what you and Gavin did all those times you left Krunk and I alone?" Nicholas asked.

"What do you mean?"

"I mean is this what you two did? Walk blindly into traps?"

Takeo snorted. "Firstly, we're not blind. Qing is scouting ahead, and my sword did not grant any supernatural abilities related to stealth. If Botan and his men are still there, she'll know. Secondly, trap or not, we're going. Gavin was seen."

"That's not the rumors we heard. Word is there was a golden-haired man—that's different. Anyone with a bit of dye can turn a man blond. This is a trap, Takeo, and you know it. Our armies are a day from meeting on the battlefield, and what does Botan do? He makes a personal trip out to this no-man's land between us and is *certain* that you know about it. Tell me where the smart part in all of this is?"

"It's simple," Takeo said. "I will take any risk to get my sword and Gavin back."

"And Botan knows it."

Takeo didn't deny it. He also didn't respond because, true to form, Nicholas couldn't stay silent for long. He'd change the subject rather than let silence reign. Nicholas looked around, eyeing Kuniko and Ping in the distance to make sure they were just out of earshot.

"So that elf is stuck to us?" the viking asked.

"Between Zhenzhen believing I need protection and Virote wanting to keep an eye on me, yes," Takeo confirmed. "That's okay, though, because I want things that way. With Emy gone, I could use some uncanny hearing and eyesight about. Any edge I can get I will take. Lord Botan has too many advantages on me already."

"Like a turncoat knight who knows you inside and out?"

Takeo gritted his teeth.

"Subtlety isn't your strong suit, is it, Nicholas?"

"You ever met a viking who exuded subtlety? Here, hang on, let me try being subtle. How is the Lady Zhenzhen in bed? Does she let you lead, or does she enjoy controlling the infamously uncontrollable ronin?"

10

Takeo turned his head slowly in Nicholas' direction. The viking gulped.

"I mean, come on," Nicholas said with a shrug. "You didn't think that would stay a secret for long, did you?"

The ronin sighed and dropped his warning gaze.

"No, I suppose not," he said. "How'd you find out?"

"Soldiers talk, and people gossip. It might have started just as a salacious rumor, but then someone said they could confirm it. Whether or not they could is irrelevant. Besides, I bet all the really important people knew already."

"But does the prince know?"

Nicholas shook his head and said, "Your guess is as good as mine. What would you do if he did?"

"It's not me I'm worried about. It's him. I have no idea how he'd react, or the oni for that matter. What do you think about that whole situation, anyway? Him and the oni?"

"I prefer not to."

Takeo didn't say so, but he agreed. The tangled web of lies, deceit, and subterfuge that surrounded the oni's dealings with the Hanu family unsettled someone even as grounded as Takeo. Once upon a time, he'd thought knowing the dark secrets of his shogun would benefit him, but now he wasn't so sure. The thought of working towards a future ruled by an oni was a terrifying one, yet Takeo couldn't find a way to cut the cord just yet. The oni were indispensable allies, in a time where Takeo needed all the help he could get, and the problems only started there. The real issue was that Lord Nobu, the prince, the soon-to-be emperor if Takeo was successful, was a complete and total failure. He was weak, emotional, dimwitted, and wouldn't last a month on the throne of the world. Takeo could hardly justify fighting to unite the world under such a man—no, *boy*—for surely the world would only plunge back into darkness upon his death. Takeo wanted to create something strong and enduring, and neither of those words applied to the child who was supposed to be in charge of this army. However, were he an oni, that would be different story. But was it worth the risk?

Yes, Nicholas is right. Best to think on that later, after Lord Botan is defeated.

"So, before we get to this village, I've been wanting to talk about something," Nicholas said. "I've tried before, but it's hard to get you alone these days."

"Tell me about it."

"It's about Gavin, and you, apparently. Why did you lie to me?"

Takeo sighed. He'd been dreading this conversation.

"I didn't lie, Nicholas. I just didn't tell you. There's a difference."

"Not to me. I didn't like getting caught off guard when Gavin started spilling his guts out in Kuniko's personal gardens. What in the world, Takeo? You promised never to lie to me. You said I wasn't important enough to be lied to. How could you keep a literal death pact a secret from me?"

"It's not a death pact," Takeo replied, darting his eyes at Nicholas. "It's an ominous prophecy. There's a difference."

"That sennin on the mountain didn't say one of you would die, did it? It said you two would kill each other, or that one of you would kill the other, and neither of you said a damn word to Krunk or me. Which, the ogre, I get. He'd have wanted to stop right then and there, but me? Why not me?"

"It wasn't just you, Nicholas," Takeo said. "We didn't tell anyone. We didn't even talk to each other about it, not often. That was until Yeira came along."

"Don't blame her. It wasn't her decision to keep me in the dark. That was all you."

"Now you're starting to sound like Gavin."

"And you sound like a prissy milk maid all caught up in the technicalities of the swill she's been serving at her father's inn. Damn it, woman, we just got back from a long trip out to sea! Bring out the good mead and let us have at it!"

"You're just jealous because that prophecy would make for a really great end to your legendary tale."

"You're damned right it would!"

Nicholas' voice boomed out, and Takeo gritted his teeth and shut his eyes. At least Gavin knew a thing or two about being quiet.

Meanwhile, up ahead, a frail looking girl stepped into view, only she wasn't a girl, or at least not a human one. Her name was Qing, and she was an elf, though only a few people knew that, or so he

12

assumed. For all he knew, Emy had spilled the beans to Botan and the whole world knew.

Takeo hoped Emy hadn't turned. Gavin was bad enough, but as knowledgeable as the knight thought he was, Takeo understood that Emy knew more. She was a rakshasa, and that meant she might know things about Takeo even he did not. And to think she was with his enemy now, an enemy who carried his enchanted sword, and had nearly destroyed him once already. It was enough to unnerve anyone.

Qing raised her chin as the pair approached. In the distance, Kuniko and Ping paused along with their warriors. They looked to Takeo for their next command.

"You don't have to keep them spread out," Qing said. "Botan left some time ago. I don't think he's coming back, either. Rumors are he left in a hurry."

"Not worth the risk," Takeo replied. "They stay far apart, just in case. We'll be harder to ambush that way. What did you find?"

Qing grimaced and cast her gaze to the ground. Takeo's stomach dipped.

"Gavin," he whispered. "Please, tell me you didn't find him."

"Well," Qing said, pausing. "Not all of him."

Takeo dug his heels into his mount, and his komainu responded with lightning swiftness, snarling and leaping into the air over Qing's head. A chorus of cries came up behind him, but he bent forward and spurred his beast to greater speed. It responded with equal fervor, glad to take to a full gallop. Takeo could feel its bloodlust rise, and he did nothing to quell the instinct. He couldn't breathe, or think, or hardly see, so blaring was the dread that rose within him.

Not his head. Please, please don't let it be his head. I'll kill Botan with my bare hands, I swear on Her soul.

Takeo's mount burst into the village, scaring the people there so badly they screamed in horror and ran in all directions, likely thinking a wild komainu had found them. However, seeing a rider on its back dressed in the red laminar armor of a Hanu samurai did nothing to suppress their terror. They screamed anew and fled to their homes or off into the woods, disappearing so fast that the place looked deserted by the time the rest of Takeo's group caught up.

13

Nicholas was first on scene, with Qing sharing the saddle. To have caught up with him so quickly, she must have grabbed Nicholas as he rode by and flung herself onto the mount's back. Kuniko, Ping, and the others weren't far behind, and they stormed upon the place like the small raiding party they were, and that's when the villagers truly fled.

"Damn it all," Nicholas shouted over the screams. "Didn't we just talk about this being a trap?"

"Just because I said Lord Botan isn't here, doesn't mean you can just charge off, you idiotic ronin!" Qing screeched. "That's exactly the sort of thing-"

She stopped. In fact, they all did. Takeo's gaze hadn't moved since he'd burst into the village, and as the group followed his gaze, what they saw brought a stillness to the air. Across the way, nestled on the village's outer ring, sat a small, decrepit hut that could have been abandoned. What stuck out, though, was not its derelict appearance, but the severed hand nailed to the door with golden locks of hair intertwined in its fingers.

It could be someone else, Takeo thought, yet no hope came to him. He knew in his heart it was Gavin's, and his throat swelled.

The ronin dismounted, his komainu whined because its violent charge had been curbed. That was the only sound, though, as Takeo paced toward the severed hand, until he heard the slide of leather on fur followed by a heavy thud. Nicholas followed.

"Looks like his, I'd say," Nicholas commented.

Takeo cut a hand through the air, swift and short. The viking stopped and didn't say another word. Takeo approached alone.

The hand was freshly cut, judging by its immaculate condition and the blood that ran down the door of the hut. Whoever had hammered a nail through Gavin's hand hadn't done a good job, as they'd missed the bone and drove only through the flesh. Such a thing would fall off, given time and rot. They'd taken his left hand, and although the skin was changing color, Takeo had seen that hand enough times to leave no doubt to its owner.

Takeo swore.

"I warned him," he whispered. "I should have tried harder. I should have forced him to stay."

"Yes, you should have," Qing replied.

14

Takeo glared at her. Nicholas grimaced.

"At least they didn't take his sword hand," the viking offered. "That would have been cruel."

"No, they did worse," Takeo replied. "They took his shield hand."

He reached for the limb, paused, then grabbed a cloth first. He pulled the hand free from the nail, ignoring how the flesh slid across the metal and dripped blood down the shaft, and then wrapped it up. He wasn't sure what to do with it. He couldn't keep it. The thing would just rot and become a carrier for disease, not to mention the smell would excite their mounts. It didn't feel right to just leave it, though. He looked about and noticed a campfire nearby, or at least what had once been a fire. It was just hot embers now, but that was enough. He nodded to the fire.

"Are you sure?" the viking said, approaching and taking the hand.

"No, but do it anyway."

Nicholas strode over and set the limb into the bed of ash and embers, and the cloth it was wrapped in went up in flames. The fire crackled with the new fuel. Takeo ignored the smell of burning flesh.

"Idiot Gavin. You should have stayed with us," Nicholas muttered. "I hope Krunk's okay."

The silence was solemn, dignified, and Takeo appreciated that. He didn't want to watch the flames, so he kept his gaze on the bloody nail and the trail of red that ran down the crooked door. He looked over the entire hut, actually, and couldn't help but feel a twinge of nostalgia. He'd lived in a village like this once, before his brother had them both conscripted into Lord Ichiro's army. It was one of the few times Takeo had gotten to be a child, if even for a short while, playing with Mako, and his friend, Lei. He even learned a thing or two about the simple life, one outside war, torture, and death.

"Botan could have placed Gavin's hand anywhere. Why here?" he muttered. "Kuniko."

"My lord?"

"Gather the villagers. Find out what happened here and what's so special about this hut."

"Sir!" she shouted.

"I'm not sure if there's anyone left, Takeo," Nicholas said.

At the mention of the ronin's name, a muffled cry came from inside the hut. The sound was so unexpected that it cut short the flurry of activity Kuniko and the others were about to commence. They all went still, and Takeo fixated on the door. He paused, listening, but the hut had gone silent again. Cautiously, he raised a hand and knocked. No one answered.

"Tiny place," Nicholas whispered, scratching the back of his neck where his maul rested. "Surely whoever is inside heard that."

"My lord?" Kuniko asked.

"Do as I said."

Kuniko nodded and then motioned to the other samurai. They hesitated before dismounting and dispersing about the place. Meanwhile, Takeo rested his right hand on the pommel of his katana and reached with his left to open the door.

It wasn't locked, or even latched. The door hung so crooked that the bottom dragged in the dirt, and Takeo had to exert some effort to wrench it open. From inside, he heard a gasp, but he could see nothing but darkness at first. As his eyes adjusted, the thin frame of an older woman materialized in the small hut. She sat on the floor, atop an old mat made of large leaves and thin sticks. There was little else in the place, minus a topless chest filled with a small array of cooking and pottery tools. Takeo scanned once again to be sure no one else was inside before taking the woman in.

She was dressed simply, in what Takeo could only describe as an old dress long past its allotted time in this world. Her hair was straight, long, and unbound, with mostly black strands broken by rivers of silver. Her lips were thin, and she was short of stature, which Takeo could tell even though she was sitting down. Her eyes were dark in the low light.

As his eyes fell on the woman, her lips parted, and she stared back at him unblinking. She seemed poised yet frozen, as if she could up and dash away at any moment, yet also might collapse if she tried. She wasn't breathing, or even moving, as Takeo eyed her. He didn't know what to expect when he opened the door, but somehow this wasn't it.

He scanned the room one more time to be sure he hadn't missed anything. Botan had chosen this hut for a reason. Gavin only had two hands. There lay a message here somewhere, or an assassin.

16

"Do you know who I am?" Takeo asked, eyes still darting about the place.

"Yes," she replied breathlessly, then hastily added, "I mean, everyone knows who you are."

"There was a lord who came by here," he went on, "Lord Botan Katsu to be specific, the shogun of these lands until I rip them from his cold, dead fingers. Do you know what happened here, just outside your door?"

She nodded. She was breathing now, if in shallow waves.

"He . . . he came with his guard, and a handsome foreigner," she said. "I caught a glimpse of them before I shut the door. I heard screams and hissing flesh, and then they nailed something to my door. I didn't know that it was a hand until I heard the others talking about it outside. I was terrified, to be honest, but not as scared as I was when he opened my door and came inside."

Takeo, satisfied that nothing was inside the hut, stepped in. His head brushed the top of the shallow hut, and from outside Nicholas peered in like a cyclops outside a goblin's cave. Takeo knelt down to stare at the woman, and he noted that as his eyes adjusted, nothing about her brightened. Her features remained dark, untouched by the light. He also noticed there was a musty, shut-in smell to place, like something left to die in an ocean of self-loathing.

"Lord Botan spoke to you?" he asked.

She nodded.

Most commoners, most people in general, couldn't hold a gaze with Takeo. His reputation preceded him, and his presence was enough to make hardened veterans avert their eyes. This woman though, could not get enough of him. No matter the gaze he put on her, she stared right back, unfazed.

"What did he say?" he asked. "Why you? Did he give you anything?"

"We had tea," she said. "His guards tried to bring in a chair, but he shooed them off and sat on the floor with me. He was actually quite friendly, even if he didn't say much. Mostly he just asked me questions about myself."

"Such as? Answer them as you did for him."

"He asked me my name, and how long I've lived in this village. I answered as best I could, telling him my name was Dhyana, and that

I'd been here ever since I'd had my son. He asked me what happened to my son, and I told him that I lost him at a young age. He gave his condolences, and only then introduced himself. He told me that you would be coming soon, and that was all. After the tea was finished, he left."

"You knew I was coming, and you didn't run?"

"Of course not," she said. "Actually, I thought he was you when I first saw him, as I'd never seen this lord, but then I realized he was too old."

Takeo looked back at Nicholas. The viking shrugged.

"Why?" Takeo asked. "Why would you think he was me? Wouldn't you recognize his blue Katsu colors? Wouldn't you notice his hair wasn't cut like a ronin's? The age difference?"

"I was willing to overlook all those things, at first," she said, "because of the sword he carried."

Takeo's heart skipped. Whatever attention he had directed elsewhere fell away as he focused in on the old woman. She met gaze with equal intensity. She blinked once.

"What would you, a poor commoner who's never seen her own shogun, know of the sword he carried?" Takeo asked.

"He never drew the blade, but I would recognize that sheath anywhere. Black, smooth, simple and efficient, untouched by time. I think most have heard rumors of what the Karaoshi family sword looks like, but I think precious few know what it's made of. In fact, I got the impression even Lord Botan didn't know. After all, hardly anyone has ever heard of treantwood."

Takeo was silent. A daze fell over him until a sense of wonder and suspicion swept it away.

"How could you possibly know that, with nothing but a glance in the dark?" he asked. "I'm not even sure my own brother knew."

Takeo's demand flew over her, and she seemed to gain confidence from his tone. It was as if she were the one asking questions, as if he weren't armed and close, as if he weren't a dangerous man to contend with. His temper flared.

"Answer me. How do you know this? Tell me."

"I was told all about that sword," she replied, smoothly, "by your father."

Takeo's heart stopped. His blood went cold.

"Who are you?" he whispered.

"Oh my dear, boy. Haven't you figured it out yet? I'm your mother."

Chapter 2

They searched her. They searched her hut, her old chest, her withered bed, even the dirt beneath them. They searched the ground and trees surrounding her hut, and then searched those huts close by. Finding nothing, they didn't stop until every home in that village had been inspected. Once that was done, they divided up the villagers, separated them from each other, and asked question after question about the old woman who had supposedly been here so long that few remembered a time before her.

"She's always been very quiet," one man explained, then added quickly, "lord. Good to the children and excellent with a needle and thread. She doesn't talk much about herself, though. Never has."

"Yeah, I know her," another explained, a young mother with a baby in her arms and her stomach round with another. "Thinks she's above all of us, I think. Lingers around here, never married, just flirts with the men like some old yuki-onna. I wish she'd just die already—my lord."

They didn't get anything useful until they got to one of the village elders, a real withered ancient of a woman with five great-grandchildren running about the place.

"Oh, I remember her coming here," the woman explained, voice weak yet eager. Her children, old themselves, stood close by to catch her if she leaned too far to one side. "Must have been a few decades by now. She was beautiful then—still is, I say—and young, with a baby. I remember because it was so strange. I thought for sure her parents had cast her out, and the child's father had abandoned her, if she even knew whom he was. I took pity on her and shared our family's food. I forced my husband to build her that hut. Oh, he was mad at me for an age, I tell you, may he rest in peace. He thought like most the others, that she ought to get out, as nobody wanted some vagrant outcast taking up residence in our little village. He didn't understand what it's like to be a mother, to give birth. I knew if we didn't do anything, that poor child of hers would starve, and she'd die, too, most like. I couldn't sleep at night just thinking about it.

"But that wasn't even the worst of it. Oh, poor Dhyana, she lost the baby, did you know? We never learned of what, but one day, he was just gone! Can you believe that? She cried for years, *years*, my lord. To think what she's been through."

Meanwhile, the woman in question—Dhyana—stood several paces off from the komainu, surrounded by some half dozen samurai who looked just as baffled as Takeo felt. They were probably wondering why it took so many of them to guard a single old woman, but Takeo didn't know what else to do with her. He didn't trust a word anyone said. For all he knew, she was a rakshasa in disguise, just waiting to rip his throat out, though he had no idea how Botan got a rakshasa. Perhaps this was Emy, and she'd finally turned on him, but no, that couldn't be. He'd recognize her in any form.

"Qadir, then?" Qing offered, as he shared his thoughts out loud. "No, can't be. You mutilated him to prevent this exact thing."

It was just the three of them now: Takeo, Nicholas, and the ninja. They were at the edge of the village, hopefully out of earshot of anyone or anything, though Takeo dared not go further for fear of letting the old woman out of his sight. He didn't care how many guards he'd put on her.

"I mean, I suppose there's a possibility it's a third rakshasa?" Nicholas said.

"No," Takeo replied, shaking his head. He did so not to add to his words, but to try and clear the dense fog that seemed to fill his mind. "She can't be a Botan assassin. Who else would know about my sheath, about the treantwood? And we already confirmed her story with the other villagers. This woman, who claims to be my mother, has been here for decades, alone, and lost her child."

"Could be someone else's mother, though?" Qing whispered. "Perhaps he swapped this woman with another—a fake mother, in the attempt to get close to you. That seems the most plausible thing, in comparison to the other options."

She stopped, as if the other options were obvious. Takeo blinked at her, though she went on staring like he knew what she was talking about. Takeo couldn't think of anything, though. His mind kept blaring, over and over again, that he had a mother, that she knew his father, and maybe even his brother. He didn't know what to think

21

about any of this. It was overwhelming enough to have such thoughts at all.

"What other options?" Takeo demanded.

Qing frowned.

"That she's actually your mother," she said, shaking her head. "Then none of this makes sense. Why would Botan go through the monumental ordeal of uncovering one of your relatives, just to lead you to her, and then leave? This would have been the perfect ambush, yet he's gone. He didn't even leave anything with her. No weapons, no poison, nothing of note. What benefit could this possibly bring Botan?"

"True," Nicholas added. "I mean, if his intention was to get you to care about her so he could use her, then why leave? He can't threaten her while she's in your care. You think she's a spy?"

Takeo huffed. "Piss poor spy at that. I'll have her under guard night and day."

"So, it's personal, then, it has to be," Qing said. "She's on Katsu land. Is it possible this is a last-ditch effort to get you to switch sides? He has Gavin and the ogre, one of which he's just maimed. Perhaps that was a threat to stop, and now he's giving you another reason to leave it all behind? Reminding you that you're a Katsu native?"

Takeo shook his head, arms wrapped tightly about his chest.

"To get you to grow a conscience, maybe?" Nicholas said. "Or to distract you? We are on the eve of battle out here. Our armies are mere days from clashing."

"I say we leave her," Qing put in.

"No," Takeo snapped. "No, not a chance. What if she is my mother? What if? We can't leave her here. People will know now. Word will get out. What will happen then? Perhaps that's what he wants? Botan wants people to know my mother was a lowborn villager, and that I carry the Karaoshi name only in bastard fashion. I'm not sure, but I can't control something beyond my reach. She comes with us."

Takeo's eyes kept flicking to the old woman surrounded by samurai. He thought of her that way, as just an old woman, in his head. He couldn't call her by name, not even to think it. Not yet, and

22

he knew why. Doing so would humanize her, which would make her difficult to kill.

"We've spent too much time here," Takeo said. "Just because this wasn't an ambush doesn't mean it couldn't become one. Let's go. I have a shogun to conquer."

He ripped away from the other two, and they paused before following. Takeo was certain they doubted his judgment, but he didn't care. He was doing everything possible to think about nothing at all because, every time he tried to conjure a thought, his mind fell down an endless pit of questions.

How did Botan find her? What has she been doing here all this time? Who was his father? Was Okamoto even his brother? Were they step-brothers, perhaps, if even that? No, that couldn't be. Okamoto was his brother. He knew it, everyone knew it, even that old withering hag, Lady Xuan Nguyen, had known it before he'd murdered her. Yes, that was true. His faith couldn't be shaken there. Okamoto had been his brother, and he had not stolen Takeo away in the night. It just couldn't be true. Takeo wouldn't accept it. The fact that he'd once been a child, with a parent, who perhaps cared about him, he just couldn't fathom, or accept, or even dream. The thought terrified him, even. What did that say about him? How could he accept whom he was anymore, knowing these things? He'd always believed his path had been predetermined, destined, yet now there seemed—

Stop! Stop it, damn it! Focus, you idiot. You have a war to end. Nothing has changed. Nothing . . . has . . . changed.

He reached his small band of warriors, and those surrounding his would-be-mother. His eyes darted from samurai to samurai, doing everything possible to avoid the woman, but he still noticed her in the peripheral, and she held no such reservations about him. Her dark eyes, so dark that the light of the day would not touch them, honed in on him with rapt attention. She should have been unremarkable, what with her short stature and simple dress, but the features she bore drew eyes from all. Her thin lips, paired with dark hair, and those pupils, were features few had seen, and that Takeo had only seen in his reflection.

23

As the entire group stood there in silence, waiting for their commander to speak, Takeo's will failed him and his gaze fell on Dhyana. She did not flinch.

All doubt fell from him. This woman was his mother.

"Ping," Takeo said.

A young man stepped forward, tall with broad shoulders and a clean-shaven face. He was of the Sun family and was a prodigy with the blade. Combined with Takeo's training, he'd surpassed the abilities of all his peers. His loyalty was also above reproach. There was a reason Kuniko had made him her right hand.

"My lord?" he asked, bowing.

"She rides with you," Takeo said.

Ping rose up, eyes wide. If there was any question lingering in the back of his throat, it died as Takeo climbed onto his mount. The rest of the samurai were quick to follow. Ping looked to Dhyana, and she to him, for once peeling her gaze from her son, and Ping stammered all over again. It was as if her gaze unsettled him more than Takeo's. The boy recovered by retrieving his mount and bringing it over to her. He paused, seemingly unsure whether to help her up first or climb up and then offer a hand. The awkwardness of it all intensified under the scrutiny of the warband, and Ping in the end decided to climb up first. He reached down, took her by the arm, and went to pull her into the seat behind him.

"No," Takeo said. "Put her in front, where you can watch her hands."

Ping blinked but obeyed. Dhyana smirked.

I'm making a mistake, but I can't help it. I don't know what else to do. I . . . I wish Gavin was here.

Takeo looked back to the village, to that old withered hut with a nail slammed into the crooked door. The blood that ran down had trouble seeping into the old wood, and it shined brilliantly in the afternoon sun. The fire where Gavin's hand had been cremated still flickered from the meager fuel.

Yes, focus on that. I'll save you, my old friend, even if you want nothing to do with me. I finally understand what love is, I think. It's when you care for someone no matter what, even if they don't love you back.

24

When he turned his gaze back to his samurai, he instead found the old woman again, sitting comfortably in the shadow of Ping's large figure. The look on her face showed no fear that she was soon to leave her home, but instead bore a touch of understanding.

Takeo shook his head to free his mind and then spurred his mount. The rest followed.

* * *

They rode hard, partly because they were in enemy territory, partly because Takeo always rode hard. If he had stopped to admit it, he also would have said it was to prove to himself that nothing had changed. He wasn't about to slow his pace or change course just because a relative had been uncovered. He was still Takeo Karaoshi, the infamous ronin, and he had a destiny to fulfill. Not his destiny, no, but Hers, the most—the *only* important woman in his life. It was that line of thought that restored his sanity.

He remembered that time in the forest clearing, where she'd cut his hair. He'd never allowed it to grow long again. He remembered the cold nights in The North, and the battle of Lucifan. He remembered everything he could about her, from the freckles, to the smile, to the smell of her hair, everything that the jinni hadn't taken from him. It was enough. He remembered the woman who had chosen him above all others, through no obligation of blood or expectation of reward. The thought alone strengthened him, restored his confidence and his steadiness. Nothing could pull him away, he realized, not even something like this, so long as he remembered what mattered.

In fact, by the time they returned to the Hanu encampment, Takeo felt very much restored to his old self. If anyone had asked him about his mother in that exact moment, he would have given them a puzzled glance. It helped that he refused to look back the entire trip home, and this mentality went uninterrupted right up until the whispers started.

From a distance, the Hanu army was a sea of red on the edge of Juatwa's southeastern plains. However, all armies, whether a thousand, ten thousand, or one-hundred thousand, seemed the same once one entered the ranks—rows of tents packed with bored bodies, waiting around for their next set of orders. Takeo and his warband took one of the main thoroughfares towards his tent. As expected, his arrival did not go unnoticed. Although Takeo dressed like a common samurai, he was infamous enough to be recognized on sight, and men and women on all sides scurried to bow before him as he passed through the camp. Not on his order, of course. Takeo wasn't a lord by Juatwa standards, as he didn't own land with which to cultivate taxes and samurai sworn to his name, but that didn't seem to bother the common ranks. Yet all this attention did have a downside. Takeo had become a subject of gossip.

Out of the corner of his eyes, he watched the curious glances the Hanu ranks gave Dhyana. They were as subtle as could be, whispering faintly only after Takeo had passed, and using sparing looks rather than dead-eyed stares. Unfortunately, when an entire camp is whispering, the purpose is defeated. Although they didn't know whom she was yet, Takeo's heart sunk as realized it was only a matter of time.

Given solitude and an iron will, Takeo could forget this woman existed. After all, she hadn't been a part of his life for over three decades. But forget her among an army's gossip? He wasn't so sure.

He picked up the pace.

Unlike his previous campaign, Takeo now had a sizable tent to his name. Lady Zhenzhen insisted on it once she'd heard that Takeo had been sleeping in what amounted to a single sheet draped over a wire. Despite explaining that he preferred it that way, she would not let it stand. Now that Takeo had proved his worth, again, he was to be treated like any general in her army, and thus he was furnished with a lavishly sized tent and placed among the daimyo's quarters. Takeo was now both easy to distinguish and easy to find, and placed side-by-side with all those who hated him—royalty.

As they reached the outskirts of the royal encampment, nested within the beating heart of the army, servants met them to take their komainu away. Takeo was offered food and wine on silver platters—and Nicholas, too, because the servants didn't know whom to offer and whom not, lest they offend someone and find themselves on the chopping block. Takeo waved them away, as always, while Nicholas indulged himself with as much as he could carry, as always. Kuniko did as she did best and took care of all the logistics. She ordered most of the troops away, assigning a courier in case she needed to get a hold of them again, and ordered a half dozen of the finest warriors to follow Takeo back to his tent for guard duty. There was a time when he would have preferred to be alone, but Takeo didn't trust the daimyo he was stationed alongside. He saw the guards as protection from spies.

As for Ping, he looked to Takeo and back to Dhyana, hoping for some direction, but Takeo gave none. The ronin walked off as if none of this was happening to him because he truly wished it wasn't. In the end, Ping carried out his last given order and escorted Dhyana off the komainu and towards the tent.

Qing fell into step with Takeo.

"You are going to send her away, right?" she whispered.

"I don't know yet," he replied, flatly. "I need to focus on the coming battle."

"My point exactly. It's bad enough you brought the other woman, but now this? You can't pawn these two off as servants. They are distractions."

"I can handle a few distractions. War is where my heart lies. This is my purpose."

They reached Takeo's tent, a massive thing that was tall enough for an oni, wide enough for an oni gathering, and worth more coin than Takeo had seen in his lifetime. Along with it, Lady Zhenzhen had shipped a small treasure hoard worth of trinkets that were to be strewn about inside, all of which Takeo denied. Perhaps his shogun saw such measures as a sign of wealth, but all Takeo saw were places for people to hide. He wanted his tent barren as could be. That was comfortable, familiar, and safe. He could only bend to his shogun's will so much. She wanted him to have servants, however, so he'd relented there, in his own way.

Mako Tamura pulled back the flaps and peeked out. One could have sworn she was hiding something the way she did so, with embarrassing hesitation, but Takeo knew it just the way she was. Mako, though tall and beautiful, would struggle to be noticed in an empty room, and would be entirely missed at a royal party. To Takeo, this was endearing.

"You're back," she said with a modest smile, deflecting her gaze. "I . . . I,"

27

"Was worried again?" he asked.

She blushed. "I know I shouldn't be. This is war. You're going to be gone a lot. But I can't help it. I worry about you every time you leave."

Mako pulled back the flaps for Takeo, but he stopped in the entry way. He gave her a warm smile, not just for her, but for himself.

"I'm not going to tell you how to feel, Mako," he said. "If you want to worry about me, you can, but know that it won't help anything. Try to keep busy while I'm gone. I worry about you, too. You're my sister, after all."

"In-law," she added.

"Makes no difference to me. We were the only people who knew Okamoto, and that's a bond I share with no one else, not even Emily."

Mako's smile grew. She stopped staring at her feet, lifting her head and stepping out into the light. Her eyes found Takeo's guards spreading out and surrounding the tent. They found Qing, nearby and wearing her trademark look of aggravation and annoyance. They found Nicholas licking his fingers after having just devoured a meal that would have fed a small family. They found Ping and Kuniko approaching with a short, older woman who was smiling, too.

"Takeo," Mako said, nodding. "Who's this?"

His mood soured.

"My, uh, mother," he mumbled, and rushed into the tent.

Mako's gasp followed him, along with an all-too-loud, "Your mother?"

Takeo didn't reply. The tent flap fell closed behind him, and he was swallowed into its stuffy confines. He busied himself immediately, searching for his tools to sharpen and oil his sword—not *his* sword, he remembered. His sword didn't need such maintenance, but this borrowed one did. Yet that didn't aggravate him because he needed a distraction. Any moment now, Mako or someone else was going to bash into the tent and demand answers, and it churned his stomach just thinking about it.

Yet something much worse occurred.

"You're Takeo's mother, truly?" came Mako's muffled voice through the tent wall.

"I am," came the reply.

"None of us can believe it either," Nicholas jumped in with boisterous enthusiasm. "It's a good thing Krunk isn't here. He and I had a running bet. Krunk believed Takeo's parents were dead, like his, but I assured him Takeo's mother was alive and well."

"Wait, how is that a good thing? Wouldn't you have won the bet?" someone asked, who Takeo couldn't tell.

"True, except I bet there was no way Takeo was human. I wagered he was the offspring of a strange love affair between a satyr and a minotaur."

Laughter surrounded the tent, unforced, for one painful second. Takeo clenched his teeth so hard they threatened to crack.

"Well, that aside, I'm pleased to meet you. Takeo is very dear to me, you see," Mako said. "You'll have to excuse Nicholas, here. He's Takeo's brother-in-law."

There was a pause, a calculated one.

"Pleased to meet you, too, but if you're his sister-in-law, and this man is his brother-in-law," Dhyana started, "and it's clear this viking isn't related to you, my dear, then that must mean my son is married."

"Well, not exactly," Nicholas began.

Takeo bolted to his feet and dashed out of the tent, ripping the flap open. No one had moved from their positions since he'd gone inside, but they all went still at the violence of his exit. Everyone deflected their gaze as if they'd all been caught scheming behind his back—all but Dhyana.

As his gaze fell on her, she didn't appear injured or threatened, ashamed or regretful. Her eyes spoke of something deeper, something Takeo was not familiar with. Her eyes had a glimmer to them that Takeo found unsettling.

"I'd heard rumors," she whispered. "Common people don't like to talk about you much, as if doing so will summon you to their bedside, but I gathered all the information I could. I'd heard you'd loved and lost. Your wife? I'm so sorry I wasn't there for that, to see you fall in love, and to see you lose the one you cared about. I know how that feels. I lost your father. I'm sorry, so sorry I wasn't there for you. It wasn't my choice."

The anger in Takeo's heart suffocated and went out. As his mother stared at him, teary-eyed and unafraid, Takeo's aura of

29

certainty fell away. He stood stunned, not knowing what to think or feel, as he encountered a situation he'd never prepared for. The whole day might have gone on this way, with him just staring like an idiot, if he'd not been saved by the appearance of a small entourage of heavily decorated samurai, surrounding a familiar face.

They came marching from deep within the daimyo encampment, a good dozen strong and decorated for war. For a moment, Takeo thought they were coming to kill him, but that faded when a tall man with a slight gut strode out to the front. Lord Yoshida was a difficult man to miss, what with his graying goatee and long eyebrows.

He didn't look happy, either.

"Takeo," the man said, shaking his head. "Must you vex me at every turn? I've been waiting an age for you. Don't you know better than to leave on your own accord when we're so close to the enemy?"

On instinct more than manners, Takeo bowed to the lord, deep and low. Yoshida acknowledged the show of respect with a nod.

"It was urgent, my lord," Takeo replied. "I assure you I wouldn't have done so if it hadn't been important."

Lord Yoshida's eyes swept the scene and quickly deduced the oddity of an old woman standing so close by, surrounded by soldiers. She didn't look like a royal servant, what with her ragged clothes, and Lord Yoshida was too smart a man not to ignore the situation. Takeo cringed.

"Well, that can wait," the lord said, cautiously. "Grab a dozen of your guard and follow me. Lord Botan's army is approaching. Battle looms."

Chapter 3

Lord Yoshida led their large war party out onto the plains. They didn't go far, just a hair outside bow range from the army, though they still rode komainu to do it. Lord Yoshida didn't walk far if he could help it. In fact, none of the daimyo did, and Takeo was growing accustomed to riding thanks to his proximity to Juatwa's upper echelon.

Once beyond the camp, Yoshida commanded the troops to surround them and spread out, beyond earshot. The guards did so only once Takeo gave his nod of approval. Yoshida scoffed at that, seeming to take offense, and Takeo couldn't blame him.

"My lord, what is this about?" Takeo asked. "This is a hefty guard for just a conversation. I'd have been suspicious if you hadn't commanded me to bring my own."

"That's why I did it," Yoshida replied. "Also, we could use the extra protection. One can't be too careful in times like these. I still recall with vivid clarity that messenger stabbing you mere paces from myself. No, no, Takeo, I will not be taking any more chances. I don't even take a piss on my own anymore, not with Lord Botan so close."

"What is this about?" Takeo asked, pointedly. "We're not out here to discuss battle strategy, are we?"

The two were still mounted at this point, atop a small hill that gave a pleasant view of the surrounding grassy fields. At least, it would have been pleasant, if not for the sea of red troops and white tents filling the area, trampling the place into dust.

Lord Yoshida frowned over the mass and sighed. To Takeo's surprise, he dismounted, and the ronin hurried to do the same. They stood close by, facing each other, their mounts surrounding and shielding them from view, and Lord Yoshida struck out his hand.

Takeo stared at it and blinked.

"I know, it's a bit personal, but please accept it," the lord said.

Slowly, hesitantly, Takeo extended his own hand and grasped Yoshida's. They shook once and let go.

To an outsider, like Gavin or Nicholas, what just occurred might have gone unnoticed. Handshakes, smiles, even hugs, were handed out with ease in most of the world, but Juatwa shunned such things. Showing emotion was a sign of weakness, even between close friends. On top of this, Lord Yoshida was a daimyo, and a high-ranking one at that, with connections, wealth, and power that rivaled a shogun. Meanwhile, Takeo was still a ronin, even if a valuable one, considered to harbor some unseen disease. To acknowledge Takeo's existence at all was considered by some royalty to be beneath them. To shake his hand, though? Takeo was almost as stunned as when he'd found out he had a mother.

"My lord?" he managed to say.

"We haven't had a chance to talk privately since defeating Lord Pircha," Yoshida explained. "I feel I owe you an apology. I know we disagreed on how to handle the late shogun, but I want you to know I harbor no ill will towards you. I am aware that we would be dead or imprisoned were it not for you, and I thank you for that."

As grateful as Takeo was to hear his deeds being acknowledged for once, he couldn't help but remark, "You had to wait to say that in private? I'm still that much of an outcast?"

Lord Yoshida ran two fingers along his goatee but didn't appear amused.

"We're not out here for that," he said. "If I'd wanted privacy, I wouldn't have brought gossiping guards. And, no, Takeo, you aren't an outcast anymore. It's becoming well known that the common ranks hold a measure of respect for you, and I would be a fool to ignore it. It's time you were treated as an equal. That's why I brought you here, to make sure we're on the same page."

Takeo balked. His heart beat irregularly, skipping at odd intervals while his stomach flipped. He couldn't believe the words he was hearing, so much so that his mind instantly turned against them.

"An equal?" Takeo stuttered. "What game are you playing at? I only have one purpose, my lord: victory."

"As I've noticed. That's exactly the page I'm talking about, trust me."

"No offense, lord, but I don't trust easy. I've been betrayed my whole life. It will take more than a handshake and a promise to change that."

Lord Yoshida sighed again and put his hands behind his back. He cocked his head at the army in the distance.

"Just as I suspected," the lord said. "You distrust me even more now for my actions, don't you? Well, let me be frank with you, then. Do you see that army, Karaoshi? Anything you notice about it?"

Takeo reluctantly glanced at the army, but no inspection was required. He knew the answer.

"It's small," the ronin said. "I expected more to invade the Katsu lands. We need more."

"And you're right. We should have more, about a good quarter more to be precise. You see, when Lady Zhenzhen made you an adviser to Lord Nobu, she did so discreetly and with little notice. All the daimyo had pledged their forces for the fight against Lord Pircha by the time your involvement was revealed. They hadn't time to protest. Now, though, the jig is up, and many aren't happy about it. Many daimyo have withdrawn their troops in protest of you."

"Protest of what? I saved their lives."

"Well, if you'll recall, you were unconscious for that last battle. Also, there is no immediate threat to their lives. You see, when the Hanu lands are being invaded, you'll find the protests against you will lessen. When we invade, however? Well, many will find an excuse to sit this one out. If you fail, nothing will happen to them."

Takeo fumed but only a little. In truth, he wasn't surprised. That's just the sort of cowardly inaction he expected his enemies to take, even those who were supposed to be his allies.

"I'm surprised Lady Zhenzhen tolerates this," Takeo said.

"She won't if she finds out."

Takeo cocked an eyebrow. Yoshida sighed.

"Listen Takeo, you and I are about to have an honest conversation, one with potentially lethal consequences," the lord whispered. "Well, for me at least, because I seek victory like you do, and we won't win if we're fighting each other and Botan at the same time. Yes, Takeo, I am protecting those protesting lords and ladies from our lady's wrath. She would surely see their actions as traitorous, and it's only a matter of time before her uncle, Lord Virote, finds out what I'm doing and consequences come my way. However, I'd wager you're a smart enough man to see my side of things. Don't disappoint me."

Takeo faltered in place. This conversation was jolting in more ways than one as Lord Yoshida jumped from subject to subject, from one absurdity to the next. It was enough to question the man's sanity, had Takeo not already had a measure of respect for this old lord. Yoshida, along with being sound of mind, had an impressive military record. He'd fought side by side with the first Hanu shogun, Lady Zhenzhen's father-in-law, and had more than earned a level of respect. Still, to ask Takeo to defend his detractors? The ronin recoiled at the thought.

And yet he was also a realist. When offered a problem, his mind found a solution.

"You're protecting Lady Zhenzhen from herself," Takeo thought out loud. "She would take revenge on those protesting daimyo, immediately, and plunge the Hanu army into a civil war. Then our assault on the Katsus would surely fail, and we'd only leave ourselves weaker while our enemies regained their strength."

Yoshida grinned.

"You see?" the lord said. "It's better to let these daimyo have their protest and either deal with them after or watch as they fall in line when we return victorious. Either way, this is only temporary. If you succeed here, the Katsus will fall under Zhenzhen's command, and Juatwa will be one step closer to being united. Is that not the better way? Wouldn't you agree?"

Admittedly, Takeo hadn't thought of that until Yoshida had forced the question. He was used to the late Ichiro Katsu's style of command: that of an iron fist.

Takeo sighed.

"You're a clever man, Lord Yoshida," he said. "No wonder you haven't been assassinated yet."

"Politics is a battle all its own, and it pays to be good at it."

"This still doesn't address our immediate problem, though," Takeo replied. "How are we to bring down the Katsu fortress with a quarter of the army missing?"

"We're going to supplement our numbers with akki."

Takeo balked.

Akki were the underlings of the oni. Small, lanky, and red-skinned, their cruelty was only outmatched by their cowardice.

34

"My lord, that's absurd. There's a reason we only use the akki for raids and scouting. They break and run at the first sign of trouble, assuming they follow orders at all."

"True, but we have no other options. It will take a resourceful general to turn them from a liability into an asset. That's why I'm turning the army over to you."

Takeo, against all odds, found himself stunned once again. His jaw dropped as he stared at Yoshida.

"My lord?" he asked.

"Effective immediately, you will have total control of this army," Yoshida went on, crossing his arms over his chest. "Your every order will be obeyed without question, and anyone found disobeying your orders will be held for treason. You can request advice, of course, but you are under no obligation to accept it. You'll answer solely to our shogun and her heir, and you'll be treated as a manifestation of her direct will upon the battlefield. You'll have first pick of any spoils of war, and full credit for the outcome of this battle. You will be addressed as General, so that all will know to whom they are speaking."

Takeo remained frozen, except to blink.

"I told you that we were going to have a dangerously honest conversation," the lord continued. "Lord Nobu may be in line for the throne and slated for immortality, but his ineptitude will be a stumbling block every step of the way. He's young, impressionable, and naive. He cannot lead. As for me, well, I could try, but I will not take such chances. You've stood against Lord Botan once already, heavily outnumbered, and survived. You led us to victory against a rakshasa, winning while unconscious and dying of blood loss, mind you. I have no doubts about your abilities now. Lord Nobu will go along with this, we both know, as he's oddly infatuated with your reputation. As for the other daimyo, those who hate you most are absent and the others I will keep in line. Do what you do best, Karaoshi: win."

Takeo, to the best of his ability, could not regain control of his basic functions. He was fully aware that he looked like an idiot, standing there with mouth agape and eyes bulging, but he couldn't seem to do anything about it. Lord Yoshida gazed back, idly, and appeared to contemplate saying more. He thought better though, and turned away from the ronin, mounting his komainu.

"Take what time you need to process this and formulate a plan," Lord Yoshida said, turning his mount away and signaling to his guards. "I'll meet you at Lord Nobu's tent when you're ready."

Yoshida made to canter off, and only then did Takeo finally find his voice.

"My lord!" he shouted.

The man stopped and looked over his shoulder, raising an eyebrow. Takeo reddened, as there had been no need to shout. Yoshida hadn't left yet.

"My lord, I have something to confess," he said. "This morning, when I left, I found, well—I found my mother. And I brought her back to our camp."

Takeo couldn't explain why he said this. There was nothing logical about it. Yoshida didn't need to know this, and probably didn't care, yet Takeo felt the urge to say something. The confession had tumbled out before he could retract it, and he stood there, feeling more embarrassed than before.

"Your mother? Truly?"

Takeo could only nod. Yoshida smiled.

"That's wonderful," he said. "Good for you."

"It is?" Takeo replied.

"Of course. What I'd give to have my mother alive again. You're a lucky man, Takeo."

And with that, Lord Yoshida rode off, taking with him a measure of respect from a hard, cynical ronin.

No, not a ronin—a general.

* * *

"By Valhalla," Nicholas said with a gleam in his eye. "You did it!"

Takeo ducked to avoid the viking snatching him up in a lung-crushing hug. Although the two were alone in Takeo's tent, relatively speaking, it was still an embarrassing maneuver for the ronin, and he eyed Nicholas.

"I thought Gavin got overly excited about things," he said.

36

"Excited! How can you be anything but?" Nicholas countered. "This is it! This is what you've been fighting for. An army, command, the chance to prove yourself. This is great news, Takeo. We should get drunk."

"We should dress for war. Lord Botan is approaching."

"All the more reason to drink. You know anyone foolish enough to fight sober? I've known a few, but well, they don't last long. It's well known a good drink helps loosen the muscles. I mean, only an idiot would fight sober, and you're not an idiot, are you?"

Takeo didn't answer, other than to finish gathering his things to meet Lord Nobu. Nicholas sighed.

"Boring," the viking muttered. "Hopelessly boring."

Outside, a sharp cheer rose up and then went silent. Takeo even recognized some of the voices. He quickly deduced that Kuniko had spread word to the others. He'd told just her, Nicholas, and Qing upon his return because Ping had disappeared with Dhyana to fetch provisions for the old woman. For some strange reason, Mako had gone with them, but Takeo didn't have time to question that now.

"I have to wonder," Nicholas said, keeping his voice low as if talking to himself, yet loud enough for the opposite to be just as true. "Which news do you think will spread faster? The fact that Takeo Karaoshi has a mother or that he's now the general of this army? I mean, really, both warrant a shock to the system."

"I'm sure no one is interested in my parentage," Takeo answered. "They've never been before. Why start now?"

"Hm, good point."

"We need to meet Lord Nobu and Lord Yoshida, soon, and I do mean we. Sellsword or not, you're my right hand until I can save Gavin. I want my every thought examined by a mind outside the collective culture of Juatwa."

Nicholas did a mock bow, and replied, "I'm honored that I only out rate the traitorous ex-knight because he isn't present."

"Don't get used to it. Do you have your maul?"

"Are trolls ugly?"

They beat a steady pace to Lord Nobu's tent. It wasn't far by any means as Takeo was now a permanent resident of the daimyo camp, but that didn't stop the pair from drawing attention. Wherever Takeo went, silence followed, along with open gawking right up until he

37

looked in the gawker's direction. He also received everything from respectful nods to full bows from samurai guards and soldiers, accompanied with either sly smiles or wide grins. A couple of servants even went to their knees as he walked by, heads pressed to the ground.

"And I thought word traveled fast on a viking ship," Nicholas muttered as they walked.

"Lord Yoshida's guard must have spread the news," Takeo surmised. "They returned before I did, and now the whole world knows. Chances are even Botan will hear of it before we meet. As furious as the royalty probably are, at least the warriors seem happy with it."

"Of course, they are. Every warrior loves to win, no matter their proclamations on honor and tradition, and with you as the general, they now know victory is assured. They'll sleep easy and follow your orders without hesitation. This is what the daimyo were afraid of all along, and exactly why vikings don't have royalty."

Takeo frowned.

"But wait, don't you? What are jarls if not royalty?"

"Jarls aren't royalty." Nicholas huffed. "Jarl is just a title, like the one just bestowed to you, and it is earned and fought for every day. Like ogres, vikings only follow the strongest."

"Ah, I see. So that's why you never became a jarl."

Nicholas howled his laughter, startling those nearby.

True to his word, Yoshida had readied Lord Nobu for Takeo's arrival. Unlike the previous campaign, they met in a closed tent and without the heavy entourage of lords and ladies attempting a dinner party. Inside were only Lord Nobu, Lord Yoshida, Qing, and the guards of the former two. Yoshida had two heavily armed samurai by his side, while Nobu had his oni: Tokhta and Borota.

Upon Takeo's entrance, Tokhta gave the slightest glare ever conceived. In oni body language, this was akin to a mortal threat.

Not that the ronin was surprised. He expected as much, given recent events. Tokhta had shared with Takeo and Gavin the great conspiracy to transform Lord Nobu into an oni. It had taken Gavin less than a month to betray that trust and spill the secret to Botan, whom then spread word as far and wide as he could, trying to persuade loyal Hanu daimyo to defect. Combined with Takeo's recent promotion, this would deal a serious blow to the Hanus, given time. Fortunately, the rumors were just that for now, as Lord Virote was busy falsifying the claims as best he could. Considering the source of the news was a turncoat sellsword, and the news itself was shocking and difficult to believe, most were willing to brush the conspiracy off as nothing more than bold propaganda.

They had but one shot at solidifying Hanu control before the whole chain of command broke into a civil war, and it hinged on Botan's head.

"And here he is, the last of my mother's generals," Nobu said, slouching in his chair, head tilted as it rested on an open palm. "Here to tell me what to do? Honestly, do I have to be here for this? You two don't need me."

That last part was murmured, quiet enough that it would have been missed were not the tent removed from the ruckus of the surrounding army.

"My lord, it's important you attend and listen," Yoshida offered, bowing as he did so. "Takeo and I will not always be around, and it's to your benefit to learn from our wisdom. When we go out to meet Lord Botan, you should endeavor to think better of yourself. Saying such things will only embolden our enemy."

"If it's so important to intimidate him, why don't I just stay here?" Nobu asked, swiveling his gaze in the old lord's direction. "That way it will look like I'm so confident that I didn't even bother speaking with him."

"That would be rude, my lord," Yoshida replied. "The best ruler is one who conquers without insulting."

Nobu scoffed and rolled his eyes. "It's not like he could think any less of me anyway. He already knows what's supposed to happen to me."

Takeo and Nicholas exchanged looks, but nothing more. They bowed.

"I heard the news," the prince went on, speaking to Takeo now. "Did you really find your mother out there?"

"So it would seem," Takeo replied, "but I wouldn't trouble yourself with it. Trust me when I say I won't let it affect me."

"I hear she was overcome with joy to see you," Nobu went on, leaning up off his palm. "Isn't that something? You've been gone all this time from her, all these rumors about you, but the moment you come back, all is forgiven. That's insane, isn't it, in the best sort of way? You must be happy."

"My lord, if you please," Takeo said through clenched teeth, pointing at the map on the table. "Time is of the essence."

"I mean, what's she like? Have you two talked much?"

"My lord."

"Do you think I could meet her?"

Yoshida coughed.

"My lord," the old man said, "he's right. That's a topic for another time."

"It won't take but a moment."

"My lord, Botan's army is approaching," Qing whispered from the corner.

"Really, let me just send a servant. Then, afterwards—"

"My lord!" the trio of voices came in unison.

Nobu clammed up for several seconds, then slouched, defeated. His eyes paired with a frown and fell to the table. A moment's silence passed before everyone else convened around it.

One glance over the placement and markers told Takeo all he needed to know.

"This is the last report from our scouts?" he asked.

Qing nodded.

"So then, we don't have the numbers we should," Takeo said, "and because of that, Lord Botan is striking out to meet us rather than hide in his keep. He'll have his komainu army, which is more substantial than ours, and he aims to use that to his advantage out here on the eastern plains. We have akki to supplement our numbers."

He paused and glanced at Tokhta, but the oni stayed motionless. Takeo knew this was the creature's way of confirming, so Takeo went on.

"But they're a cowardly bunch of animals who can't hold the line against normal samurai, let alone a stampede of komainu. In addition, we have a half dozen oni that we can scatter about to bolster our forces, but they can only do so much. We have a tall hill to our west, forest to the north, and a shallow gorge to the east, none

40

of which will be close enough to prevent Botan from maneuvering around us. Have I missed anything?"

Silence met his question. The situation looked dire by any normal means, but none doubted Takeo's abilities, not even enough to offer a suggestion. He continued.

"Let me be clear, I don't want Botan to retreat, not even as a rout. If he can't be killed, then at worst, I want his army annihilated. Every soldier we kill today is one less to harass us at the walls. I see only one way to do this."

He tapped the gorge.

"We use the akki to our advantage. Place their large numbers in the front lines as fodder for Botan's komainu, and when they break, make them flee to the gorge by having our eastern side heavy in their numbers. Botan will follow them inside while we keep our own komainu hidden in the forest. Once his army has entered and he can no longer outmaneuver us, we'll instead encircle him and mire this gorge in Katsu blood."

Yoshida and Nicholas both gave a single nod. Qing folded her arms.

"And your plan to make sure Katsu falls for the trap?" she asked.

"I'll be sure to be seen among the akki and in retreat," he answered. "Although he may still sense my intent, I doubt he'll resist the temptation to end me."

"Excellent plan," Yoshida commented. "I'll head the komainu forces to bolster you. I won't be late."

Takeo hesitated, looking at the gorge. *Excellent* was not the term he'd have used. This plan still had the potential to cut both ways. That's the only way it would work, but what choice did he have?

"Be sure that you aren't," he said.

Chapter 4

As the two armies situated themselves opposite each other, the generals prepared to ride out and meet in the center. Lords Nobu and Yoshida each had personal mounts to use, but Takeo and Qing had to fetch communal ones from the komainu master. Takeo decided four people were enough, and Nicholas should sit this one out, while Kuniko and Ping were set to task readying their forces.

Along the way to pick up their komainu, the ronin and the ninja found themselves walking alone in total silence, avoiding eye contact, and hardly breathing if they could help it.

"Not that it bothers me, but are you always going to be like this?" he asked.

"Like what?" she replied.

"Resentful."

"That depends. Do you know why?"

"It's because I used you," he said without hesitation. "You stuck your neck out to save me from the oni, and I didn't once reflect on it, or even seem to care when it came time to choose between Gavin and Lady Zhenzhen."

"And do you regret this decision?"

"No."

"Then I don't see any reason for my opinion to change. It's clear to me that you aren't here to serve Lady Zhenzhen. You're here to serve yourself, and you will only follow her commands so long as it suits you. It's exactly as I suspected."

Their conversation took a sharp pause as they passed a small crowd. Through the gaps between people, Takeo spied an intense dice game being played, judging by the vigorous movements of the players and the silence of the crowd. The two were noticed as they walked by, and the game took a pause as the group bowed low to Takeo and acknowledged him with various titles such as "My lord, General, Sir."

Takeo nodded to them.

"Well," he whispered to Qing, "I don't think you've discovered anything there. Everyone suspects I'm only out to serve myself, even our lady."

"Yes, but everyone else is human and therefore doesn't understand the concept of time. I'm almost one hundred years old, Takeo. That's still young to an elf, yet I've seen more than most humans ever will. I've lived with humans long enough to realize their fleeting nature, and to also realize their numbness to the concept. Lady Zhenzhen and the others are probably dimly aware that you will one day betray them, but they don't think about it because they assume that fateful day is, perhaps, a decade out at least. A decade is a long time to a human, but it feels like tomorrow to an elf. All these others see only what they stand to gain in the short term, while all I can think of is the woe you will bring afterwards. Resentful doesn't begin to describe it."

"And yet you're helping me."

Qing snarled.

"Firstly, I'm not helping you. I'm doing as my lady commands and furthering her cause. I won't let my hatred of you blind me. I obey her orders. I'm not here to serve myself."

"Believe it or not, neither am I."

They obtained their mounts and set them at a trot along the main road through the Hanu camp. Takeo turned heads everywhere he went, and the army bowed to him in various degrees as they traveled. Some put their hands together, as if in prayer, while others crossed their chests with enclosed fists, all depending on their personal view of showing respect. Takeo nodded to them at first, but soon grew weary of that and stopped. He realized that if he nodded to every person who bowed to him, he'd never lift his head.

"News travels fast," he commented.

"And why shouldn't it?" Qing replied. "Nothing interests a soldier like whom the new commander is. Like a slave, their lives are in your hands."

"There's something I've been meaning to ask you, Qing, and I hope our mutual disgust for each other means you will be honest with me."

"One can only hope."

"How did you end up serving Lady Zhenzhen? Why does she trust you so much?"

Qing stiffened atop her mount and bit her lower lip. She was some time in answering, which Takeo thought unfortunate because they hadn't much time before they met up with Lord Nobu and Lord Yoshida.

"Fine, the whole story, then. You might as well know the beginning," she whispered. "I had been traveling for some time before arriving in Juatwa. I was young and naive at the age of fifty, angry that the elven boy I loved had been arranged to be someone else's partner. In the throes of passion, I claimed I didn't want to be an elf anymore and cut the tips off my ears. If you know anything about elven culture, you'll know my kind makes Juatwa natives look like vikings. My emotional outburst was considered a sign of severe mental instability, and my village disowned me. So, I left, deciding to make better use of my life traveling the world. I went to see Lucifan, Savara, and many more places, thinking I'd find happiness there.

"As you can tell, I was impressionable then. I fell in with a ninja clan when I first arrived in Juatwa, as I found them in the forest, and they were quite impressed with me. They taught me a lot, and I taught them a few things, too. Before this, I'd never stayed anywhere for long lest my elven nature be discovered. I didn't want anyone to cast me out. I never wanted to feel ostracized again. However, I liked this clan and stayed with them, and they trusted me with some of the most difficult assignments due to my abilities. Then they gave me a unique job, what would become my last job with them.

"At this time, Lady Zhenzhen and Lord Nobu were still prisoners of Lady Xuan Nguyen. Nobu's grandmother, Lady Ki, was acting as shogun for the Hanu clan, which was fractured at this point because few wanted to serve a dying old woman whose line of succession was in the hands of another. Officially, the Hanus were vassals of the Nguyen empire, but that was recent and Lord Pircha Nguyen was faring poorly against the Katsus. Lady Ki saw an opportunity to regain Hanu independence if only she could free her grandson—and she did mean *only* her grandson. This wasn't just a rescue mission, but an assassination, too.

44

"The plan was for me to slip in, kill Lady Zhenzhen, and then rescue Lord Nobu. Due to the timing of the servants and guards, I'd have to spend a quarter of an hour in Lady Zhenzhen's room before I could leave for Lord Nobu's. In order to keep her quiet and complacent, my plan was to mislead her that I was there to rescue them both, and then murder her at the last moment.

"Somehow she saw right through me.

"To this day, I don't know what gave it away. Perhaps when I mentioned Lady Ki had set the rescue up? Either way, Lady Zhenzhen knew two things within a minute of my entry: one, that I was there to kill her; two, that I had an overwhelming lust for her.

"Surely, you've noticed how beautiful she is, Takeo, how sensual. Her curves are almost on par with Yeira's, and I surely gawked in that room. Lady Zhenzhen made me an offer; before I killed her, she would give me a session of pleasure sure to change my mind. I laughed at the boast, but I was willing to let her try. What would ten minutes amount to?"

Qing paused as a shudder went through her, and she sighed.

"An hour," she continued. "We were in that room for an hour, and she touched me in ways I'd never known I could be touched. It was on that day that I realized not every weapon has a sharp edge. She is amazing, in every sense of the word, and at the end of the hour, I was hers, and she knew it.

"I disobeyed my orders by saving both Nobu and his mother that night, but in exchange, I earned a place at a shogun's side, and the everlasting hope that one day she'll invite me back into her bed."

Takeo was left no time to reply because Qing ended her story right as the two reached the edge of the Hanu camp where the samurai were gathering in large numbers, ready for war. Lord Yoshida and Lord Nobu stood tall and slouched, respectively, waiting on their mounts. The four exchanged meager pleasantries.

Across the plains at the edge of their vision marched a sea of blue soldiers, ever encroaching and making the horizon shimmer as the light reflected off their armor.

They waited until a small group of komainu broke off from the ocean and headed straight toward them.

"Shall we?" Lord Yoshida said.

Nobu gulped by nodded. They spurred their mounts.

45

It hadn't been long since Takeo had last seen Lord Botan Katsu, or at least not long enough for two enemies such as themselves, and so Takeo picked out the man from a distance.

All else aside, Botan had one thing going for him: an aura of respect. His straight spine paired well with the sharp edges of his face, and the look the man could bestow upon people reeked of natural born command. In some ways, Takeo saw him as the rightful successor to Lord Ichiro Katsu, Takeo's former lord, who also had an ability to speak as if he were above being questioned. That being said, Takeo knew full well that Lord Botan was only part ruler, as command over the Katsu hoard was shared by two. The other was Botan's cousin, a certain Lady Anagarika whom Takeo had yet to meet.

And it seemed she wasn't here today either, as the two groups met on the open field and Takeo saw that Lord Botan was accompanied by only men. Lord Botan eyed Takeo and the others, setting his gaze longest on Qing. Doubtless he knew whom she was from reports, but he would also wonder what she was doing at this meeting. He had no idea it was Takeo who commanded her presence. He certainly didn't fear an assassination, though, because he carried at his side the Karaoshi blade.

Takeo's gaze honed in on Botan like a predator to his prey.

"Lord Yoshida," Botan began. "It's an honor to see you again."

"Likewise," Yoshida replied.

"However, I'm surprised to see an esteemed general such as yourself sully your good name by associating with this one. Surely it wasn't your decision to invite him to this meeting?"

Botan didn't indicate whom he spoke of. There was no need.

"On the contrary," Yoshida replied. "It was his decision to invite me. As acting general, he has that power, so long as it doesn't override our prince."

Botan's face turned red, and a vein pulsed against the skin of his neck. Takeo let a wicked smirk stain his face.

"How dismaying," Botan said. "I assumed the Hanu line's depravity would stop at some point, but it continues to be a bottomless well."

Yoshida shrugged and replied, "His command is only necessary because you refuse to yield. I'm sure were you to make your terms of surrender, Takeo would not be needed. Lady Zhenzhen would surely accept them. Think of the lives you would save."

"And hand Juatwa over to the oni?" Botan said, darting a spiteful glare at Nobu, his first glance in that direction, then swiveled back to Yoshida. "No. I think not."

Lord Nobu sunk further in his saddle, his spine now fully curved and his nose dipping below his neck.

"You're going to pay for what you did to Gavin," Takeo said. "I don't know what you're planning, but it won't save you. I promise you that."

Lord Botan finally turned to acknowledge Takeo. The disdain on his face deepened.

"Gavin is only the beginning," the lord began, "I have more in store for you, and when it comes, know that you deserved it."

"And what does any of that have to do with digging up my lost family?"

Botan smiled.

"Haven't killed her yet, have you?" he said.

"No," Takeo said with a snarl. "And why would I do that? If I was half the monster everyone thought I was, I wouldn't have friends to threaten. I don't make this offer often, my lord, but I'm making an exception just this once. Surrender, now. You aren't a fool. You have to know that so long as I have a reason to storm your keep and cut off your head, I will find a way. Bend to Lady Zhenzhen and let me set my gaze upon Qadir."

Botan placed a hand on his sword, Takeo's family sword, and shook his head. For the first time, Takeo noticed Botan was wearing a glove on that hand.

"Well, now that you've made your offer, allow me to make mine," Botan replied. "No matter the outcome of this battle, if you want your friends to survive it, you will perform seppuku before me. Your life for his, that's the deal. Secondly, you will return the rakshasa to me, or I will execute the ogre."

Takeo, Yoshida, and even Nobu, balked. Qing stayed deceptively still but did turn her head ever so slightly to Takeo. Yoshida and Nobu soon followed suit, raising eyebrows. The ronin stared wide-eyed at Botan.

47

"I have no idea what you're talking-" he stopped, then glared. "You lost the rakshasa?"

"I didn't lose her," Botan spat back. "She escaped! And I know she ran to you. I still have the ogre though, so return her or I'll gut him. I know she cares for the creature."

"Well, well," Takeo replied, folding his arms across his chest. "Nicely done, my lord. You couldn't hold her for even half a year, and now she's gone. No, you idiot, she didn't come to me."

"You lie," he said.

"I wish I was lying," Takeo replied. "That would be preferable to the more likely scenario: that she ran off to the Nguyens. Now we're all in serious danger if she and Qadir mate, let alone the threat she poses if she decides to go on a killing spree first. I've been training myself against her for this exact scenario, but you? Or Nobu? Or anyone else? She'll make every ninja assassination attempt seem like child's play. She could climb a smooth stone wall, creep into your room, and strangle you to death without ever making a sound, all while your wife slept soundly by your side. As I said, nicely done."

The redness in Lord Botan's face went a touch pale, and he swallowed. The grip he held on his sword tightened.

"Return her," Botan warned. "Or else."

Takeo rolled his eyes and looked to Yoshida and Nobu.

"I assure you, my lords, she's not among us," he said. "I trained myself to recognize her movements, and I can spot her even when she's changed her appearance. Lord Botan's threat is useless, anyway, as all threats are coming from men condemned to die."

Lord Botan narrowed gaze, but it was the silence afterwards that spoke loudest. Takeo had expected his insult to be met in kind, but it seemed he'd struck a nerve.

"I believe this meeting is over," Lord Botan said through clenched teeth.

He turned his mount and galloped away. Takeo and the others did the same, though they left at a slower pace, following Takeo's lead. He wanted time to think before he returned to the army and begun issuing orders. Specifically, he wondered about Emy.

It didn't surprise him that she'd slipped from Botan's grasp. He'd realized long ago that few cages could hold their kind, and that the only thing keeping her from running was her own free will. That

48

was the whole point of keeping her close by all those years, not to keep her trapped, but so that if she did run, he'd be as close as possible to hunt her down.

He was surprised, though, that Emy would leave Krunk. What did that mean? Had she finally outgrown her strange orphan insecurities? Or, worse perhaps, had Krunk's mental state degenerated to the point where either he didn't recognize her, or she decided he was on his deathbed anyway? That was a strong possibility, as Krunk had been losing his mind month by month last Takeo had seen him. That hurt just to think about. In a way, Krunk had always been the spirit of their little group. With him around, they'd felt less like a band of mercenaries and more like a brotherhood.

At least, that's what Takeo wanted to believe.

"You have interesting methods," Lord Yoshida commented as they rode along, interrupting Takeo's thoughts, "but they do appear effective."

"Uh, if I may ask," Nobu piped up, "What was the point of offering him to surrender if you were just going to threaten to kill him? I don't understand."

"Takeo aimed to infuriate him, my lord," Qing answered. "These pre-battle meetings are rarely about avoiding bloodshed. Most of the time, it's about getting into your opponent's head or tempting them to slip you some vital information. With Lord Botan, Takeo has managed to do both."

"What did he say as he rode away?" Takeo asked.

"The exact words?" Qing replied.

Takeo nodded.

"I don't care the cost," Qing said. "Kill that man."

Chapter 5

The trap was set.

The Hanu army marched out onto the plains, or at least those on foot anyway, while Lord Yoshida and Nicholas took the komainu and fled into the nearby woods. They did their best to mask the attempt by sending them out in small bands as it was inevitable that they would be noticed. Hopefully the numbers would seem small enough to keep their plans hidden.

All others accompanied Takeo, including a large number of spear warriors meant for Lord Botan. Although Takeo doubted the shogun would sully himself in combat, he couldn't be sure. If the man did decide to join the fray, the army needed a way to fight the awesome power of the Karaoshi blade, and that meant spears. Takeo knew this from experience. It helped that the akki were all spear-wielding creatures, and they sure did have a lot of those.

The Hanu army positioned itself on the plains, but in such a fashion that the gorge and its accompanying stream were placed some distance to the northeast. No commander would think to retreat into something like that, but Takeo made sure it would happen by arranging his army with the contingent of akki funneled between his most solid troops. The gorge thus became the only direction they could flee, assuming his entire army didn't break first. As for Takeo himself, he stood in the heart of it all, surrounded by akki, and for that, he was furious.

Takeo hated few things more than akki.

Only rising as high as a man's stomach, the creatures were comical at first glance. Their bodies were tight balls with long limbs stretching out, along with exceptionally long, hooked noses that came to a point at a level either at or below their chins. They only had three digits per extremity, and their skin was red with a scaly yet bumpy look to it. Their piercing blue eyes were a crazed sort that matched their mentality. These creatures were less sentient than most, lacking any sort of hygiene or sense of decency. They tortured for fun, laughed in maniacal high-pitched voices, and even ran like beasts, often on all fours, or at least skittering off to the side.

Perhaps what offended Takeo most in this moment, though, was their smell.

They stunk, and he wasn't the only one to notice.

As the akki weaved into the human troops, the men and women crinkled their noses and stifled their coughs. Some breathed with their mouths open, while others tried to mask the stench by covering their nostrils. A few teared up, the smell was so bad, and all pulled away from the beady-eyed creatures that scampered about their ranks.

The akki didn't seem offended. Far from it, they seemed elated. They chattered like komainu on the hunt, fought and shoved each other for better rank, and fidgeted in place like children. Their spears swayed, knocking into people, and a fight broke out somewhere. Takeo sent Kuniko to deal with it.

Takeo looked to Borota, the oni assigned to them by the ever so generous Tokhta, and shook his head.

"This is going to be a disaster," Takeo said. "Why do you put up with these creatures?"

"We don't," Borota replied, face as placid as always, despite the chaos of the akki. "You are the one trying to put them into ranks. We just let them run wild and direct their fury."

"How can you direct anything with them? They can hardly talk, let alone understand."

"Words, perhaps, they struggle," the oni admitted. "But we don't speak to them in that language. Brutality is our only command, and that they understand."

Takeo searched for Kuniko in the crowd. He couldn't find her, despite a portion of his army being only waist-high. The sounds of fighting weren't so loud now, so he assumed she was doing well.

Qing pulled down the cloth from around her nose and mouth to speak.

"She succeeded," the ninja said. "It took her some effort, though. She would have had an easier time with Ping at her side."

"Ping's turn will have to wait," Takeo replied. "I'll not leave that old woman alone. Besides myself, and perhaps you and Nicholas, Ping is the best warrior in my command. I'm not sure what she or Botan is scheming; for all I know, he's going to send ninjas to kill

51

her right this moment, just to taunt me. Ping is there for her safety and as much as my own."

"You're such a thoughtful son," Qing muttered.

Horns sounded in the distance, ones more familiar to Takeo than he cared to admit. Having served in the Katsu army for a good portion of his life, Takeo recognized the long, low blast that signaled a unified charge of both foot soldiers and mounted komainu troops. Accompanying the horn came a howl of voices echoing across the sky. A stillness swept through the Hanu ranks, quelling even the fidgeting akki for a few seconds.

"This is good," Qing said. "He's sending everyone. Lord Yoshida successfully hid his troops."

Takeo hoped that was the case.

Ever wary of betrayal, the thought had not escaped Takeo that this would be the perfect opportunity for Yoshida to leave the ronin to die. In fact, that's why Takeo had sent Nicholas with the old man, just in case this plan went poorly. The only reason Takeo had agreed to it was because if Yoshida did betray him, the Hanu army would be obliterated, and Takeo didn't think the old general could benefit from such a loss.

"Remember the plan," he shouted to his troops. "Hold the line."

The human part of the army had been recently informed of its intent to retreat to the gorge. With luck, this would prevent spies from passing the information to Botan in time. The secret had only been revealed at all because Takeo needed his troops to funnel the retreating akki in the desired direction.

"You're not going to kill me this time around, are you?" Takeo asked of Borota.

The oni scoffed.

"I want to," it admitted. "But Tokhta believes you will be useful in putting Nobu on the throne. After that is done, I will kill you."

The oni leaned on its club, which it had propped against the ground like a massive walking stick. At the sight of the blue Katsu ranks peeking over the edge of the grassy knoll ahead, though, Borota swung the club up on his shoulders. The enemy hoard roared its challenge anew, and the Hanu army replied in kind, yelling and drawing together, preparing for the charge.

Takeo was calm, motionless even, as his heart beat rhythmically in his chest. He'd been in this exact spot so many times that it was difficult to feel anything at all, until he realized this time was different. He'd never been a general before, never had to command or inspire many. Victory now carried more than a second chance at life; it carried opportunity.

Takeo drew his sword and leveled it vertically before him. He didn't anticipate needing it soon, as he'd barricaded himself in the center of the mass, but he felt more comfortable holding a blade.

Around him, Kuniko had reappeared, and she and the other samurai mimicked his actions. The akki began to hoot and jump in place, waving their spears. They pushed forward, eager for action, but it wasn't long before the wave pushed back.

Takeo heard more than saw the Katsu ranks slam into the Hanu. The howls turned to screams as the first victims were run through, and the clash of steel rang out sharply in the crisp air. The Hanu army was forced back a pace on impact, and that motioned passed through the rest of the troops like a shock wave, jostling Takeo and everyone else in place. Cold sweat dripped from the pores of soldiers all around, and a silence fell over those waiting to die that was so complete it mocked a graveyard. For a moment, all that could be heard was noises in the distance, of clashing steel, triumphant howls, and dying screams.

Although Takeo couldn't see the front line, he could make out glimpses of the Katsu mounted troops above the fray. As expected, Lord Botan had a healthy contingent of them, and he would use their supreme maneuverability coupled with terrifying power to flank the Hanu lines. It was a favored tactic of the Katsus, no matter the general, because it was so hard to counter. Komainu were devastating on the battlefield, especially when properly trained and directed. The screams of the dying slowly expanded in a semi-circle around Takeo's location, signaling that his army was being encased. Without good training and solid experience, the men were sure to buckle and flee.

And that's where the akki came in.

The creatures howled and yipped like the animals they were. Their chattering alone was enough to make one's jaw clench. Then the lines collided and the chatter turned into an uproar. They vaulted about on their stilt-like legs, bouncing back and forth, climbing on top of one another to get a better view and waving their long limbs in the air. They swiveled and jostled in place, unconcerned with the way their hooked noses would slam into those around them, especially as the press of bodies packed them in together. Their beady blue eyes winked in the sea of red, scaly skin, as they thrusted their spears into the sky with so much eagerness.

The screams didn't even seem to bother them at first. They seemed invigorated by the pain and suffering, laughing at the cruelty of it all. The sound of an akki in the distance letting out one horrified, shrill shriek didn't even disturb them, not until there was a second and a third, and then the akki screams began to mix solidly with those of humans, and among it all one could hear the deep howl of a komainu in a rage.

Takeo watched with a keen eye as the akki around him stopped waving their spears so much. Their bouncing lessened, and those sitting atop their friends went wide eyed as they gaped off into the distance. He could hear hushed conversations in their raspy, broken voices, and with this sudden silence came the unfiltered sounds of those being slaughtered, human and akki alike.

Takeo had seen men break before. He'd seen how a retreat, or even a rout, started, both as the one attacking and as the one fleeing. It was well known that to keep cowards in line, it was important to put them side-by-side with the brave because they were less likely to run in that case.

Akki, it seemed, had no such tendencies.

Those sitting atop their friends that could see the carnage coming their way, relayed it by screaming and vaulting to the ground, then pushing their way through the crowd. Takeo followed the gaze to see the komainu on their right flank making wicked good progress into their ranks, having now found the akki masses. The front most komainu had caught one in its teeth and whipped it about, the akki's long legs flailing about like red, limp sticks. The akki screamed, shrill and piercing, unnerving even Takeo, and he wished the beast would stop playing with its food.

The akki howls around him turned to panicked hoots. They looked at their friends trying so hard to push through the crowd, looked at each other, looked at Borota, who hadn't moved an inch since the battle had started, and made the decision to run.

"Sound the retreat," Takeo ordered.

Kuniko pulled out a horn and blew two sharp blasts. The akki broke and ran like a red river towards the gorge, funneled by the Hanu troops. As for Takeo himself, he stayed put, letting the sea part around him.

This was the most dangerous part of his plan.

Armies in a rout were like animals to the slaughter, especially when hounded by komainu. When retreating soldiers showed their backs, the enemy could get among them and kill with impunity. Takeo's entire army might be wrecked before it could reach the gorge if at least some didn't stay and fight.

That was why Takeo had concentrated his most experienced soldiers in the middle ranks, saving them for the retreat.

"Time to prove your worth, oni," Takeo shouted, so eager for a fight that he strode forward through the tide of akki screaming and fleeing about him.

Borota swung his kanabo off his shoulder and twisted the handle with hands as large as a man's head. The oni grumbled something unintelligible and trudged on, as did those others chosen for this gruesome task.

"Take the lead," Takeo commanded.

Borota snarled but obeyed, picking up his pace and plowing through the retreating akki. One particular komainu caught his eye; the beast was steeped in bloodlust, ripping akki in half with its jaws while its claws raked through those unfortunate enough to be within reach. The rider was equally enthralled, letting her mount run wild and paying little attention to her surroundings.

She never stood a chance.

The oni darted in, bounding over the last few akki and slamming the kanabo down with all his might in one grand over-head swing. The woman screamed before being clobbered, her body offering little resistance as the hunk of wood and metal crashed down on the komainu as well. The beast's spine snapped, and it collapsed, howling in pain but now crippled and flailing on the ground. Borota reeled up for another swing, clashing down on the animal's head and ending its suffering.

Similar howls echoed out down the Hanu line, and Takeo risked a glance to be sure everything was going according to plan. Borota wasn't the only oni afforded to the Hanu ranks. Bringing their akki underlings in tow, a full dozen had been summoned for this campaign, and Takeo had been sure to spread their number about his ranks to counter the komainu. He only ever had eleven, though, as Tokhta had made it clear he'd never leave Nobu's side, and Nobu was not fit to be anywhere near a battlefield.

Not that there was time to dwell on that now.

Borota swung at the next komainu to come charging in, and Takeo leapt into the fray. The komainu dodged the oni attack, deftly pausing just before the swing, only to have a fearless ronin fly into its face, sword point first. Takeo's blade pierced the komainu's eyesocket so deeply that the creature died instantly. It crumpled, and Takeo ripped his blade free and approached the rider. The man had fallen with his mount, his leg pinned under the beast, broken for sure, judging by the man's screams. He saw Takeo approach and begged for the mercy he would not receive.

"Don't get caught in a fight!" Takeo shouted down his line, ripping his sword free of the man. "Continue to fall back!"

The akki were making swift progress, their long legs perfect for eating up the distance, despite their short height. Those with space added their arms to the retreat, scampering on all fours like little red orcs. It was a struggle to keep up with them and hold back the Katsu hoard, but the Hanu managed, thanks in no small part to the oni. The creatures' massive size and huge clubs meant they could command a large swath of land, and all it took was a few dead komainu for the enemy to pause in its eagerness. Yet still, the Katsu ranks did not relent, for victory was within their grasps.

The gorge lay ahead with the first few akki reaching its mouth. The small contingent Takeo had hidden among the rocks there stormed out of their hiding places to entrench themselves at the narrowest part. Their first task was to stop the akki from fleeing further, by force if they must, and Takeo could only hope they would succeed. If not, the entire plan would fall apart, as the akki would rush through the gorge and out the other end.

"Takeo!" Qing shouted.

The ronin finished ramming his blade through an overconfident samurai and, getting it stuck in the man's ribs, had to kick him off. Takeo risked a glance around, spotting Qing astride an oni's shoulders, leaning out with a hand gripping one of its horns. With the other, she pointed into the distance with her wakizashi, which dripped blood down the oni's back. Takeo followed her gaze but could see nothing over the chaos. He found Borota and shouted at the oni only enough to get its attention, then clambered onto Borota's upper back, wrapping an arm around the oni's neck. Borota snarled, but Takeo ignored him.

Takeo was high enough to see over the carnage, but it was difficult as the oni swiveled from side to side, raking the battlefield with the kanabo. A moment's pause allowed Takeo to look in the direction Qing had pointed, to the woods to the north, where Lord Yoshida and his komainu troops were supposed to have gathered and stayed hidden.

That was the plan, anyway, for Takeo clearly saw glimpses of red troops sticking out among the green trees. It wasn't many, but just enough that any intelligent general would sense a trap. This couldn't be by accident. Lord Yoshida was up to something, as Takeo's mind raced through the possibilities, he could only come to one conclusion.

"What do you see, human?" Borota asked, irked to no small degree. "Are you going to get off my back, or am I going to have to rip you off?"

"You might as well," Takeo replied. "We're being betrayed."

Chapter 6

"Run!" Takeo yelled, leaping from Borota's back. "Full retreat into the gorge!"

Kuniko, always nearby, heard the command and didn't hesitate to rip out her horn and give it two more sharp blasts. The first she'd given some time ago had been more a signal to the troops than an actual retreat, but the second would let them know that the situation had changed.

"My lord, what is it?" Kuniko asked, stowing the horn and joining her general in his sprint.

A half second later, Qing darted into view beside them.

"You saw?" the ninja asked.

"Lord Yoshida has allowed himself to be seen," Takeo said. "Intentionally, I'm certain."

"How can you know that?" Qing demanded.

"Regardless, the outcome is the same. Botan will direct troops to impede Yoshida now, and Yoshida won't be able to aid us, if he ever intended to. We're on our own. The gorge is our only hope now, as it will prevent us from being flanked."

"But we'll be trapped," Qing countered.

"I know!" Takeo shouted back but did not slow his pace.

Damn that Yoshida! That slimy, good-for-nothing politician. I'll bet he gave me this position just so I'd let my guard down, and so that he could pin the loss on my corpse. A two-for-one stroke, eliminating his competition while deflecting any blame. What a fool I was to trust him. One would think I'd have learned by now.

The Hanu ranks funneled into the gorge, this time in great haste. The akki had already sprinted far ahead, and Takeo had to push his way into the ranks to get a look at the back of his army. He wanted to be sure the akki had been stopped and breathed a sigh of relief to see the mass of red bodies pushing up against a solid wall of samurai. The akki surely would have kept fleeing otherwise, despite the Katsu ranks giving pause. Yoshida had been noticed, and there was a delay as that information slithered its way through the Katsu army. Takeo knew it wouldn't last, though, for he'd made sure of it.

Botan wanted him dead.

A horn blast sounded, loud and low to signal the charge should continue. From within the low line of the gorge, Takeo could no longer see the open plains above, as the gorge descended some forty feet below level, but he could make out some of the Katsu riders splitting off from the main mass toward Yoshida's position. Meanwhile, the Katsu infantry leveled their weapons, cheered, and descended into the soon-to-be cauldron of blood and death.

Takeo swore.

"All the oni to the front," he commanded.

Borota scoffed and replied, "You are not Nobu. We will not die for a losing battle."

"We'll only lose if you don't get your fat red masses to the front," Takeo spit back.

"I stay," Borota said, then added with a smile, "to ensure Botan does not take you alive."

The cries of the enemy horde vibrated off the jagged rock walls, making the ground shake along with the thunder of so many feet slamming into the ground, weighed down with armor and weapons. The soldiers under Takeo's command grimaced and tightened the grip on their weapons, and a profound stillness washed over them. They looked to Takeo from all directions, drawing strength from his presence. Hanu troops were used to fighting alongside their commander, as this had been the way of things until Lady Zhenzhen had come along. Takeo could see in their faces that they took solace in the fact that as grim as things were, their commander shared their fate. They would not break.

The akki felt differently.

As the Katsu ranks slammed into the Hanu ranks once more, another shudder ran through the press of bodies. Screams and the clashing of steel filled the air again, this time twice as loud, as the sounds echoed off the rock walls and reached an ear-splitting volume. A heartbeat later, the sounds were matched by the squabbling and screeching of the akki, as they broke into a panic. They scrambled over one another, pushed and shoved against the back rank, but Takeo's men held firm. He'd chosen the largest of his soldiers for this task, and they beat the smaller akki back with ease. Some of the red creatures became so bold, or perhaps so terrified, that they tried to attack their allies, but a quick kick to the face ended those attempts. Takeo's soldiers held no sympathy for these beings. Few humans did.

"Fine, die here if you wish," Takeo shouted to Borota. "But at least command the akki to take your place. Quickly, lest I send you back to the realm you call home—in pieces."

"Order them yourself. Haven't I told you this already?" Borota mumbled. "They respond to brutality. Must I repeat myself at every turn?"

The Katsu lines pressed in, and Takeo watched in horror as a line of red troops began to skirt the upper ridge, headed for the back end. The Hanu mass was about to be flanked, as originally intended by both Botan and Takeo, but the results were soon to play out to the former's favor. Takeo didn't like the odds, and neither did the akki.

"Takeo, look!" Kuniko shouted.

He ripped his gaze from the oni to see the little red creatures had taken to the rock walls. They reached with long limbs, strengthened with terror, grabbing ledges and scrambling up. Takeo glanced back to his line of troops engaged with the Katsu, where the battle was fierce and soldiers on both sides pressed closer than lovers. It was only a matter of time until one side gained the upper hand. Takeo wouldn't let his soldiers fall alone.

"Tear them off the walls!" the ronin yelled.

Human hands flew up the rock walls to grab akki limbs and yank the little creatures back into the fray. They yelped and screamed, but there were too few within reach. So many had begun to climb the walls that the brown and gray rocks now looked a sea of red, as the akki fanned out like a burst of blood from a wound. They screeched and howled their triumph, those in the back emboldened by those ahead. Their long limbs made them ferocious climbers, scampering almost as fast as they could run.

All the while humans died.

I won't let them escape. I can't! These wretched creatures get to live while samurai die. Worthless bunch, all of them. Worse than worthless. They are a plague, and I will treat them as such.

"You want brutality," Takeo shouted at Borota. "I'll show you brutality."

He looked at the spear warriors that surrounded him, those intended to stop Botan, and ripped the weapon out the hands of the nearest one. The man gaped, but Takeo ignored him and scanned the mountain side. He found the akki nearest to the top, leveled the spear, and then hurled with all his might.

The weapon sailed true, piercing the air with ease until it struck hard against a little red scaly ball of flesh. There was enough weight behind the spear to ram straight through the akki and stick into the crevices of the rocks. The akki died instantly, releasing its grip and falling back onto the spear. It didn't have enough weight to rip the weapon free, instead wedging the tip further into place. There the corpse hung, over the Hanu and Katsu line, dripping blood along its shaft.

The akki just below stopped and screamed when the dead one's leg smacked it in the face. The cry made others look, all pausing to gape, and a hoard of blue eyes and hooked noses swiveled to Takeo. The ronin yanked another spear from one of his soldiers and leveled it at the next highest akki.

"One more step and you join him!" the ronin shouted, unsure if his voice would pierce the uproar.

The akki Takeo locked eyes with cackled and feinted a move upwards, but like a child testing the boundaries of their parents' tempers, didn't actually move.

Takeo didn't hesitate.

His second throw struck truer than the first, sticking the akki dead center of its ball-shaped body and splattering the rocks behind it with akki blood. The spear tip bounced off the rocks this time around, and the akki plummeted to the ground, striking two other akki along the way and almost knocking them off the wall.

Takeo grabbed another spear and looked for his next victim.

"Fight or die!" he yelled.

Or maybe I'll just kill you all anyway. Worthless scum, the lot of you, I'll butcher your entire race if I make it out of this alive.

The next akki in line met Takeo's dark gaze and then looked up to the pinned corpse just above. Blood dripped onto its forehead, and Takeo waited for the thing to try and scamper up the mountainside. That seemed the inevitable thing, as he was only one man and the akki were many. He couldn't hope to kill but a handful while hundreds would flow up over the wall. Any creature with a basic level of survival, sentience, and sanity would take the risk and continue fleeing.

Borota laughed.

"Well done," it grumbled.

The akki beneath the pinned one reached up a long arm and slapped the dangling foot of its dead cohort, which flopped lifelessly. The living one giggled manically. The giggle then turned to a cackle as it smeared the blood dripping on its forehead across its face. It shook its head, splattering those close by, and the cackling spread and turned into a high-pitched laugh. A few started hooting, at odds at first, but then their voices collated into a pattern, and they waved their spears about. Those at the second rank from the top poked at the ones above, pointing at the dead akki and laughing. Those at the top snarled at this, as no creature with an aptitude for pain appreciates being stuck with a spear, and they attacked back. The laughter increased from those below, while angry chatters mixed from above. One got so mad that it hurled its spear, but the throw was so poorly aimed that it sailed out into the open and struck some random soldier, judging by the scream that followed the weapon's landing. It had landed somewhere close to the Hanu and Katsu line, so it could have been anyone, but Takeo was so angered that he went to throw another spear when he was interrupted by the oni laughing again.

"Akki only know two states of mind, fear and mayhem," Borota said. "And those can never coexist. This is going to be fun."

The akki on the walls pointed at the unfortunate soul on the ground and howled. One of them with an eager smile on its face tapped it closest friend and leveled its own spear for a throw, eyes crazed. Others mimicked, and Takeo shouted.

"The enemy, you idiots," he yelled and pointed. "The ones in blue!"

The many akki glanced his way, sighed or snarled, and then raised their spears just a little higher. One let out a triumphant cry and then hurled its spear, the weapon sailing through the air and piercing some soldier deep in the Katsu ranks. The man screamed, and the akki howled their laughter. Spears began to pour in from all around, the akki turning to feverish enthusiasm to impale as many

Katsu soldiers as possible. Takeo heard one of the Katsu leaders shouting at his men to take cover, but an akki spear snatched him right off his mount. The akki found this particular death so hilarious that some fell from the walls, gripping their sides, which only caused the others to laugh harder. All the while, men and women fought and died beneath them.

Some of the akki pointed to their fallen comrades and raised their spears, but one thought it funny enough to imitate the others by leaping off the wall altogether. He did so in epic style, spear in both hands, legs and arms back, and screamed all the way down until it landed on the top of some poor Katsu samurai's head, piercing the short spear into the man's skull. Other akki, not to be outdone, soon followed suit, screaming and leaping from the walls as insanity took hold. All but a heartbeat later the sky darkened as a flood of red akki bodies rained down upon the battlefield.

"Ah, this is why we keep the akki!" Borota roared, raising his kanabo. "Look how fearless they fight when given over to bedlam. Haha!"

"Well don't celebrate yet," Qing shouted. "Look!"

Takeo followed her gaze and found the Katsu ranks had finished encircling them. A line of blue troops was visible up above, fighting with those akki who'd climbed the walls to attack. Still more had reached the back end of the gorge and were pouring in like a small wave. Takeo knew Botan's forces weren't large enough to encase the gorge, which meant the shogun had split his forces to cut off the ronin's retreat. There could be no escape now, and trapped as they were, it was only a matter of time before the Katsu ranks overwhelmed the akki above and started raining projectiles and boulders down upon them. Takeo had hoped for more time to make a retreat. He'd hoped Botan would hesitate to divide up his forces, but it was not so.

The infamous ronin had made a mistake.

The Katsu ranks roared as they flooded down into the gorge from the other side, slamming into the Hanu ranks like a typhoon. The shudder went through everyone, and the sounds of battle doubled in their intensity. Takeo was pressed so tightly against those around him that it was all he could do to keep his sword free. Now more than ever was he glad he put his strongest troops in the rear.

"My lord," Kuniko said, grunting as the press of bodies threatened to suffocate her. "What do we do?"

"Please tell me you've got a plan," Qing added.

Deep, murderous laughter danced across the stone walls nearby, and Takeo saw Borota had reached the Katsu ranks and was swinging that kanabo to deadly effect. The tightly packed formations on both sides meant there was nowhere for the oni's victims to run, and his swings launched multiple men into the air. Meanwhile, the little akki moved like knives in the water, darting between the legs of their victims and stabbing with impunity. The Katsu ranks that had first assaulted them began to weaken under the violent chaos that ensued.

"We fight our way out," Takeo shouted, pushing through the crowd. "Follow the oni."

Takeo had never felt so useless in a battle. He was used to fighting in the front lines where his martial prowess could help turn the tide of battle. Yet now he had to issue orders, and that meant being somewhere less active, so that he could observe all sides at once. He needed to win this fight, to escape, to flee even, to kill that traitorous Yoshida. How could he do any of that in this mass of allies, with no enemies nearby to strike down? His very life now boiled down to his troops' ability to fight, and he never felt so helpless.

He pushed through the ranks, those ahead trying but failing to part when they saw him approach. There was nowhere to go. The oni and akki ahead weren't pushing so hard anymore. The tide was turning back against them, and Takeo felt raw fear pulse through his body.

It won't be enough. We're going to die.

A horn sounded, muffled though it was over the heavy ringing of combat and shouting. It took a heartbeat for Takeo to recognize it as a Katsu one, and a moment longer for him to understand it was something akin to retreat or at least something defensive. Either way, it wasn't the rousing call to charge that Takeo expected, and he stopped trying to shove through his men long enough to look around. He couldn't see much, but his ears picked up on a sharp cry behind him. His head swiveled to find the flood of blue Katsu samurai that had encircled them where now fighting a double-edged battle of their own: Takeo's men on one side, and a bulging line of Hanu komainu on the other.

Leading the charge was Yoshida, surrounded by elite warriors, plus Nicholas, swinging his maul like an oni through the Katsu ranks.

It took one second for the rest of Takeo's troops to see this, too, and a massive cheer erupted.

Lord Botan's army, divided three ways and turned inwards to annihilate Takeo, was ill-prepared to deal with a mass komainu attack. Yoshida's assault was both brutal and swift, striking a deadly blow not just in numbers but in morale. The enemy ranks crumbled, and the Katsu horn was blown again, this time signaling a full retreat. Only one third of the Katsu numbers could escape untouched, another third was harassed and suffered heavy casualties, while the last third was captured in the gorge just like Takeo had been. The attackers became the defenders, and the Katsu ranks were annihilated nearly to the man.

Before the killing was finished, yet once the battle was certainly over, Lord Yoshida cut his way to Takeo. The ronin couldn't help himself as he looked up at the old general, atop his blood-splattered komainu, and grinned.

Yoshida scowled.

"Do you mind telling me what in the world you were thinking?" the lord started, one vein pulsing against the skin of his neck.

Takeo's grin fell.

"You never sounded the horn!" Yoshida shouted, ignoring all the looks he gathered. "I waited and waited for the signal, but it never came. Finally, I just charged in. How long were you going to wait?"

"What, me?" Takeo stammered. "You were the one who got noticed. You were supposed to stay hidden."

"And what does that have to do with anything? It was a last-minute change to help you. Firstly, it looked like you were having trouble, so I exposed a few troops to make Botan hesitate. Secondly, I could see he was holding back reserves for just such a trap, so I let him think he found our plan. Then, thirdly, I altered my own position to attack from the other end, thus ensuring a retreat for you. I thought for sure you'd see the wisdom in the move. Yet none of what I've said explains why you didn't signal me. We almost lost the battle!"

Takeo blinked and his mouth fell open. He hadn't thought of any of that. Yoshida had increased their tactical advantage by baiting Botan with false information. The only problem was that Takeo fell for it, too.

"I," Takeo started, pausing. "I thought you intended to retreat."

Lord Yoshida gaped. A silence fell over them, minus the screams and clashing taking place in the distance.

"Retreat?" the lord repeated. "You mean, you thought I was going to leave you to die?"

Takeo went to reply but stopped. He'd been about to make some excuse, something along the lines that such a thing wasn't so crazy in his world, but he couldn't form it into words. His gaze fell.

"I made a mistake," Takeo said.

Yoshida swore and straightened in his saddle.

"I knew you were a cynic, but I didn't think the problem stretched this far. Why wouldn't you at least give the horn a try? Signal me anyway? You were so convinced, that easily, that I'd betrayed you, that you almost died."

Yoshida paused and sighed.

"Takeo, if you continue to act this way, you're going to doom this campaign. No general, no matter how clever, survives a battle where he doesn't trust those under his command."

"I," Takeo stuttered, "I'm sorry, my lord."

The words slipped out before Takeo realized the damage they would do. He was supposed to be the general here, not Yoshida. Why was he apologizing? He looked weak.

"Don't apologize," Yoshida replied. "Do better. And you can start by pursuing Botan all the way back to his fortress. The real fight hasn't even started."

Chapter 7

The more Takeo thought about it, the worst he felt. Lord Yoshida's question kept repeating over and over in his mind, asking how Takeo could have been so certain of betrayal—off so little a change in the battlefield—that he'd almost marched their army into the jaws of death without flinching. Even the slightest glimpse of hope in his mind would have prompted him to sound the horn, but it never occurred to him. Takeo had been that certain, and this bothered him to no small extent.

It wasn't his skepticism that was the problem, though. The fact that Takeo had been willing to accuse Yoshida of betrayal wasn't considered a weakness in Takeo's mind. The ronin relied too heavily on that instinct to start trusting people wholeheartedly. What bothered him was a certain blindness, so to speak, the fact that Takeo had been unable to see any possibility beyond betrayal. He limited his options and almost paid the ultimate price for it.

Thinking on this brought back a memory of his time with Emily. Right after the colossus joined her, she'd used the creation to broker a deal with a viking jarl. She requested safe passage at sea in exchange for a favor to the jarl; to which, the man had howled with laughter. The viking couldn't understand why Emily was trying to broker a deal at all when she could, quite literally, strong arm the entire village into doing her bidding. Emily had been shocked not at the brutality of the statement, but that the thought had never occurred to her.

It seemed Takeo had the same problem, but from the opposite perspective.

He hadn't been granted a colossus to control, but he now had an army. That was a rare privilege few could claim, and like Emily, Takeo's first use of it had been a half-minded attempt hampered by his old habits. He couldn't afford to be blind to any option in the coming battles, not against Botan, and certainly not against Qadir. To do anything else was not only foolish, but deadly.

Takeo thought all these things in only scattered fragments in the aftermath of the battle. As the acting general, he had a fair bit of logistics to undertake. Before Botan could be properly pursued, there were the dead to strip, a camp to strike, messages to be dispatched, scouts to be sent out, and so much more, not to mention the injured to consider. Not that any of this slowed Takeo down. He had served indecisive commanders before and knew that the only thing worse than a bad decision was no decision at all. He handled every inquiry to the best of his knowledge as he made his way back to the camp.

Combining this with Nicholas' ceaseless chatter, it was a wonder Takeo had the time to reflect on anything at all.

"Battles here are so strange," Nicholas wondered aloud between messengers running to and from Takeo. "We won, didn't we? Why are we running down Botan right now? I mean, how is each side quitting the battlefield just to return and pack up their camps? I mean, can I just ask what in Valhalla is going on here? Our camp be damned, why aren't we chasing that shogun down right now?"

"Many reasons," Qing butted in. "You must remember that battles in Juatwa aren't like those in The North. This many soldiers requires a small city of supplies, which means assaulting a camp is like assaulting a small city. If we were to attack Botan now, we'd do so on his terms, against his fortifications, and against the rest of his reserves, which might turn our victory into defeat. Also, since we didn't capture Botan at the battle, we're unlikely to catch him at camp. He can break off from his baggage train and disappear from our grasp, making us risk much to gain nothing. The tactic to winning a war is patience. Don't bite off more than you can chew. We'll pursue Botan when we're good and ready, specifically when we're well supplied for a long trek into enemy territory."

Nicholas frowned.

"Oh," he said, then looked to Takeo. "Why don't you explain things like her, huh?"

"Because I don't have the patience."

"It's because you find me too handsome and get distracted, isn't it?" Nicholas replied.

"No. I literally just told you the reason."

"Don't worry, my friend. I know I'm beautiful. I have this sort of effect on everyone."

Takeo sighed.

68

The camp was a flurry of activity upon their return. The orders Takeo dispatched were carried out, and the entire place was brought down in a hurry. In truth, the camp was already half-struck, as it was known prior to the battle that the army would be moving one way or another fairly soon. Botan's place would be the same, and both armies would be mobile in no time.

Takeo knew he wouldn't catch Lord Botan before the man made it back to his fortress. This was Katsu territory, so they could afford to pack light and move fast. If Takeo had his sword—his enchanted sword—he might entertain the idea of assassinating Botan in the night as the man's army traveled, but as the opposite was true, that was out of the question.

Unfortunately, a siege was inevitable.

As he neared his tent, his thoughts were interrupted by three loud giggles, one of which he recognized as belonging to Mako. He focused his attention, and a conversation drifted to him on the wind.

"This is too much, too much!" a voice said.

It took Takeo a moment to realize it was Lord Nobu.

"No, it's true!" replied another, older, female, and Takeo's heart raced as he realized it could only belong to one person. "He was an adorable baby, so eager to walk. He used to push himself up and start sprinting, trying to get his feet out in front of him, but then smack! He'd fall face first on the ground."

"I just can't imagine it," Nobu said, laughing. "Tiny baby Takeo, crawling in the dirt and drooling all over the place."

"It's easy to forget, but everyone was a baby once," Mako jumped in.

"That's true," Dhyana continued. "He's all grown up now, but I still remember having to clean his little baby booty, and not to mention trying to breastfeed while he was teething. Ooohh, that was not fun."

Nobu huffed, and replied, "I don't think my mother ever cleaned me, or breastfed me, or much of anything really. We had servants for that."

Takeo stormed into view. His eyes revealed what his ears had told him, that Lord Nobu was having a tea party with Takeo's mother and sister-in-law, surrounded inevitably by Ping, a few others of Takeo's personal guard, Nobu's personal guard, and the oni, Tokhta. All were well within earshot to hear the entire ordeal, plus whatever had certainly occurred prior to Takeo's interruption.

His presence summoned the attention of every soul in view, and the silence was deafening. Mako went red, Nobu went pale, Tokhta grinned, and Dhyana smiled.

"Ah, there he is," she said with those thin lips. "My son returns victorious, as usual, or so I hear. You must be proud, my lord."

This last part she addressed to Nobu, adding a bow of respect. The prince forced a grin and a nod, then rose swiftly.

"We'll have to speak again sometime," the prince said. "I wish everyone could be so lucky as Takeo here, to have a mother so loving. You make me a jealous man."

"Your lordship is too kind," Dhyana replied, nodding again.

Lord Nobu beat a hasty retreat, taking with him his oni and human guard, sparing Takeo but a fleeting glance as he left. There wasn't much embarrassment in the look, not as Takeo expected, more of a vapid expression. Takeo got the feeling Nobu wasn't fleeing the ronin's wrath so much as he was fleeing an argument. Either way, Takeo paid little mind. He was focused on the short old woman with eyes as dark and unflinching as his own.

Mako was the first to rise and come to him.

"Don't be mad," she whispered, which was useless with the silence all around them. "She was only answering our lord's questions."

"My lord, the prince demanded an audience," Ping said, rising and bowing.

"I want everyone to leave," Takeo commanded, eyes on Dhyana. "Everyone but you."

The order was swiftly obeyed, and when they were alone, Takeo went to his tent, pulled back a flap, and gestured inside. Dhyana went in and Takeo followed. The interior was darkened yet hot from the afternoon sun. Neither complained as Takeo began to strip off his battle gear. Outside, he heard Kuniko approach and intercept a stream of messengers looking for the general.

He thought of a million things to say yet couldn't choose one well enough to make words. Takeo took off his laminar armor in pieces, dropping each to the ground to remind himself they needed to be cleaned before being stowed. Meanwhile, Dhyana clasped her hands and stood with back slightly hunched, like any good peasant was expected to do. Takeo couldn't tell if she was thinking like him, her head swirling with a mountain of unsaid words. He assumed so.

"What am I going to do with you?" he said, more to himself than her.

She didn't reply.

"I spoke with Botan before the battle," he continued, finding a thought to latch onto. "He's got some plan for you by which he means to hurt me."

"Whatever it is, I know not what, my son," she said.

"Don't call me that."

"Oh? Excuse me, but I think I will. You didn't pop out of thin air, like everyone seems to think. I gave birth to you. That makes you my son and me your mother."

"Mothers don't abandon their children."

Dhyana's head fell and her shoulders slumped, which Takeo only noticed out of the corner of his vision. He couldn't bring himself to look at her.

"So that's what you're angry about," she whispered. "What am I saying? Of course, you are. Your brother never mentioned me, did he?"

Takeo paused before answering, "No."

"Well, if he had, he would have told you the truth. I didn't abandon you. I never, ever would have abandoned you."

"Evidence speaks otherwise."

Silence fell between them. Dhyana's eyes continued to admire the ground while Takeo looked intently at his gear. He bent down and began to clean the pieces, which was something he shouldn't have time for as the general of an army, yet he needed something to do with his hands. They itched for his sword, his only source of comfort in the past many years.

"You," Dhyana started, paused, then pressed on after a large breath, "you were three, when I lost you. That's not old enough for a child to have memories yet, but that's when it happened. I'd only met your brother once before that, in your father's presence, but that one time was enough to make an impression. I saw how there was no empathy in him, a cruel creature void of emotion. Your father knew it, too, but he was a blithe sort of man. Not that it bothered me, I wasn't exactly looking for a husband either, not in my profession."

Takeo scoffed. "So, it's true, then. I am the son of a whore."

"Yes," Dhyana replied flatly.

Her tone made them both raise their heads. The look they shared was one of cold, calculated understanding. Takeo was the first to look away.

"Though I was only called a whore as an insult," she said. "We preferred the term *hostess*, but I knew that was only for the clientele, to make them feel more comfortable. I'd never deluded myself into thinking I was anything above a common prostitute, and as such, we had methods of ensuring we didn't get pregnant. That's never good for business, you see, but sometimes accidents can happen, and we had procedures for that, too, but, well, that's not what happened with you. When you came out, you were my first, and my world changed.

"It probably sounds cliché to you because so many mothers say that, but it's true. I didn't realize how unhappy I was until I saw you, and I knew instantly that I wanted a better life for you. Boys in whorehouses don't amount to much, you can imagine. They can only find work as hired thugs or conscripted soldiers, both considered fodder for royalty. I knew I couldn't give you to your father either, as I feared you'd end up like your brother. There were few options, really, but that just made the choice clear.

"I left. I ran away. I wrapped you up in my arms, took what I could, and escaped from the clutches of my mistress. I was lucky she wasn't the type to search me out. She was old and relied on more passive ways to get her whores to return to her, things like starvation and lack of work. Most hostesses that try to flee find common whoring a poor experience at best, dangerous at worst. Thankfully, I had other ideas.

"Village after village I scoured, Takeo, looking for a home, someone to take me in. You know how insular the common village can be, right? Well the problem is tenfold when you're a young, pretty woman. I was seen as a threat by the women, a victim to manipulate by the men, an unwanted mouth to feed by both. I don't know what I would have done if that one woman hadn't taken pity on me. I settled in as best I could, and I raised you with all the love I wished I'd had growing up. You were my world, Takeo. I fed you, I

72

cared for you, I named you. I taught you to walk, I taught you your first words, and we were going to do so much more together. I was so happy those years, oh so happy.

"Until he came."

Dhyana paused as her voice began to tremble. She took in one calming breath, held it, then released it slowly. The tears forming in her eyes stopped. Takeo realized his mouth had fallen open at some point.

"At that time, I didn't understand why Okamoto had come," she continued. "It was only later I would find out that Lord Ichiro's parents had been killed, and that Ichiro had almost died, too. I later discovered that it was some samurai close to him that made the attempt, and I eventually was able to piece the puzzle together. Your father had tried and failed to complete a dangerous mission, and Okamoto felt the need to flee Juatwa. I don't know why he wanted to take you, a baby with no connection to the event, whose existence was known by so few, but I didn't get the chance to argue the point.

"He came at night, sword drawn and in hand. He looked at me; I'll never forget that look. Oh, how it scared me. No one that young should have that look, but I knew instantly that he would kill me without hesitation. He wouldn't care about the villagers who may or may not come to my aid. He wouldn't care how loudly I screamed. He'd forget about me before my corpse hit the ground. Meanwhile you were sleeping so peacefully, right there, in my arms.

"I didn't know what to do. I didn't know what he wanted, at first. Fear kept me silent as he came over and grabbed your little arm. It was all I could do not to fight. He held that blade over my head—not a single threat in the action, just necessity. It was like I was a liability he was just waiting for an excuse to end. He pulled you from my arms, and the only thing that kept me frozen wasn't the fear of death, but the fear of leaving you alone forever. I realized in that moment that I couldn't stop Okamoto from taking you, and I would die if I tried. If I ever wanted to see you again, if I ever wanted to hold you in my arms once more, I had to let you go.

"You were too young to remember, but you woke up and looked at me as Okamoto carried you off. I thought you would cry, but you didn't. You just stared back at me, trusting me that because I was standing still, there was nothing to be afraid of. You went back to sleep without a care in the world, and I cried for us both.

"I didn't abandon you, Takeo. You were stolen."

Dhyana reached up and wiped tenderly beneath her eyes. A single sniff escaped her otherwise calm demeanor as she then clasped her hands in front of her, awaiting judgment.

As for Takeo, he didn't feel much of anything beyond a tingling numbness that permeated his entire body. He'd stopped cleaning his armor at some point, his hands frozen in the air, yet he was only dimly aware of it. He was motionless because Dhyana's description of Okamoto had brought back many, many memories of his brother, none of which he'd thought about in quite some time.

Being a skeptic at heart, Takeo's first impulse was to doubt his mother's story. There was no one alive to confirm it, no witnesses she could name. Even if the story was partially true, she could have warped sections of it to be sympathetic to her. In fact, Takeo expected it, and despite his heart's yearnings, his mind urged caution towards this supposed tale of a mother's love and loss. However, one thing was clear.

Dhyana knew Okamoto.

Chapter 8

"That has got to be one of the most insane stories I've ever heard," Nicholas said. "And here I thought I knew every rotten thing your brother did to you. What a madman. Makes me both wish I'd met him and thankful I didn't."

The two were traveling with a fair bit of space between them and the army. The Hanu horde was on the move, traveling across the eastern Juatwa plains to hunt down Lord Botan. Not that they would catch him before he reached the safety of his keep. The Katsu army was beating a hasty retreat, unburdened by heavy baggage, siege supplies, and a hostile populace. Takeo didn't bother to force his army along. He wanted them to arrive at the Katsu fortress well rested and in high spirits.

In the meantime, Takeo had taken Nicholas out for a stroll ahead of his army and made sure Qing was scouting somewhere so far away that even an elf couldn't hear his words. He'd ordered her to and had said it exactly like that, just to see her glare and obey. Some distance behind them, Dhyana traveled side-by-side with Ping, an endless conversation passing between them.

Takeo was interested in that, but not so interested as to stop it. Not yet. If Dhyana was going to gossip, at least let her do so to only one individual, he figured.

"What do you mean you can't believe it?" Takeo asked. "Honestly, that sounds like my brother. And I haven't told you everything. I still haven't told you the worse thing he ever did to me."

"I don't know, Takeo, this one sounds pretty bad. In viking culture, there's nothing so insulting as robbing someone of their destiny. Your mother went through leaps and bounds to set you on this particular course, and Okamoto stole the decision right out of your hands. You weren't like me. I got to choose a life of war. Violence was forced upon you, and not by necessity. Far from it, war sought you out."

"Maybe that's because this is my destiny," Takeo replied. "My mother fought so hard to save me from the life of a samurai, and in the end, she was powerless against fate."

"Still doesn't change the fact that your brother literally ripped you from your mother's grasp. Damn, just think about how she felt. It's enough to make me think of my own mother. At least I left her willingly, you know? Wait, is that better? I think it's better. Maybe it's not? It has to be. Hm, I'm confused now. Thanks, Takeo. You're as helpful as always."

"Likewise," the ronin replied, adding a sigh.

And this is why I miss Gavin. He'd know what to do, what to think, in a situation like this. I might not have agreed with his moral compass, but at least he had one. Nicholas and I are like two blind men arguing over color.

"I wonder how my mother is doing," Nicholas muttered. "And my father. And by Valhalla, Abraham. Oh, and my nephew! William, that was his name. How could I forget? Huh, he must be, what? Close to a decade old? Wow, that can't be true. Did time really go that fast? Do you think he knows I exist? What am I talking about, of course he does. Abraham had to have told him about me. I should see him one day, teach him to fight. That's what a good uncle would do. I know none of the others are doing it. Oh, Takeo, I could be the first one to take him to Lucifan! Wow, wouldn't that be something. I can already hear Mother getting furious, yelling at me. Ha! That'd be something. I'd be the greatest uncle ever. Don't you think?"

"I'm going to be honest, Nicholas. I'm doing as little thinking as possible lately. I'm beginning to see that Botan's plan really was to throw me off balance, and I'll be damned if this isn't a good effort. Less than one week in and I'm on the verge of throwing my entire world into question. I can't falter, not now. I can't afford this. Maybe Qing is right. Maybe I should just send the old woman back to the Hanu keep and deal with her when I return."

"Well, I don't think it's a bad idea, but you have to ask yourself one thing," Nicholas replied. "Do you trust Lady Zhenzhen with your newfound mother? Or that other woman, Lady Ki?"

Takeo's blood went cold.

"Damn," he whispered. "I suppose she stays, then. This is what I get for joining a band of liars and schemers. I suppose I'll have to quarantine her some way, then."

"In an army?"

"Are you going to question everything I say? I don't need another nagging voice telling me I'm treading water. I need solutions, or at least ideas. You can contemplate your problems and homesickness on your own time, Nicholas. Right now, I need to win a war."

"You do realize I don't work like Gavin, right? See, what you're doing right now, with that comment, is trying to push me away. For whatever reason, Gavin was only intrigued by that and would chase after you harder than ever, right up until he found a new love, and you pushed him straight into her arms. Now Gavin is sitting in a prison, unable to count past five without taking off his shoes. You think I want to end up like Gavin? No, you moron. You're not pushing me anywhere. When I leave, I'll do so of my own free will, and not a moment sooner. So here, let's try again. You said something really stupid like, 'Hey Nicholas, what if I tried to keep my mother away from everyone in a tightly packed camp? I mean, surely nothing could go wrong with that plan, and if you suggest otherwise, in any subtle way, I'll say something even stupider. Watch me!' And then I replied, eloquently and full of wisdom, in a manner most becoming of a legendary being. Oh, you want me to repeat it? Of course, my simpleton friend, anything for you. I've dealt with ogres before. I repeat:

"In an army?"

Takeo swiveled a look at Nicholas. The viking ignored him, except for a wide grin that stained the big man's face.

"When you retell this conversation, don't break your arm patting yourself on the back," Takeo said.

"Are you kidding me?" Nicholas replied. "I'm going to break both my arms."

Takeo spent the rest of the journey to the Katsu fortress avoiding Dhyana at all costs, which wasn't difficult to do with his newfound position. The constant monitoring of the army's every facet was an exhausting, ceaseless task, that was just too much for any one person to tackle. Takeo quickly understood why generals were apt to

77

delegate duties, but he had an added problem that few other generals needed to face: laissez faire insurgency.

See, in Juatwa armies, daimyo did more than supply the war effort with taxation, samurai, and conscripts. They also took on auxiliary duties, such as being in charge of field reports, or supplies, or food, or scouting, etc. Thus, a massive war effort could be undertaken, and the many moving parts contributed to the whole. This was done mostly on a voluntary basis, as royals wanted to undertake these tasks for any number of benefits, from a larger cut of the spoils to better connections in the Juatwa upper echelon.

So, when it was announced that Takeo was now the general, there was suddenly a vast dearth of volunteers.

The problem was twofold. While Lord Yoshida was certainly doing his part to keep the remaining daimyo from taking their troops and abandoning the army, he couldn't make them excited about staying. There was nothing written about daimyo having to help the general beyond being present, and the daimyo saw nothing to gain by associating with the ronin over Yoshida. They led a silent protest by making themselves scarce. The second part of the problem was that Takeo did nothing to stop this. He wasn't about to force a bunch of people he perceived as lazy to run his war effort. The way he saw it, they'd do a terrible job at best, intentionally ruin him at worst.

Lord Yoshida took over as many duties as possible, but there was just too much, even for two people. Takeo ended up breaking the unwritten code of ethics a step further by assigning many of these semi-honorable duties to normal samurai, or at a bare minimum those with at least some lordly blood, such as Kuniko. Surprising no one, she rose to the task admirably, and Takeo soon found himself delegating tasks to her, just so she could turn around and delegate them to others. If he wanted that forest scouted, she knew whom to send and how many. When he expected camp to be struck, it was done. So many problems that could have been massive hurdles were quickly brought to heel by a combination of necessity and innate ability on Kuniko's part.

Thus, the situation evolved that by the time the Hanu army appeared before the Katsu walls, Takeo was back to doing solely what he did best—determining how to crush his enemies.

The entire journey had caused distant, sometimes painful memories to surface in Takeo's mind as he'd spent a fair amount of his life in service to the Katsu empire, but all of them paled in comparison to the rush that hit him upon seeing the fortress itself.

Takeo did not know how old the Katsu fortress was or who built it, but he reckoned the man or woman in charge of its construction had suffered the two mental illnesses of vanity and genius.

For the genius side, the Katsu fortress was built on one of the eastern most reaches of the Juatwa peninsula, on a section of the sea cliffs that jutted out in a sharp triangle. This made the fortress assailable by land from only one direction. Then, in an impressive feat of engineering and expendable labor, a massive moat had been dug out of the hard ground, connecting from one part of the ocean to the next, so that the fortress was made to set off on its own little raised island. Only a single drawbridge, which could be raised up to become part of the wall, connected the fortress to the mainland. To assault the Katsu keep, an invading army would have to do more than scale walls; they'd have to cross a river that swayed with the tide, all while under constant attack from enemy projectiles.

For the vanity side, the designer wasn't content with having one of the most difficult fortresses in Juatwa to assault. No. That person wanted everyone to know it. The Katsu fortress was an unrivaled work of art. Its towers and walls were built tall enough that they could be seen a full day's travel away on a clear day. A mixture of stone and wood was used to achieve this impressive height in an economic fashion, but that didn't mean the Katsu keep appeared poor. Quite the contrary, no expense had been spared when it came to decorating and painting the place. Every pillar was a sculpture, every beam an artifact, and every wall a painting. The entire place was a mosaic of color, and those parts that weren't painted were only left bare because they were made of naturally beautiful elements, such as gold, marble, or ivory.

The last Takeo had seen this place, it had been under attack by seaborne siege engines. Although a clever idea, the attacks had been mostly a distraction as floating weapons were atrociously difficult to aim. While the late Lord Ichiro had sent forces to deal with the ships, the true Nguyen assault had come at the walls, overwhelming the exhausted defenders and capturing the place. The walls had since been repaired, the towers standing tall and the paintings retouched.

Or so it appeared from a distance.

The Hanu army stopped a ways before Katsu fortress. The defenders would no doubt have siege weaponry of their own to hurl death upon the attackers, so the place was given a wide berth. In typical fashion, the Hanu army spread out around the fortress, doing its best to cut the place off. There was still the sea to contend with, but that was in another daimyo's hands. Yoshida had assigned the naval blockade to someone long before Takeo had any control, and that woman's only job was to blockade the Katsu. It was always understood this was to be a victory by land.

While all this was happening, Takeo issued his first orders.

"Make sure the tents are set up with wide channels. I want good lines of communication throughout the camp. Start digging latrines, securing water sources, and collecting the food. Put the akki somewhere out in the open, away from us. I don't want half the camp crippled by disease within a month. I want scout reports of everything within two days journey from here. Find all villages, towns, houses, cottages, clearings, caves; I don't care. If there's a peculiar blade of grass within two days ride, I want it on a map in my tent as soon as possible. Kuniko, look there. You see the small city outside the fortress? It should be abandoned, but I want that place scoured, then burned to the ground. Come victory or defeat, that will hinder the Katsu's ability to recover from this war, and it will send the message I want everyone to hear. I did not come for peace. I came to conquer.

"After you're through relaying that, fetch us mounts. I'll rely on the scouts' reports for the countryside, but the fortress I will see with my own eyes."

"Yes, my lord," came the reply, and he was obeyed.

While Kuniko was getting the mounts, Takeo busied himself by assisting the servants in erecting his tent. They tried to insist he take a seat, but Takeo was too anxious to sit still. He needed to do something besides grind his teeth, and he'd set up his own tent so many times in the past that he thought nothing of doing it now, the title of 'General' be damned. He only paused when Dhyana and Ping showed up.

Takeo expected Dhyana to approach, but to his astonishment, she instead looked to Ping and gave him a subtle nod. Ping took a deep breath and marched forward, chest out. Takeo narrowed one eye.

"My lord," Ping started, taking a knee.

Even at this level, Ping neared Takeo's chest in height. Ping was tall and broad, rivaling Nicholas in mass, which was a rare thing for a Juatwa native, or rather any normal human not bred and raised by viking standards. While height and weight were always advantageous to a fighter, Ping went the extra mile by being naturally gifted with the blade, using his innate athleticism to become a terror on the battlefield. Adding Takeo's personal training on top of this, Ping Sun was one of the deadliest fighters in Takeo's army, and perhaps would one day outpace the ronin himself. In fact, Takeo suspected that day was soon to pass, and it worried him how many other Ping-types were out there just waiting to meet him in combat.

Hence Takeo needed his sword back.

"What is it?" he asked.

"My lord, I heard you're going to inspect the Katsu walls. I request to accompany you."

"I believe I've already assigned you a task, Ping," Takeo replied. "Is it too much for you to handle?"

"No, my lord, of course not," he stuttered.

Ping shook his head, never raising it. He looked back at Dhyana, and she nodded and swept a hand forward, urging him on. She ignored the glare Takeo gave her.

"My lord," Ping started again, and it seemed to Takeo the man was using the title as a crutch to stop from stuttering. "I don't want to miss this opportunity. This is the first fortress I'll have the honor to assault, and under your command. I know you're taking Kuniko, and I have no doubt it's to mentor her. With all due respect, I want to be there, to learn, as well. I . . . I think I've . . . earned that right, my lord."

Takeo had yet to let his eyes fall from Dhyana. All he could think throughout Ping's short speech was to wonder what game she was playing at. She couldn't make her intent any clearer, and that bothered him. He expected at least some subtlety in a move like this.

81

"You've earned it how? By your particular skillset?" Takeo asked.

"That and more, my lord. I may not command as openly as Kuniko does, but I've done nothing less than be a trusted servant to you. Please, grant my request."

"Stand up, Ping."

He obeyed, rising above Takeo, and met his general's gaze.

"I do trust you," Takeo said. "And it's that trust combined with your skills that makes your current task so important. Like guarding the food in that ruined fortress, you remember? This is the most dangerous time for, well, her, and you. We've only just arrived, and Botan could have left behind any number of traps. Until we've scouted this place, I need you to be on your guard. This won't be the last fortress I assault, Ping. I'll be sure to mentor you next time."

Ping hung his head, but then recovered by turning the movement into a nod. For a moment Takeo thought he'd have to command the boy to leave, but Ping was not Kuniko. He did not persist so boldly. Ping left without another word, and Takeo departed, as well, for he saw Kuniko approaching with their mounts.

Time to see what Lord Botan has in store for me.

Chapter 9

Four riders set out into the open plains. As with anything in life, Takeo chose his companions with purpose. He selected Qing for her elven eyes, Nicholas for his bohemian mind, and Kuniko for her astute obedience. He wanted his underling to know precisely where and what he was referring to when he started giving her orders.

They tore into the mix of weeds, grass, and flowers that grew tall in this part of the Juatwa. The plains danced in the breeze that constantly blew in from the ocean, and only a few sparse rocky outcroppings and lone trees dotted the land. It reminded Takeo of the Great Plains, in a way, except for the stark color difference. Nothing was yellow in Juatwa, while the Great Plains had been only that.

They entered siege weapon range but made sure to stay far beyond the reach of bows. Fast as they were on their komainu, they'd have time enough to avoid any flying rocks, but arrows were another story. Takeo directed his party to the right first, circling around the southern side of the fortress where the abandoned town outside the walls was being put to the flame. If need be, Takeo would scorch all the land within a day's march of this place just to set an example.

"Botan knows we have to assault him," Takeo explained. "We don't have the time to starve him out. Our blockade isn't strong enough to prevent some other daimyo from eventually sending Botan supplies, and the Nguyen were not injured enough to delay their next move. Qadir will consolidate power and invade as soon as he can, knowing we'll be at our weakest right now with most of our forces deep in enemy territory. I estimate that if this fortress doesn't fall in two months, we're done for. We'll need at least half that time to build siege equipment, even shoddy ones, at a backbreaking pace. Make no mistake, our losses may be substantial."

They turned about and cantered at a steady pace in a wide half-circle about the fortress, heading west, then north, then east. They studied the walls, towers, sentries, and everything else in silent, concentrated fashion.

Well mostly.

"My lord," Kuniko spoke up, halfway through. "There's something I have to say."

"So, say it."

"It's not my place to question you, but, well, that woman—the one claiming to be your mother—I don't trust her."

Takeo smirked.

"I don't think anyone does," Qing quibbled.

"I wasn't talking to you," Kuniko snapped, then whispered none too quietly, "heretic."

Nicholas straightened in his saddle and glanced at Takeo, but the look was ignored.

"She's poisoning the ranks," Kuniko went on, emboldened by Takeo's silence. "Her comments about your childhood aren't just unwelcome, they are insulting. She shouldn't be here for the same reason Lord Nobu doesn't bring his mother to the battlefield."

"I agree," Takeo replied, "but she's more than that. She's a trap set by Lord Botan, and I can't avoid a trap I can't see. I appreciate your skepticism, Kuniko. Do me another favor and keep an eye on Ping. If she is trying to poison the ranks, that's where she'll start."

Kuniko's chest swelled with pride, and she glared triumphantly at Qing. The ninja rolled her eyes and huffed.

They came to a stop about three-quarters of the way around, not far from a small rock outcropping atop a shallow hill. Takeo nodded into the distance to one part of the wall.

"You see it?" he asked.

"Aye," Nicholas commented. "Between the second and third turret. Wall seems off."

"They're still finishing the repairs or trying to fortify the wall," Takeo went on. "That's Botan's weakest point and where we'll concentrate our forces. He'll do the same, but it's still our best shot. Qing, do you see anything we don't?"

"No," she replied, though her eyes searched the grass. "I do, however, hear something. We're being watched."

A heartbeat went by before all four drew weapons, and they instinctively tugged at their mounts to close into a circle, facing out. Takeo scanned the waist-high grass dancing in the wind, looking for any patch that didn't move so enthusiastically. Meanwhile he risked a glance out at his army still trying to make its way out about the area. Reinforcements weren't far off, but that wasn't what worried him. He listened for a bow string being drawn taut.

Qing pulled out a throwing star with her off hand and closed her eyes.

"There," she said and threw the projectile into the grass perhaps four paces from Takeo.

As it disappeared from view, no sound rang out. No thud of hitting flesh or dirt, as if the star simply ceased to exist. A moment later and the star returned, tossed in a wide, slow arc toward Takeo.

He caught it and lowered his katana.

"How long have you been there?" he called out.

"In this exact spot?" Emy replied, still fully submerged in the tall grass. "I've only just arrived. I've been creeping along ever since I saw you approach. I knew you'd inspect the walls yourself. As for how long I've been waiting for you to arrive? Days."

"Show yourself," Kuniko demanded.

"She can't," Takeo said, nodding to the fortress. "It's certain we're being watched. Botan will want a full report on my every move. Right now, he doesn't know where Emy is. If she stands, he knows, even if she changes form. No one was here before we arrived, so no one should be here still."

Even though Takeo couldn't see the rakshasa, he could feel her eyes on him, and also her smile.

"Tell me everything," Takeo commanded. "How and why you escaped, what it's like in there, if anyone is dead. You know what I want."

"I had hoped for a private audience," she replied.

"It's too late for that," Takeo answered. "These three know you're out here, and if any of them slips the information, Botan will know that I have in-depth knowledge of his fortress. Besides, they'll say nothing, won't they? Not even to little old men far off at home."

Takeo spoke generally but he looked at Qing. The ninja stared back, deadpan, then nodded.

"Start at the beginning," he said.

"As you wish," she answered. "I escaped because Botan tried to play nice in the beginning, but not nice enough. He kept us—or rather, me—out of the fortress, in the town, which I knew was to

85

prevent me from studying the place. He knew I'd have worked up a thorough escape plan if I wandered within the walls, even under guard. I worked up a plan to get Krunk and myself out anyway, when the time came. I knew betrayal was a possibility, but I became certain when the army left to challenge you and Gavin left with them. I wasn't sure he would return, honestly. I knew Krunk and I had to run."

"But you left him. Why?"

The silence that met him spoke louder than words. Takeo understood what happened before she continued.

"I tried," she said, softly. "But Father, his mind . . . he's losing his grip on reality. He says whatever comes to mind now, and Botan has had his guards listening eagerly. They know about the oni and their betrayal of you. They know how you got your enchanted sword. They know about the sennin at the mountain, about Kuniko, and how Lord Eun died. Even though Krunk wasn't there, Gavin told him mostly everything, as they were close. It's not good, Takeo. Krunk is in a bad way, and I couldn't get him to leave. He didn't understand. I realized that even if I freed us both, he'd only get us captured again. So, I changed my plan. I stayed, at least for a little while longer.

"They took us into the fortress and then straight to the dungeons. They blindfolded me, but I listened to the best of my abilities. I have no doubt they expected me to escape that night and so intended to triple the guard. Unfortunately, they didn't expect me to escape within the hour."

"Aren't you worried about Krunk?" Takeo asked. "Botan threatened to kill him if you don't return."

"He lies. He's afraid of you, not me. I could smell it on him. He won't kill either Gavin or Krunk until he's certain it plays to his advantage. To him, I'm a bridge further upstream. You're the one he has to cross now."

"By Valhalla," Nicholas whispered. "Poor Krunk. I shouldn't have let him go. He didn't know any better."

"How did you escape?" Takeo pressed. "Could it be done again, with help, perhaps?"

Takeo nodded in Qing's direction and assumed Emy could see the movement.

"I only escaped because, well," Emy replied, pausing, "I didn't, really. Not at first. After scaling the fortress walls, I came back inside. The komainu they used to track me down kept losing me after crossing the river twice. The komainu likely know I went back in, but the riders just think they lost the scent. Only later did I truly leave, to find you."

"I assume you made good use of your time inside," Takeo said. "What's the situation in there? Best place to attack? Weak points, strong points, I need everything."

"Botan is smart," Emy replied, lightning fast, needing no time to gather her thoughts. "He spoke time and again about how you once served this Ichiro for years and thus would be knowledgeable about the fortress. He resolved to change everything he could, and he's been doing so for a long while. Old access tunnels have been collapsed. New wells have been dug. Locks changed, armories moved, even new windows put in place. He's paranoid to the point of nearly switching out the fortress brick by brick. And like I said, he's been doing this for some time, preparing for you. I think it was always his intention to bring you here."

Takeo glanced to the Katsu fortress, taking it in along with a deep breath.

"So that crumbling wall?" he asked.

"Trapped," Emy said. "He's baiting you to attack there with heavy defenses in place."

"The other walls?"

"None less fortified."

"The gatehouse?"

"Guard is tripled, windows walled up, the door locked in place."

"He what? If something happens in there, he won't be able to open the gate. He might very well trap himself."

Silence was the reply.

Takeo swore.

"Well, I have to give him credit," Qing said. "The man learns. He already lost to you once, badly. He's not leaving anything to chance this time around."

"I think I preferred it when everyone thought I was an inept scoundrel," Takeo muttered.

Nicholas scoffed. "Oh, don't worry. I'm sure he still thinks you're a scoundrel."

Takeo scanned the walls again and noted the subtle shifts in the catapults' positions atop some of the turrets. They were taking aim, practicing perhaps. The group of four hadn't moved in some time, and it seemed the commander on the walls was debating taking a shot at them. It was a useless gamble, perhaps a one in thousand chance to hit, but that was worth it for a target such as the infamous ronin.

"Any weaknesses you noticed?" Takeo asked. "Something, I hope."

"If there is, I missed it," she replied. "I may be smart, but I'm not a sennin, and I've never laid siege to a fortress before. Also, I couldn't get into every place. In fact, I couldn't get into most places. I have to disguise myself as someone in the fortress, which makes moving about risky."

Takeo hung his head. No part of him thought this task was going to be easy, but he had hoped for some slight advantage over Botan. But no, not only were his numbers less than ideal with a good chunk of his army made up of cowardly demons, the foe he had to face was paranoid, the walls he had to scale were in good shape, and the only point of access was across a moat.

Oh, and let's not forget my lack of time. Damn it all.

"Hey Takeo," Nicholas piped up. "You know I love a hard fight as much as the next viking, but you think maybe just once we could have an easy one? You know, for fun?"

"I'll work on that," Takeo replied, rubbing his forehead.

"Hey Emy," Nicholas went on. "How's Krunk? You know, how are they all being treated?"

"I don't know much, only what I've overheard, as they separated me from the others upon entry to the fortress. Botan fancies himself an honorable man, so although Gavin and Yeira are under lock and key, they're given royal accommodations. Pleiades is even given free range of the place, but only because she's a child. Gavin doesn't let her go much, but Botan seems to have taken a liking to her. He takes her on walks, I think to remind Gavin of his place. Krunk, though, isn't so lucky. Father has been locked in their strongest cell, the one they'll put me in if they catch me again. I'm sure Gavin has requested Krunk to join him, but Botan thinks Father is a danger. I don't think he's being treated well."

She didn't plead that Takeo hurry to save them. She knew he was working as fast as he could, and no urging from her would help. She didn't ask for orders, either, because she knew Takeo was thinking on that, as well. The two communicated silently better than most communicated with words.

"You want to know where you'll be most useful to me," he said. "That depends, though. How certain are you that you could get back inside that fortress unnoticed?"

"Very certain."

"Could you remain hidden for weeks, or even months?"

"Somewhat likely."

"If you were captured, could you break out one last time?"

"Doubtful."

"Well then, you better not get caught," he said. "Watch and wait. If the situation changes, find a way to let me know. If I need you, I'll loose a flaming arrow off of the north side of the fortress. Come immediately."

A soft purr, eager and excited, came from the grass. Takeo heard a tail swish over the wind.

"As you wish," Emy replied.

Takeo heard nothing else after that. He scanned the grass again but discerned nothing.

"She's gone," Qing said after a moment.

"Let's continue our scouting trip," Takeo said. "We've already drawn enough suspicion just standing here, and those catapults atop the walls are being loaded. Hopefully Botan thinks I'm very interested in his trapped wall. I need any element of surprise at this point."

Off they went, and Takeo cast one more fruitless glance into the grassy plains, knowing Emy was too good for him to catch, too quiet for him to hear.

If I had an army of her instead of akki, even half as many, I could capture this fortress by nightfall.

Chapter 10

Assaulting castles was horrible, bloody, nightmarish work, avoided at all costs by defenders and attackers alike. Assaults were done only by necessity, as the death toll would be atrocious on either side. The nature of the work, sending hordes of men against stone and siege works, meant that the faster a place was captured, the more dead there were. Lengthy sieges produced the fewest casualties, but could take up to a year, while ladder assaults could bring down a walled city within a day, but, well, it was best not to speak of the result.

Which is why the Hanu army worked in silence building ladders.

To add to the difficulty, the Katsu fortress had no nearby forests. Attacking armies didn't usually bring their own siege equipment, or at least not all of it. Doing so impeded movement, slowed the army down, and put extra strain on the men and komainu to haul everything. The ideal situation was to build the ladders, catapults, or trebuchets on the spot, using surrounding trees. Some defending castles did what they could to prevent this by burning entire forests down, but such a thing was difficult to do in Juatwa's lush, wet landscape.

The Katsu fortress had no such problem, though, being surrounded by plains. The closest forest was almost a day away, and it was a meager one with few strong timbers. The Hanu ladders would have to be built in pieces, lugged to the camp in teams, and then lashed together. This would weaken their strength and make the ladders prone to breaking, which would limit the number of men that could climb them at once. That played to the defenders' advantage, and everyone knew it. The Hanu soldiers did their absolute best lashing those ladders together because it would mean certain death otherwise.

To bolster spirits, Takeo made it known he would join the charge, and he walked the ladder-building scene often to show his investment in the assault. Sometimes he had company.

"Come now, this madness," Lord Yoshida commented now. "Generals do not lead ladder assaults. That's dangerous work, and

90

you're too valuable to be wasted on this sort of carnage. Being present is good enough, and the men know it."

"I appreciate your concern, lord," Takeo said, "but this isn't my first siege. I've been on the ladders before, and I'll not command anyone to do a task I cannot do myself."

He spoke at a level volume but kept his chin up so that his voice carried. He saw the soldiers that heard grin and work with purpose. Takeo used to hate drawing any attention to himself, but he realized that those under his command appreciated his background. They liked that he was an experienced warrior and drew strength from his involvement. If they fought better with him around, then so be it.

"Just don't be the first one up, that's all I'm asking at this point," Yoshida said, speaking at much lower tones but still overheard. "Let the younger men have a chance at glory. To make a name for themselves as you did."

Although they'd never spoken about it, Takeo knew why the old lord was having this conversation now. Politically skilled as he was, Yoshida was giving Takeo the chance to back out of his promise without appearing to be a coward. In the presence of so many, Takeo could lessen his role in the assault and deflect the blame onto Yoshida, showing that it was strongly insisted and wisely advised he sit this one out as acting general. On the other hand, if Takeo held fast, his presence would only bolster morale further.

Takeo made a mental note to thank the lord in private. He had proven to be an asset.

"My decision stands," Takeo said.

"Well, if you won't listen to reason, then perhaps you'll yield to emotion. Think about your mother. You've only just met her, and she's been forced into this army. You think she's waited all this time to see you again just to watch you die?"

Damn, this man will not quit.

Takeo just shook his head.

The two paused as a group carrying freshly cut timber came their way. It wasn't to get out of the group's way, of course, as they were a lord and a general, and so they yielded to no one. They stopped because they wanted to inspect the wood, Takeo especially. The group carrying the load set the timbers down and bowed. A couple moments and Takeo nodded to them, letting them continue on their way.

"Let's leave my mother out of this, lord," Takeo said. "She's not been a part of anything for some time."

"What a cruel thing to say," Yoshida replied, gaping. "Have some heart, Takeo. I'm sure it wasn't her choice. Life is too fleeting to hold a grudge."

"Grudge? How can I hold a grudge against someone I don't even know?"

"Don't ask me. I'm not the one holding a grudge."

Takeo sighed. They stopped another work crew, who bowed upon noticing they were being watched. Takeo and Yoshida nodded back.

"You're starting to sound like Nicholas."

"Family is important. No one else in the world should be able to love you like family, and those that miss that lesson are doomed to struggle. My mother was my rock growing up. She taught me lessons at the table that were far more important than those on the battlefield. If I had the opportunity to speak to her again, like you do now, I would not miss it for the world."

"Okay, I take that back. Now you sound nothing like Nicholas. I have to ask, why are you so interested in my mother, lord? I don't see you suggesting anyone else head home and kiss their creator on the lips. Why me?"

"This may shock you, Takeo, but I want you to be happy. Unlike so many other daimyo who hold their position in precarious fashion, I am quite secure. I don't see you as a threat, but as a fellow who could be quite useful, even loyal if given the chance. I've come to realize your reputation as a habitual murderer is undeserved, and you've only traveled that road because you've been forced to beyond your control. Truth be told, I even enjoy your company.

"I'm being frank with you again, you see, and I'm not bothered by how many overhear it. I'll not lie. You have amazing potential, similar goals as myself, and I see no reason that we should be enemies. Quite the opposite, we should be allies. In time, perhaps even friends. It's not so crazy, and if I had a friend who'd never known his parents, then suddenly discovered one of them, I'd recommend that friend do all in his power to make up for lost time."

92

Takeo stopped in his tracks. Lord Yoshida turned to face the ronin. A paternal smile crossed the old man's lips, but Takeo just stared, lips apart and eyebrows furrowed.

"I," Takeo started, pausing. "I don't know what to say."

"You don't trust me, I know," Yoshida replied. "And that's okay. A komainu who has only been beaten does not warm to human touch so easily. Judge me on your terms, Takeo. I ask for no special treatment. However, I will say this. If you're determined to lead the ladder assault, then go make the best of your time right now. The men have seen you enough, and they'll see you again when it matters most. Go find out what your friend lost his hand for."

Takeo bowed, more out of automation than agreement. He was reeling from Yoshida's short speech, so thrown off center that he didn't know what to think, let alone do. His soldier side took over in the absence, and he followed his lord's order.

It was also a great excuse to leave the conversation. What had first been a simple discussion of tactics had quickly taken a personal turn that Takeo was unfamiliar and uncomfortable with. He left without any direction, though he soon found himself on the road leading back to his tent. Calls of respect fell upon him as he walked, as did samurai and soldiers bow.

Nothing made Takeo more wary than kindness. He hated kindness because kindness could be a mask. People who were kind wanted something; that's how the world worked. Villagers were nice to their lords because lords had power over their lives. Soldiers were nice to their commanders for the same reason. Kindness was simply a side effect of the direction of power. Only dumb, unambitious people were kind for no reason, like Krunk. That wasn't an insult, not the way Takeo thought of things, but simply an observation. Kindness was an expense, a show of weakness in a cruel world that devoured all it could. A man like Yoshida would be aware of that, would understand that, would use that to his advantage. Kindness, to Takeo's eye, was a lie.

Yet he couldn't be sure that Yoshida was lying to him. After all, hadn't the man explained what he wanted? Hadn't he just said that he wanted Takeo at his side, at his command, and kindness was his payment? Wasn't he speaking Takeo's language in the most clear and direct manner possible?

He had, and perhaps that's what unsettled Takeo. Most deals offered to the ronin were easy to resist, poorly devised and issued in half-mocking tones—the Lady Ki and Lord Eun came to mind. Lord Yoshida, though? Takeo had to hand it to him. That man knew how to read people.

One thing remained uncertain. If Yoshida really had seen down to Takeo's soul, then why hadn't the old lord turned away in horror?

That question was put on hold as Takeo came upon his tent. He nodded to the guards and went inside, only to find Mako alone. She turned red.

"Where's my mother?" Takeo demanded.

"Oh, don't be mad," she said, coming towards him. "You can't blame her."

"Please don't defend her."

"I think you'd be surprised if you talked to her. When we talk, she only wants to know about you. Don't be mad, please. She didn't have a choice."

"Mako, where is she?"

Takeo said this firmly, though only by a hair. Too much and the fragile widow would break, but Takeo had gone too far. Mako teared up, and Takeo sighed.

"Lord Nobu summoned her," she whispered.

Takeo burst back outside.

"You have to promise not to be angry with her!" Mako pleaded and ran after him.

The two zipped through the camp. Takeo did his best to keep to a walking pace, but that was hard with his blood boiling and with the knowledge that he was racing against time. He didn't want to draw attention, not any more than his mere presence already did, but what else could he do? Mako was hot on his heels with red eyes and a solemn disposition.

"What else could she do? Deny the prince?" Mako continued. "You have to give her a chance, Takeo. You've treated her like she failed, and I guess she did in a way, but don't you see how both of you suffered?"

"So, she's told you the same story, I see," Takeo replied. "You do realize that was your husband she was talking about."

94

Mako choked on her next words but kept stride with the ronin. They stopped at one of the many, many tents dedicated to Lord Nobu's maternally enforced hobbies only to find him absent. Takeo cursed and pressed on.

How is this still a problem? I'm the general of this army now. Shouldn't Nobu's location always be known to me? I should have foreseen this. I should have known after he visited her during that battle, he would try again when he knew I was away.

"Just because I loved Okamoto doesn't mean he was flawless," Mako continued. "I think of you in the same way. Okamoto was just looking out for you, afraid Lord Ichiro would turn vengeful, but that doesn't mean it was right to take you. Sure, you lost your mother that night, but you gained a brother, and she lost her son. How is your pain different from hers?"

Because she wasn't beaten over and over and over in a foreign land with no one else to turn to.

By chance, the two burst into a tent with the one servant who'd seen Nobu recently. At the sharp command in Takeo's voice, the servant fell to her knees and thrust her forehead to the ground, then shouted that the young lord was in his private cook's tent. Takeo rushed off without another word.

Mako remained quiet the rest of the journey to Nobu.

Takeo knew he'd found the right place when he came across a tent surrounded by servants, guards, and two towering oni. Or at least, they would have been towering if they hadn't been sitting in the grass, slouched over. He thought that perhaps he should order the oni to stand at all times so that Nobu could always be found by the sets of horns milling above the tents. Also, it would annoy the oni, but they would never obey.

Takeo's rapid pace and direct approach caught the attention of the servants wandering about outside, and once he was noticed, the whole place snapped into activity. Servants darted out of his way and fell to their knees. Guards bowed low enough to kiss the ground. Music stopped and the tent flaps were yanked aside for him. Takeo never had to break his stride until he charged inside, Mako less than a pace behind him.

The scene within fulfilled Takeo's expectations and fears all at once. Lord Nobu and Dhyana sat across from each other on large, fluffy pillows, for the cook's tent had no tables suitable for dining, or at least not for a prince. The cook and his servants were feverishly working away, brewing tea, cutting meat, boiling vegetables, filling the place with a thick and pleasant aroma. Nobu was leaning forward, supporting himself with elbows on crisscrossed knees, eyes wide and focused on Takeo's mother for a split second before all attention fell on the ronin. As the place went quiet, Dhyana tensed without ever turning around. She cut short whatever she'd been saying and hung her head. Ping was seated on the ground close by, while Nobu's guards filled the tent's corners, and they all went rigid. Even the cooks froze, and one could hear nothing but silence beyond the dim, muffled voices of the camp that echoed in the distance.

With Dhyana refusing to turn around, Takeo's gaze fell on Nobu. The ronin expected the prince to show some degree of shame, perhaps look away and turn red. Instead, the prince gazed back, eyes wide and unblinking. Out of the corner of his vision, Takeo spied sweat accumulating on Ping's forehead.

"My lord, have you visited the ladder builders today?" Takeo asked.

"Well, no," Nobu answered, innocently.

"Have you visited them ever?"

"Well, uh, no," Nobu replied, hesitantly.

"Those men are going to fight and die for you soon. Don't you think it would be prudent to visit and encourage them?"

"Well, yes, but," Nobu started, paused, and then pointed to Dhyana with a smile. "I have company. You should join us."

Judging by the mood in the tent, no one else thought that was a good idea. Takeo's face was so stern, it could have been made of marble.

"I mean, really, we're having a fascinating conversation," Nobu continued, now sweating as badly as Ping. "You know, I've never talked with commoners much and your mother has just been relating all the troubles she went through in life. Did you know how hard peasant life is? And trying to raise a child at the same time? It's crazy, Takeo, I mean, you have to hear it. Did you know she went a week without food, giving everything she had to you instead, just to keep up your strength? I mean, the most basic thing here, food, was hard for her to find. Can you imagine? You should hear the emotion when she tells the story, it's really something. I think that's what love really is, you know? I think, anyway. I've been trying to imagine that sort of thing, that need or desire, but it's just hard to care, you know, about, well, anything. I don't think anyone would do something like that for me. I'm not exactly spilling any secret here. I mean, let's be honest, I'm a bit of a burden, aren't I? I don't know why you want me to go out there and talk to the soldiers anyway. It's not like they'll care. It's not like anyone would care."

Nobu's speech, which had started so strongly, decayed into mumbles by the end, none of which Takeo heard over the anger pulsing through his veins. Nobu sighed and seemed about to continue when Takeo cut in.

"My lord, if you're so interested in peasant life, then why not talk to one of your many servants? Who knows? Perhaps they'll have better, more reliable stories."

Nobu mumbled something unintelligible, and his eyes started to turn red.

Damn it, he's going to cry again.

"My lord, visiting the soldiers isn't about you; it's about them."

"You know, I am your prince," Nobu muttered, voice shaking. "I could just order you to sit down."

Takeo remained standing, gaze unflinching.

Nobu sighed again.

"Fine," the lord whimpered, standing and brushing one eye with the cuff of his wrist, "I'll go visit the soldiers."

Takeo stepped out of the way, waiting until the lord had left before casting his gaze on those onlookers who still hung around. Most left with prince, including his guards, servants, and oni. Some stayed, and to those, one glance let them know they were unwanted. The place cleared out within moments, minus Mako, Ping, and of course, Dhyana. The old woman still hadn't turned in Takeo's direction.

"Do you enjoy spreading rumors about me?" Takeo asked.

"Do you enjoy calling your mother a liar?" she replied.

Takeo startled at the venom in that response. He hadn't expected it, and his blood rose higher. He marched over and sat in Nobu's former spot, forcing her to meet his gaze. Ping and Mako drew back.

"I don't enjoy it, but I have yet to hear evidence to the contrary," Takeo said.

"Ah, so I'm guilty until proven innocent," Dhyana said, nodding. "Did you know that mothers will often talk about how selfish children are? I always said I wish I'd gotten the chance to find out. For the first time in my life, I'm not so sure anymore."

"What do you mean? Is that comment supposed to draw out my sympathy?"

"No, I suppose not. I guess I was just thinking out loud. I don't know what you want from me. You don't want to talk to me, yet you don't want me to talk to others. I'm not sure what to do here, or even why I'm here at all. This isn't what I expected."

Dhyana's gaze dropped. She looked at the floor, then the sides of the tent, at her knees, then at Takeo's hands. It wasn't his gaze she was avoiding because there was no fear in those eyes, just regret. Takeo knew that for certain. He was quite familiar with regret.

Takeo wanted to remain angry. He had walked over here angrily, burst into the tent angrily, and reprimanded Nobu angrily. His pulse still beat with fury, but its strength was fading. Dhyana was not proving a worthy object of ire for some reason.

"And what did you expect?" Takeo asked.

"Well, I was hoping this time would go better than the last, honestly," she said.

"Last time what? You're drawing this out on purpose. Don't play me for a fool. What is it?"

Dhyana pursed her lips and rubbed just below her ear. Her gaze continued to drift everywhere but in Takeo's direction, despite his piercing stare.

"I hear you're leading the ladder charge tomorrow," she said. "That's dangerous work. I know what you're going to say, that you've been in them before—I've heard the tales—but a gambler's luck is not built on past success. I've already mourned you once. I'm terrified to do it again."

"Yes, so you've told me. My brother stole me away, and you let it happen."

"No, not that. I didn't mourn then, not in the true sense. I knew there was a chance you were still alive. I had hope. I meant the time when Lord Ichiro claimed you'd died."

Takeo blinked. He'd forgotten about that. When Ichiro had sold Takeo into slavery in Savara, the late lord had lied to his subjects that Takeo had died. The reason he'd done this was not known, and the lord had taken the secret with him to his grave.

"You see, after I lost you the first time," Dhyana continued, "I waited and hoped for your return. I had no idea where Okamoto took you and no means to follow. I asked about you, though, every time I visited the Katsu fortress. I think that may have been how Botan found me, from my past inquiries about you. I thought I was being careful then, but I suppose we can only hide so much, hm?

"Then after so many years, you did return. Rumors wormed their way to my village, and I was overcome with joy. You were alive! And you were here! I rushed to the city as often as I could in the hopes of finding you again. I didn't announce myself; I couldn't. And honestly, I was afraid to. You were still a child then, and I didn't know how you'd react to me. Would you reject me? Would you shun me? Not that I cared, but I wanted to see you in person first. I waited this long, what was just a little longer?

"Through part luck, part persistence, I arrived at the same time you and your brother returned from a battle. You were just two in a sea of soldiers, and the streets were packed as all the villagers came out to cheer Lord Ichiro's return. I searched and searched until I found you, walking with your head hung, standing in Okamoto's shadow. I hadn't seen you in so long, but I knew it was you, and my heart soared. I pushed my way through the crowd, yelling for you, but you must have been deep in thought because you didn't hear me. Your brother did.

"I'd heard he'd gotten married recently. Prior to this, I dared hope that age had softened that boy who came to my hut so long ago. However, that day proved otherwise. He heard my voice and found me in the crowd, and the gaze he put on me would have frozen a yuki-onna. He put one hand on his sword, lightly, and my heart stopped. I knew nothing had changed.

"What could I do? Defy him and rush out? What would happen if I told you the truth right then and there? Would you believe me? Even if you had, would that have changed anything when Okamoto drew his sword? You know Juatwa. You know there is no protection for a woman like me. Old, forgotten, poor, abandoned. As one of

99

Ichiro's trusted samurai, Okamoto would need no justification for my death. To be a peasant is to be powerless. Even if I could convince you, all I'd do is scar you for life as you watched your brother cut your mother down. I couldn't do that, not to either of us. It took some time, but I eventually found solace in knowing that you were okay. Better than okay, you were a trusted servant of the shogun. You didn't need me. You were probably better, even, without me. I knew when the winter months came you would not starve. I knew you would have shelter from the rains whenever you asked. Sure, you were a soldier, exactly what I didn't want for you, but at least you had your health and your needs were provided for. You weren't alone either. You had your brother. I did my best to take comfort in that.

"Then Okamoto died, and you followed him across the sea before I could find you again. That would be my greatest regret because it wasn't long before news arrived that you'd died, too. Lord Ichiro returned without you, and I cannot explain in words the pain that brought."

Dhyana paused. Her voice had grown shaky, and she had to steady herself with deep breaths. Her eyes moistened, but she did not cry.

"I mourned you, Takeo. You didn't know, you didn't see, but you were mourned when you died. I cried for so long, so often, all my regrets and sorrow falling away with no hope left to shore them up. I thought about suicide. What was left for me here, now that you were gone? That was everything I'd lived for, to see you be happy and healthy.

"Luckily, before I worked up the courage to see my death through, a miracle occurred. You came back! I couldn't believe it. Your death had been a rumor! The joy that I experienced, you can only imagine. I still worried for you, though. You were branded a ronin, and I feared the trouble that would cause you. I resolved to find you again, but before I could figure out where to start, you disappeared again. Rumors abounded that you'd left Juatwa forever, sold off as a slave. I didn't know what to think, or even where to look. I could only trust that you would return, and so you have.

"I was going to come and find you one day, Takeo, I was. I didn't know how or where; I don't travel so easily anymore, and it takes time for news to reach me. I was still working out how you were tied to the Hanu and if and when I could find you there. I had no idea that you would come to me. I never dreamed, not in my wildest imagination, that you would find me first.

"But you did, Takeo. Sure, it was Botan's doing, but you did! I don't care if he's your enemy; I am nothing but thankful. Everything else is trivial to me because I'm looking at you and speaking to you, and it's all I ever wanted. This, and for you to know that you were loved—that you are loved. And it breaks my heart because the other thing I never imagined is that you would be afraid of that."

Dhyana took another steadying breath and looked to Takeo's hands. He had them stretched out and resting on his legs in front of him, and her gaze fixated there long enough for Takeo to take note.

She reached out a hand for his. He pulled back just a hair out of reflex, and she paused. A moment crept by in utter silence, and she tried again. This time he didn't pull away as her hand came to rest on one of his. She lifted her eyes to stare into his.

"The last time I was this honest, you left without saying a word," she whispered. "I'm not going to tell you what to do. You're a man now, and you got here without any help from me, despite all my wishes to the contrary. All I ask is that you consider that you might die tomorrow, something I'm thinking about right now. I know you don't know me, but all I'm asking is that you survive tomorrow and give me a chance."

Dhyana's gaze did not fade, and this time it was Takeo who looked away first. His attention fell to her hand—his mother's hand—placed so gently atop his. The warmth of her blood could be felt through the thin yet leathery skin, worn by time and peasantry. Age made the veins stark, and her fingers bony, but they still had their strength.

Takeo wasn't thinking. He knew it, in a distant sort of way. His mind was too well practiced in shutting down emotional upheaval for Dhyana's words to penetrate his heart, yet that could only mean one thing: they almost had. It was that realization that struck him, that he could not respond because his brain refused to work. Without help from this logical machine, he had only his feelings to go off of, and that meant doing what felt right.

101

Slowly, achingly, Takeo rotated his hand beneath Dhyana's, then one by one wrapped his fingers around hers. He squeezed, and she squeezed back. He didn't say anything; his mouth was so dry he didn't want to. Yet also, somewhere amidst all this, warmth spread over him that he hadn't felt in ages. In a way it was terrifying, but that was okay.

Maybe, just maybe he didn't have to face it alone anymore.

Chapter 11

They didn't speak. Takeo wasn't ready for that, but he had listened, and she knew it. He held his mother's hand for some time before leaving. She didn't ask him to stay, and Mako didn't follow him out. His ears rung as he went for an aimless walk about the camp.

His attempts to stifle thought only lasted five minutes.

He wondered what life would have been like as a son to a mother in a village. He'd lived in a village once and seen what other children went through with their parents, but that didn't mean he experienced it. He also wondered why Okamoto had robbed him of that. Next, he thought about a future, if brief, where he had a mother he could turn to in times of need. He didn't even know what he would go to her for, if anything at all, as he'd never had a source of comfort like this before. Mako didn't count. He was her source, and he liked it that way. He'd felt needed because she needed him, just like she had needed Okamoto to fight the terrors that plagued her, however imaginary they were.

Dhyana needed him, too, she claimed, but in a different way, one he didn't understand. Perhaps it was because he didn't want to understand, not yet.

Not while a battle loomed.

Takeo didn't sleep well that night. He tried, for he knew sleep was important to every warrior, but he failed. He woke early and restless. Fortunately, he wasn't alone.

Not many could sleep the night before a battle, especially not when that battle would be a ladder assault. Takeo stepped out from his tent to find more than a few samurai standing outside their own, sharpening swords, polishing armor, cooking, or anything else that might distract them. Nicholas was out, too, which Takeo thought telling until he noticed the ceramic bottle in the man's hand. The viking gave the ronin a single nod before continuing his efforts to get rotten drunk.

The assault wasn't to start until midday. Since the sun rose from behind the fortress, it was best to wait so as not to blind the attackers. It wasn't like they were going to catch the Katsu off-guard anyway.

Takeo took his time eating breakfast. Takeo had a cook assigned to him that could prepare any meal he desired, but Takeo wanted nothing but the standard infantry allotment of rice and meat. He needed routine to set his mind straight. He didn't need to be a general today. The plan was a simple one, to scale the walls and slaughter everyone inside. Today he needed to be a samurai, and a good one.

Yoshida made his rounds, encouraging soldiers to fight the good fight, stopping by Takeo's tent to wish the ronin luck. Takeo didn't respond much, and the old lord took the hint and left. Kuniko was even more perceptive and avoided Takeo altogether, issuing orders to get the ladders in place and distribute supplies all on her own.

As midday approached, Takeo dressed for war. He put on his laminar armor, donned a general's helm, and sharpened his sword to a razor's edge. When he left his tent again, he found Ping waiting on the other side, equally equipped and standing rigid.

"My lord," Ping said and bowed.

Takeo looked him up and down.

"You're dressed rather fine for guard duty. Why are you alone? Where is she?"

"My lord," Ping said. "I have some of my finest warriors watching her."

"Your finest? I don't recall that being my orders. If you're here to request joining the battle again, I swear I will have great difficulty suppressing the urge to kill you. I have no use for soldiers that don't obey."

Ping swallowed and quivered in place. It was apparent he contemplated abandoning this plan, yet he stayed rooted. As the long moment drew out, Takeo realized sense would not prevail.

"My lord, I demand the right to be at your side for this battle."

Takeo cocked an eyebrow.

"I'm sorry, what did you say? Demand? I take my statement back. I'll have no issues putting you into the ground."

Ping stepped away and met Takeo's gaze. Takeo thought the boy was about to run, but instead Ping planted his feet and drew his sword. The sound of metal clearing a sheath brought attention from all around, and those guards posted outside Takeo's tent suddenly took rapt interest in the conversation. They stood and reached for their own swords, but a single wave from Takeo stayed their hands.

"I, I," Ping stuttered, sweating and gritting his teeth. "I'd like to see you try."

The guards stayed on edge, forming a thin circle about the pair. Takeo kept his hand low and out, signaling his wish to handle this had not changed. Takeo then placed his other hand on his sword and pulled it free, making sure to draw out the scraping of metal so that it rung in the air. Ping's eyes were wide, but they did not lessen in their determination.

Takeo wasn't about to admit, but he was impressed. It'd been sometime since anyone had the courage to stand toe-to-toe with him since Gavin had left.

"By what right do you challenge me? Did she put you up to this?"

"No, well, yes. Um, sort of, but I'm here for me, on my accord."

"As things are now, you stand guilty of insubordination. Worse, you've chosen to do this here, in the open, where I'll have to make an example out of you. I hope for your sake you have a good explanation for this insanity, or at least a good apology. Make it quick. I have more blood than yours to spill this day."

Ping swallowed again and faltered in his stance. Takeo dared hope the boy's sanity had returned to him.

"That is a chance I'm willing to take," Ping said. "I see now why you've always delegated guard duty to me, never granting me the opportunity to prove myself in battle, like you do with Kuniko. You respect my skill with the blade, but you've never seen me stand to adversity. Ever since you beat me that first day we met, I've buckled to your tiniest threat. You don't think I have what it takes to put my life on the line. You'll never give me the chance until I prove it to you. Well, here I am. Give me that chance, my lord. You say my life is forfeit now? What do you have to lose, then, by letting me join the fray?"

"Well, a battle for one. You're thinking too deeply about this. I honored you with a direct order and you've replied with disobedience. That's all I see."

105

"Is it disobedience? Or is it initiative? All I'm asking for is the opportunity to prove myself. I think I speak for everyone here when I say it isn't your orders that give me purpose, my lord, but your existence. Fighting for you, with you, is like nothing I've felt before. Drawing a blade beside you feels like I'm living a legend of old, fulfilling a purpose greater than myself, and striving against the impossible. No daimyo can compare to you and your vision. I saw clearly what you told us in the ruined fortress, about how the royals fight for money and power, using us like pieces on a board to enhance their status. You though? You don't fight for any of that. You don't care about money, or power, or even glory. You fight for a vision—a dream that the world can be a better place if only bent to a purpose. That's not just something to live for, my lord; that's something to die for. I'll oppose anyone for the right to fight alongside you, even yourself.

"So, condemn me if you wish. I may be terrified of you, but I'd rather die than be left behind."

Admittedly, Takeo hadn't been prepared for a speech, or a speech of that caliber. He was well aware his reputation was growing and that soldiers obeyed and respected him in a way they never had before, but he hadn't spent time dwelling on why. He'd just assumed it was because they liked to win. It had never occurred to him that some of those soldiers were doing more than their required duty. According to Ping, some out there shared Takeo's vision of a united world.

Takeo had been most unprepared for that.

"Did you get this idea from Kuniko?" Takeo asked.

"My lord?"

Takeo sheathed his sword.

"Nevermind," he said. "I suppose you're right about one thing. If you're to die, I might as well make good use of it. I'll let the enemy oversee your execution."

Ping's mouth fell open, and he beamed.

"My lord, yes sir!" he cried out and sheathed his own sword before bowing low.

"Stand up," Takeo demanded. "We'll be late to the fight at this rate. As for all you watching, don't get any ideas. Your comrade in arms here just burnt through all the patience I had for the year."

"Sir!" they shouted, and then followed the ronin out into the camp.

Takeo led them through the mostly deserted tents and out onto the battlefield, where the fields of grass were being trampled under the sweaty, armored heels of soldiers, samurai, akki, and oni. In the front and alongside the rows of soldiers lay ladders, staggered to encircle the Katsu fortress. The Hanu ranks would start scattered, better to avoid projectiles launched from the Katsu walls, and then converge as they got closer for the killing blow.

Upon Takeo's appearance, roars of enthusiasm rang out—or nervousness, depending on one's version of reality.

Not a komainu was in sight, but Takeo made certain every akki was present and pushed into the front rows. The oni had been ordered there, too, but only about half felt the urge to obey. The others hung at various places through the army, completely ignoring the orderly staging of troops. It was the best Takeo could hope for. Many souls would be taken this day, and he'd done his best to make sure that the humans wouldn't bear the brunt of it.

Takeo linked up with Kuniko, donned his helmet, and nodded. There was no need to delay any further.

Kuniko sounded the horn.

The human portion of the army roared, invigorating themselves and the mentally unstable akki before them. The ladders were hoisted in the air and the humans took off at a charge, forcing the akki to join in the stampede or be run down. As Takeo hoped, the creatures yielded to the insanity with ease, and the human roars were quickly heightened by sharp squeals and screeches. The ordered lines of the Hanu soldiers were preceded by the scampering red bodies of the akki as the creatures broke what little ranks had been forced upon them and made a mad dash for the Katsu fortress.

The enemy responded swiftly.

The moment those charging lines came into range, catapults atop the Katsu walls flung cliff-side boulders into the air. Their arcs were beautifully silent against the backdrop of Hanu roars that thundered over the valley, one flying so high that it blotted out the sun from Takeo's view before it came crashing down with the others into the akki ranks.

The ground trembled with their landing, and the boulders struck with such force that the soil could not contain the impact, and they rolled, crushing and destroying all in their path. Akki blood, screams, and bodies filled the air, and more than a few were jolted into raw states of fear, some turning back to flee until the rest of the Hanu ranks caught up with them.

Unbeknownst to the akki and oni, and on Takeo's orders, those creatures caught fleeing were skewered, and a second round of akki screams filled the air.

The akki fled toward the fortress, a good half of them propelled by fear rather than bloodlust. This was good, Takeo thought, for the worst was yet to come.

While the catapults were being reloaded, the Hanu ranks continued their charge, driving the akki before them into bow range. The Katsu forces let loose their arrows, again aimed at the akki ranks, and Takeo knew it was no accident. Just as Takeo aimed to bend the akki to the Hanu purpose, Botan aimed to the send the akki scattering. It would have worked, certainly, had Takeo not been so ruthless in his orders. As the akki ranks were decimated by arrows, those that paused were cut down by the Hanu who caught up to them.

The akki screams never ended, and they fled on towards the fortress walls.

Arrows streamed out again, this time pelting human and akki alike. A man beside Takeo took an arrow to the arm, another up ahead to her leg, the latter crashing down as she stumbled at a full sprint. The line shifted seamlessly, not at all troubled by her loss. The section of the ladder she'd carried kept on, unhindered and propelled by the insanity of war. All around, the Hanu ranks began to close in together as they neared the walls.

Over the roars and battle cries, Takeo heard the ropes of the catapults let loose, and another round of boulders filled the air.

"Right!" Takeo shouted. "Right!"

He pushed against his section of the ladder—which bowed all too much for his liking—shoving his entire line right two full paces and none-too-soon. A boulder landed just where they'd been and rolled on with deadly force, flattening dirt and grass instead of dozens of soldiers. A hail of arrows quickly followed.

Another ladder carrier in Takeo's crew was hit, and a shaft struck wood less than a hair from Takeo's hand. Adrenaline spiked through Takeo's veins at the proximity. His legs were on fire because the ladder was heavy and their pace was maddening, but he pushed harder still, for every moment spent running toward the wall was one more free shot the Katsu got to take.

The akki reached the Katsu walls first, or rather the moat that surrounded the place. Some were so terrified they dove into the water, only to be swept away in the ocean waves. Their screams died out as seawater filled their lungs, making others pause just long enough for the Hanus to reach them.

Those carrying the ladder in the front slammed their ends down into the dirt just before the stream, and those in back pushed and heaved, combining momentum and muscle to fling the ladders up on a wide arc to slam against the Katsu walls. The ground surrounding the fortress was thick now with bodies, red from either armor, skin, or blood, while arrows and rocks rained down as fast as the defenders could loose them. Screams were perpetual now, and Takeo's ears perked at every nearby whistle as yet another shaft came dangerously close to ending his life. He waited until the ladder swung up and hit the Katsu walls before pointing his sword at the nearest akki.

"You," he commanded. "Up!"

"Ack!" it shouted back. "You trick us! No!"

It went to say something else, but Takeo slammed his blade into its stomach. The creature died with shock on its face. He ripped his sword free and pointed the wet blade at the next closest, unfortunate akki.

"Up!" he yelled.

It squealed and obeyed, grabbing the rungs and flying up them as fast as its long limbs would allow.

"Up," Takeo repeated, yelling at all the creatures. "Up! I won't give you the chance to retreat. Up the ladder, now!"

All around, similar orders were being carried out in equally brutish fashion. Little red bodies scampered into the air escaping one enemy for another, and the ladders began to sag under the weight. The wood bent at the joints, creating a slight crescent moon that bent over the moat.

Takeo risked a glance up but then ducked as a storm of arrows hailed down on them. Human screams mixed with those of the akki, and Takeo cried out as a shaft buried into the fleshy part of his upper shoulder.

"My lord!" Kuniko shouted, reaching for it.

"Leave it," Takeo commanded over the roar. "It's not mortal. Rip it out now, and it will only bleed."

Pain arched up and down Takeo's right side, from fingertips to brain, but he was too well practiced to let it do anything other than feed his adrenaline. As another akki went up, Takeo grabbed the ladder and started to follow. Ping followed right behind. Off to their right somewhere in the distance, the sounds of a ladder snapping and crumbling echoed out. Either it had broken under excess weight or had been shattered by Katsu defenses. Takeo hoped it was the latter.

Takeo's ladder groaned under his added weight, the knots of rope creaking loudly over the battlefield. Takeo's heart skipped for the first time as the ladder dipped, and Takeo found himself climbing too much along the horizontal axis for his liking. He looked up just as another akki scream came from above, and a little red body with lanky limbs tumbled out of the sky, bouncing against another creature on the ladder and sending that one to the ground, too. One scaly mass hit Takeo, and he might have been knocked loose had Ping not grabbed hold of him from below. Takeo steadied himself, swallowed the searing agony rushing through his shoulder, and pushed against the akki above him.

"Climb!" he bellowed. "I said climb, or I'll ram you through!"

Takeo couldn't see the top of the ladder. That was half the reason a ladder assault ever worked. Those below couldn't see their fellows dying in droves as they tried over and over to secure a spot atop the walls. The screams could still be heard, though, along with the steady rain of corpses toppling down and splashing into the moat. Takeo heard another ladder shatter and he swore.

Takeo climbed up another body length only for his own latter to let loose a groan and sag a step further. The wood strained in his grasp, and he glanced down to see Ping had been joined from behind by several others.

"Thin out!" he yelled, but he was up too high, and the clamor was too loud for him to be heard. "Ping! Tell them to thin out! They'll snap the ladder. Back, you bastards!"

An arrow zipped by Takeo's ear, taking a few strands of hair, and then impaled some unfortunate soul through the throat. A child-sized boulder followed quickly after, grazing the ladder on its swift and terrible trajectory into the waters below.

"Up!" Takeo yelled, and he heard another ladder snap, followed by a dozen akki and human screams.

He caught sight of another ladder breaking, just a short way to his left. Bodies tumbled through the air, landing either in the water or on their fellows. He scanned the air for the offending boulder, but he found none. The ladder had broken on its own. Fear pulsed through his body.

"Hurry!" Takeo yelled and stuck the akki above him with the tip of his blade.

The akki screamed and scampered around to the other end of the ladder, facing Takeo but also protecting itself. Its long nose bumped against the rungs.

The catapults loosed again, having been adjusted to lob their loads a short distance over the moat. The boulders wouldn't have any momentum to roll, but they did their job just as well. With the Hanu packed so tightly beneath the walls, they could not miss. Screams merely preceded their impact as the boulders quickly crushed anyone below them.

Another akki tumbled down Takeo's ladder, bouncing against its comrades. Takeo clambered up the rungs, holding his sword in his arrow-struck arm and climbing with his good hand. The ladder groaned and shuddered so hard his foot missed, and he bounced against the wood. The near fall sent a wave of vertigo ripping through him because he was nearing the top and the walls were close. The sounds of the battle could be heard above, a twisted combination of akki screams and cries mixed with human grunts and cheers.

"I said to thin out!" Takeo roared and looked down.

He paled as his eyes took in the sight of the ladder half as stocked as he would have liked. His army had indeed thinned out along the ladder, spread out so much that it would impede the assault, yet still

111

the ladder was buckling under the weight. The knots strained and frayed, the entire contraption bending toward the river as if the ocean waves beckoned for it. Meanwhile the soldiers on the ground did their best to take cover from the torrent of projectiles raining down on them. They were trying to climb the ladder to join the assault as much as to get out of danger.

To his right and left, other ladders were bending just as badly. He risked a glance up, but he had no way of knowing if the akki had gained any purchase on the wall—and he wouldn't know either, not until he was at the top. His moment's pause almost cost him dearly as a nearby archer took direct aim and let loose. Takeo pulled in close to the ladder at the last second, and the arrow ricocheted off the back of his armor.

Takeo pushed up, trying to urge the akki on before the archer strung another arrow, but the ladder groaned in his grip again as yet another body joined the line. Takeo heard a violent snap and cringed, but the screams that followed came to his right and he knew it was a different ladder that broke. His relief was short lived, however, as a shadow fell over him.

He looked up just in time to see a boulder get lobbed over the side of the walls, land on the akki above him, and bash through the rungs.

The ladder snapped apart in his hands.

Chapter 12

The akki that took the brunt of the boulder's fall spiraled into the air after splattering those below with blood. Takeo followed shortly as the ladder broke at eye level, and gravity hurled the contraption forward. Takeo released the ladder on instinct, but not before he was infected with enough momentum to slam into the Katsu walls face first, dazing him as his spine folded against the unforgiving stone.

The ladder fared much worse.

It bounced against the wall for an instant before the sudden shift in weight shattered what little resilience the wood and knots had left. Takeo went into a free fall, his blurred vision returning to clarity only to find the world spinning about him, cycling between falling bodies and ladder bits. His trajectory sent him crashing into the wall again, doubling his whirling speed and forcing a howl from his throat before he slammed into the moat.

Saltwater filled his mouth and lungs. The spinning world didn't stop in its intensity as the swift tides took over, and Takeo flailed about for air before he even knew which direction was up. His hand broke free for a brief moment before a hunk of ladder crashed down on him, forcing out what little air he had left. More saltwater poured into him, and his insides burned to the point that it was all he could do not to retch. He kicked the ladder off and started for the surface again, breaking free and taking one gasp of air before being thrust under by a tide. He reached for the surface again when someone grabbed his wrist and yanked.

Ping, half submerged himself, hauled Takeo onto the shore. The ronin's body struck dirt with a wet slap, and he spit saltwater out into the grass. Ping followed a moment later and tossed himself over his lord. Arrows pelted down around them, one slamming into Ping's leg and another into his back. The man yelped but otherwise kept breathing by some form of a miracle.

"My lord!" came a shout, and Takeo looked up to see Kuniko kneeling over him. "My lord, they've spotted you. They're taking aim!"

"Stay under me, my lord," Ping said, straining from arrow wounds. "I'll protect you."

"How many?" Takeo croaked out, throat dry from the salt.

"Archers? I'm not sure."

"Ladders," he said. "How many ladders do we have left?"

"Only two remain, I think," Kuniko replied.

"Get off me," Takeo shouted. "We need to get out of here."

"My lord?"

"Sound the damned retreat!"

Takeo scampered out from beneath Ping, an arrow grazing his cheek as he did so. Kuniko grabbed the horn about her neck and gave it two mighty blows, her call ending just as the catapults released another volley, momentarily followed by another bout of screams.

The wound in Takeo's shoulder burned as the mix of saltwater and air churned against the wood, blood, and muscle. He let the pain lend him strength as he joined his army in the mad dash away from the fortress. Their retreat was hounded by enemy cheers, arrows, and boulders, and the Hanu army left behind far more than its dead.

Takeo didn't look back until they'd gotten clear of bow range, and even then, he only paused to survey the carnage.

The entire field around the fortress was littered in red: Hanu soldiers in their red armor either lying dead or running away, a flood of akki scampering off in the distance to the north, oni trudging up the rear, blood everywhere and on everyone. The fortress walls looked like borders to a mass grave, its walls untouched by the death below. Shattered ladder bits perforated the place, mixing with the dead or dying with no concern for the damage they'd caused. Takeo scanned the crowd until he found Nicholas—easily distinguishable with his height and wild hair—making his own retreat among the soldiers.

"My lord, we need to get you back to camp. You're injured," Kuniko begged.

"We lost," Takeo replied. "I need to see it with my own eyes."

One of the oni made a direct charge for the ronin, and it took Takeo a moment to see past all the arrows that pin-cushioned the creature to realize it was Borota. The oni's eyes were ablaze and its mouth twisted into a snarl.

114

"That was foolish, you human," it said, black blood oozing along red skin. "Using the akki like that. Tokhta is going to be furious."

"Really? And here I thought I was using them properly. I didn't know the oni valued akki lives so much."

"It's their obedience we need. They'll rebel again for sure after what you did. Look, they're already scampering off."

"I gave you a chance to have input when I invited Tokhta to join my battle planning. It's not my fault he didn't show."

Borota scoffed and snorted.

"Make all the excuses you want," it said. "The fact is you gambled and lost. The next hand you play will be much weaker."

Takeo knew that was true, but his pride dared not let him admit it to a creature such as this. As the oni glared at him, he glared right back until the thunder of an approaching komainu horde broke their gaze. It was Yoshida and his guards who had sat the battle out. Takeo couldn't blame him, though. Ladder assaults were no place for old men.

Borota trudged off before the daimyo joined them.

Yoshida charged right up to Takeo, looking far more concerned than angry, and Takeo felt his first measure of relief for a brief second. He wasn't in the mood for another round of scolding.

"What in the world happened?" Yoshida demanded. "I saw the ladders break in moments."

"I don't know," Takeo replied. "I thought we tested them enough. It's like the knots frayed loose or something. They all bent like twigs."

"You're injured."

"Barely. I've had worse. Ping's the one you should be surprised about."

Takeo jerked a finger at the man, and sure enough, Yoshida balked when he saw an arrow shaft protruding from that one's back.

Ping grinned.

"The akki are fleeing," Yoshida explained, unnecessarily. "They reached the camp first, but then didn't stop. They're sprinting off in all directions, though the majority are heading north. Did Borota say anything?"

"He said they're going to rebel. We've lost them—I lost them."

Yoshida swore. Kuniko straightened.

115

"We'll hunt them down, my lord," she said. "Desertion will not be tolerated, whether human or akki."

"We haven't the time," Takeo answered. "Our forces were drastically short before this assault, now we're worse off than before. I can only imagine the casualties. Botan will celebrate tonight, for sure. We didn't so much as scratch him."

The field had gone quiet on the Hanu side. The Katsu, however, had stopped lobbing rocks and arrows to cheer. Takeo could make out the walls stocked full of onlookers, whooping and throwing fists into the air in triumph. Their roars intensified for one brief second, and the crowds turned toward the gate and drew back. Three loan figures strode onto the ramparts. One was dressed as a normal samurai, but the other wore stunningly blue colors, as befit a royal of the highest status, and he stood tall above the others. The third had blonde hair, and the other two forced that one to his knees.

The Katsu cheers intensified.

"No," Takeo whispered, eyes widening and jaw going slack. "Damn it, no."

"By Valhalla," Nicholas shouted, just a short distance away. "Gavin!"

Botan drew a sword—surely Takeo's sword, though one couldn't be sure at this distance—and made sure to wave it so the steel glinted in the sunlight. Then he set it to the side of Gavin's head and began to saw away.

Takeo couldn't hear the screams, not over the Katsu army cheering and howling for blood, but he imagined them all the same. He could make out how the other soldier struggled to keep Gavin still as Botan hacked at the poor knight, cutting off what Takeo assumed to be an ear, and then held it up for all to see. The Katsu roars were maddening, and Botan held the grisly trophy aloft for several moments before flinging it carelessly over the walls.

Takeo's heart pounded in his chest.

"Another ladder assault, then?" Yoshida said, his tone implying he knew the answer.

Takeo shook his head.

"Our morale is broken, our forces reduced, and our fodder run off," Takeo said, watching as they drug Gavin off back into the bowels of the fortress. "Siege engines are all we have left. There isn't enough material for towers, or the time to build trebuchets. We'll never get a battering ram up to that gate over the moat. We'll have to build catapults, mobile ones, and push them onto the field at the time of combat. Whether we can destroy their walls or equipment before they destroy ours will be the flip of a coin, but it's all we have left. We haven't the time for anything else."

"Sounds a tad hopeless," Yoshida replied. "Don't you think?"

Takeo reach up and grabbed the arrow shaft protruding from his shoulder. He took one quick breath and then ripped it free, blood spurting out along with little bits of wood.

"I don't have hope," he said. "Just reality. Get it done."

* * *

If Takeo had written a list of all possible options for putting Botan's head on a platter, building siege engines would have resided on the bottom of that list, hastily written as an afterthought with a question mark at the end. It wasn't that siege engines were terrible ideas as a rule. Quite the contrary, they could be indispensable tools in the right situation. The problem—or rather problems—lay in the fact that there was nothing right about this situation at all.

Time, or rather the lack thereof, wasn't the only factor at play. Lengthy periods of construction brought on logistical issues, morale issues, and engineering issues, to name a few. On top of this all, the Katsu fortress' design was such that siege engines weren't truly effective anyway. Even if the Hanu army could bring one of the Katsu walls crumbling down, how would they storm the breach across the moat? Bring in a hastily erected bridge that could be easily destroyed by catapults? Try to damn up the moat while under constant assault from the defenders? These were all problems that needed to be addressed, and yet there were many more issues to conquer. After all, if the army thought they were hard pressed to build a couple of ladders, they were in real trouble trying to cobble together material for siege works. Teams had to be sent out far and wide to different forests, searching for the tallest trees to cut down and haul back so they could be cut to purpose. This vastly increased the chance of conscripted soldiers sneaking off never to be seen again, which wasn't so unreasonable considering the ladder assault had failed and the army was now on food and water rations. The Hanu hadn't brought many provisions because they weren't supposed to be needed, and not to mention, the extra weight would have just slowed them down. Botan was supposed to be defeated by now, either at the first battle, in the ladder assault, or through treachery by bribing someone on the Katsu side to lower the gate.

That hadn't worked out, though, thanks in no small part to Takeo himself. Botan's extra measures guarding the gatehouse had paid off, and the one man they'd found willing to sell his shogun out had been caught and strung up on the ramparts.

So, catapults it was, then, and that was a poor idea.

Takeo encountered all the problems Botan had faced some time ago. Time begat chance, and chance begat folly and bad luck. One of Takeo's wood-scouting teams never returned, and the party sent to investigate found the group had been set upon by a roaming komainu pack. Another team lost an entire day's work when they had to abandon their site to a gashadokuro. These problems meant less volunteers to go out beyond the safety of the camp, and less volunteers meant more forced labor, and more forced labor meant more desertions, which wouldn't have been such an issue if the Hanu army wasn't already short on able-bodied soldiers already.

As if that weren't enough, disease wrought havoc upon the camp.

It shouldn't have happened. Takeo had placed the latrines far away to prevent this exact thing, but some people were lazy and either didn't clean themselves right or just decided to relieve themselves upon a rival's tent rather than walk the distance out to the pits. Rivalries started, two men died from stab wounds, Takeo hung three more, and dozens died when the water source was contaminated. Small numbers, really, but for every one that perished, ten more were infected and put out of commission as the disease worked them over, and the Hanu doctors were run ragged trying to keep everyone alive. That meant fewer people to work, and that meant the catapults were delayed, and that meant more chances for things to go wrong. The best Takeo could hope for was that Botan was suffering similarly.

All the while, Gavin's fate weighed heavily upon him.

Every delayed day, every cowardly desertion, every missed opportunity was internalized by Takeo as a personal failure on his

118

part to save his friend. Takeo cursed himself for not having the gall to beat Gavin senseless the day the knight decided to walk off.

What was I thinking? I knew this would happen, and yet I did nothing. What stopped me? Knowing that he'd hate me for it? So what? At least he'd have his body, and his family, and a chance at life. Wasn't that the entire point of sparing Yeira? So that at least one of us—not me, not Emily, not Krunk, not Nicholas, not anyone else—at least one of us would have the chance to be happy? What stayed my hand? What a fool I was. And look who pays the price.

"Poor Gavin," Nicholas would say. "At least I was never mutilated when I was imprisoned, you know? Damn, I hope they're not doing the same to Krunk."

The viking muttered this phrase and others like it often as the weeks went by, unhelpfully and with a strong dose of melancholy. Nicholas moped about the camp like it was his job, complaining far less than Takeo would have liked. Takeo tried to alleviate this by giving him duties, like watching over the catapult construction. However, that just set the two of them further apart, and Nicholas and Takeo fought separate battles against the same enemy. Nicholas took to drink like he usually did, while Takeo tried to take to solitude but could not. He was a general now, and besides, he had help against his demons.

No one would guess by looking at her, but Mako was a lighthouse in the storm that was Takeo's life. As he struck out upon the dark and turbulent waters of the future, it gave him solace to look back to the shores of the past. Mako was everything he couldn't be—passionate, innocent, forgiving—and in a way, she represented the exact person he was trying to save. Warfare and chaos left nothing but casualties, and it was Takeo's purpose to enforce order upon the violence that had taken so much from everyone.

In the future he'd help create, there would be no need for men like his brother, or even like himself.

Mako did more than that, of course. Humble as she was, she did not mind common chores, such as keeping Takeo's tent homey and clean, reminding him to eat when his duties pressed him for time, and waking him when night terrors struck him. Surely many thought they were lovers, but Takeo ignored the gossip. The rumors prevented Mako from being harassed, at least. No one in their right mind wanted to bother the general's mistress.

Mako also became indispensable when illness struck Dhyana. Her infection shouldn't have been a surprise, considering her age and previous lifestyle. Villagers that rarely left home tended to get isolated from the diseases that assailed large populations, leaving them vulnerable when exposed later on.

Dhyana laid up in a tent near Takeo's, and Mako waited on her with the concern of a relative. In the absence of a battle, Ping had retaken his guard duties, now more enthusiastic and also showing equal concern for Dhyana's well-being. Takeo didn't visit, not often at least, though he never stopped Mako from updating him on the old woman's condition. Things didn't sound life-threatening, just a slight fever and tiredness. Word was that Qing had checked on her and then promptly disappeared. Takeo figured that was for the best. He slept better without that elf nearby.

But he did visit his mother eventually.

It took a couple weeks before the catapults were well under construction and the workload wasn't so demanding. He and Mako had their evening tea with her, sitting about like, well, a family.

It made Takeo nervous.

"Oh, it's so good to see you again," Dhyana croaked, taking a drink of her tea.

She was wrapped in a warm blanket and supported by a host of pillows Takeo had scavenged from Lord Nobu's vast supplies. He doubted the prince would notice.

"It's the least I can do," Takeo replied, unable to formulate a better response.

"You've been busy, I hear," she continued.

Takeo glanced at Mako, and the beauty took a long drink of her tea with both hands. He wasn't mad, though. It should have been obvious that information flowed both directions.

"There's a lot of work to be done," Takeo answered. "And I don't trust anyone else to do it. There's too much at stake. Too many lives."

"Including that friend of yours."

She looked at him expectantly, with sunken eyes from lack of sleep and a nose reddened by agitation. Against his instinct, Takeo couldn't help but feel a twinge of guilt at her condition.

"Yes," he said, but stopped as a coughing fit overtook Dhyana. He sipped his tea as she recovered.

"Can I—oh, excuse me—achoo!" Dhyana paused to rub her red nose. "Can I ask what that man is to you?"

Takeo looked to Mako again, but she shook her head.

"I don't know. You've never told me," she said. "I never got to meet him before he left, either. And I'll not ask the viking. He scares me."

"It's just, I can tell what's happening to him bothers you," Dhyana continued. "And he must be important for Lord Botan to torture him so. Every time we've talked, I've told you about myself, but it's you I want to hear about. I want to know my son. Maybe you're not ready to share about yourself just yet, but what about him? Who is this Gavin, a knight from Lucifan? And why did it take his severed hand for us to meet?"

Takeo took another sip of tea.

I'm hesitating to answer. Why? Isn't this what I came here for? I knew we'd talk, that she'd want to talk. Is that such a bad thing? I feel lost here, like I don't know what to do or say. But maybe that's okay.

In the silence, Lord Yoshida's advice came to mind, and Takeo decided if there was anyone's opinion to follow, it would be his. The old man had made it far in life. He must know a thing or two.

"We loved the same woman," Takeo said.

Mako blinked. Dhyana raised an eyebrow.

"From what I know of men, that sort of thing typically divides rather than unites," Dhyana said.

"It did, for a time," Takeo went on. "In fact, I almost killed him the first time we met. But then we both lost her, and I guess that pain was all we had in common."

"I'm getting the sense that shared loss creates a strong bond for you."

As she finished saying this, Dhyana took a sip of her tea and let her gaze drift to Mako. The younger woman didn't meet it.

"I never thought of it that way," Takeo admitted, "but I suppose you're right."

"This may not be the same in your eyes, but you know we share a loss, too, that of your father."

"I, uh, don't believe I'd call that a loss. After all, how can I lose something I never had?"

Dhyana smiled, which gave Takeo pause. He hadn't expected that response.

"It wasn't his decision to be absent from your life," she said.

"Actually, it's the opposite from what I hear, taking that assassination job."

"Weizhe would have cared for you if given the chance. He wasn't afraid of fatherhood. As far as the attack on the Katsu family is concerned, I don't know why he did it, but I assure you there was some measure of good in his heart when he accepted the job."

"You speak as if you knew him well. And here I thought he was just a client of yours."

"You'd be surprised."

"Maybe," Takeo said, then paused.

He'd been about to rattle off his next words without a thought, but then the weight of them hit home. He swallowed down his pride, and the steel cage he'd put around his heart opened just a little.

"Maybe one day you can tell me about him?"

Dhyana stared back, wide-eyed and unblinking.

"Yes," she said. "Maybe one day I will."

And when next Takeo visited, she did.

Chapter 13

"Making a living lying on your back has some advantages, if you're lucky," Dhyana started, fresh tea in one hand, blanket wrapped around her sickly body with the other. "Contrary to the stories, not every man who pays for the company of a woman is a knave harboring violent intentions. Many are just lonely, a bit broken and wanting someone to make them feel whole again, even if it's only for the night. Another large portion of our customers are simple free spirits looking for a good time, incapable of harming anyone intentionally. These people can be enjoyed by us just as much as we are enjoyed by them, and the line between personal and professional can blur. Your father, when I met him, fell into the latter category.

"His name was Weizhe Karaoshi, and he was handsome. That always helps. I remember that he had trouble growing facial hair so shaved himself clean because it wasn't worth the trouble, and he had a command about him that made you feel that no matter what window he fell out of, he'd always land on his feet. He was always broke and in need of money, but that's only because he spent everything he earned, as if he were living on borrowed time from the start. Of course, that didn't stop him from making outrageous claims about his wealth. The first time he saw me, he strode over, wrapped an arm about my waist and proclaimed loudly that he was going to spoil me rotten.

"I suppose in some regards, he did.

"Your father spent his time with lots of women, at first, but over time he took preference to me. He visited me more often, stopped trying to short me on coin, and brought me gifts. I couldn't say why for certain. When we spent time together, he liked to talk about himself, and perhaps that's why he came to me. I liked to listen. Your father might have been from Juatwa, but he had wanderlust in his heart.

"Weizhe told me about the world, and all the things he'd seen. How he'd sparred with kshatriya in the desert sands of Savara and dueled a pirate crew one-by-one for free passage to Lucifan. Those were his favorite stories, by the way. Weizhe was proud of his fighting skills. I don't think he ever had an aim to be the best swordsman in the world, but he did have a desire to fight them all. He loved a challenge, loved to fight, though rarely in anger. He traveled east to west, chasing the sun and dueling any worthy of the art. That's what he called it, art. I think something about sword fighting made him feel alive, even more so than gambling, drinking, or spending time with me. He was addicted to life on the edge, one could say, never more miserable than when living a life of comfort.

"Well, he made it as far as the Forest of Angor, and there he claimed to have charmed a little elf girl who taught him techniques he'd never known existed. He said after those lessons, he'd yet to be beaten, and that was the saddest part of all. Like a drunk gaining tolerance to alcohol, your father ever so slowly had to ramp up the danger he faced, just to feel that thread of life pulsing through his veins.

"I can't count the number of times he came to me wounded. I think he liked how I fussed over him, dressed the wound, and asked how it happened, just so he could tell me every detail.

"He liked to end his visits with fruitless promises, like how he'd come back and take me away, either to some village farm where we'd catch kappa or off to one of those wonderful places he visited, like Lucifan. I would entertain him, say how lovely that all sounded, but never held him to it. I knew he didn't mean it. He just said those things because he thought it's what I wanted to hear. Perhaps I was cruel not to correct him. Maybe we women just love to hear men promise to give it all up for us.

"Either way, something strange began to happen. I found myself missing him at night, after he'd gone, and waiting on edge for him to return. When I was with other men, I'd pretend they were him, or otherwise dream about him at night. I thought it was love at the time, but after having had you, Takeo, I'm not sure what it was. Something more than lust, though, and I knew I'd always remember him. That was something to say back then when I saw new faces every day. I even remember when I saw him last.

"He'd grown depressed towards the end. He'd risen quickly in the Katsu ranks, blessed as he was with his sword. It wasn't just the lack of challenge, but the nature of his duty. He couldn't say much to me directly, as a shogun's upper ranks are sworn to secrecy, but he could hint. It seemed that with his new rank, he'd gained a new level of responsibility, and also unique, grim tasks. They were tasks that made a carefree, happy man like your father lose sleep at night. He was drunk more often and didn't smile so easily. His tone grew dark whenever he spoke of the shogun, and he made mention of how he didn't like the way Okamoto took to this new profession so aptly. Your brother joined the samurai ranks young, very young, and it seemed everyone was uncomfortable about that except for the shogun and Okamoto. Weizhe's fleeting promises grew rather specific as time went on, asking me if I'd like to stay in Juatwa, but further north in Nguyen territory. I didn't take this seriously, though, until I got pregnant.

"I won't get into the details, but I knew you were his. I was terrified for you, that you might end up just like Okamoto. I may have loved your father more than most, but not as much as I loved you. So, I ran away, young and naive without giving him the chance to make things right. Sometimes I wonder if he took that assassination job because of me. Perhaps that's how Okamoto knew to find me. Weizhe had found me and it was his plan to escape that night of the assassination and take me and you away to the Nguyen lands. I don't know. All I can tell you is that it sounds like something Weizhe would do, something heroic and courageous, yet also foolish and brash. It was his last challenge, you could say, to kill a shogun, and he met his match.

"If he were here, he'd have two things to say to you. Firstly, that he'd be proud of the warrior you've become. However, secondly, he'd tell you to lighten up."

* * *

Takeo wanted to share this story with some people, but most of them were dead or unavailable. Nicholas didn't fit any of those categories, but Takeo was out of options.

"By Valhalla," Nicholas said, slurring the words as he took another drink. "Your head must be spinning."

"I will say Lord Botan made a good bet, bringing me to her," Takeo replied, taking the bottle from Nicholas to take a gulp for

125

himself. "Were I not a general with responsibilities piling on my shoulders all the time, I might crack under all this uncovered mystery. No wonder my brother sheltered me from it all. He knew none of it would change my position and would only serve to distract me. I can't believe it. My father actually sounds like a man I would have liked. He sounds like . . . he sounds like Gavin."

"See, I'm over here still thinking about your mother. I cannot believe how much like my own mother she is. I mean, it's just crazy thinking about it. Both our moms had these eventful, amazing lives—"

"My mother was a whore," Takeo said.

"Eh, whatever," Nicholas replied. "Maybe not amazing, but at least eventful. Let's agree on that, okay? So, these two women get knocked up and just give it all up. Isn't that insane? For farming of all things. Starvation, boredom, bottom-barrel hierarchy, all to spare us from the wonders of war. Then, despite all their efforts, we both rise up to become the fiercest fighters this world has ever seen. I mean, me at least. Your position is debatable, but you catch my drift. Isn't that something, though? You know, I always blamed my mother for holding me back, like she had a personal vendetta against my dreams. However, now it seems your mother was just the same way, and I don't know. It's just, it makes me question things."

Nicholas took the bottle, downed another swig, and passed it back. Takeo drunk deeply. The way the alcohol numbed his mind tempted him to keep going.

"So, is this what brings you to my humble abode, hm?" the viking asked.

He gestured around at the hastily erected tent that was about two sizes too small for him. The tent looked that way despite being put up weeks ago, nestled on the edge of the field Takeo had chosen as the catapult construction site. In fact, just a few paces away was the first such siege weapon in a long line of nearly completed ones. They were perhaps only a few days out from being tested.

Good thing, too. We've wasted more than a month cobbling the material together for these things. Reports are coming in that the Nguyens are amassing again. I've two weeks, just two weeks to end this siege or we'll have to retreat. Please, please let this work.

126

Takeo was already lining up battle plans. He'd selected which wall they were going to assault and how they were going to cross the stream—by wrecking a ship into the moat and using it as a bridge. He was going to signal Emy soon and tell her to be ready to rescue Gavin and Krunk once the wall was brought down. Takeo had increased the rations and let wine flow throughout the camp, trying to get the soldiers restless and thus eager for combat. The oni had agreed to head the charge if only to end the siege sooner, and it seemed like for once things might just line up.

However, Takeo also knew that Botan had a plan, as well. The lord wasn't just going to sit behind his walls and wait for death to come. He was going to try something, and so Takeo kept a watchful eye.

"Just checking on you and the equipment, Nicholas," Takeo said. "Nothing special. But I guess I have a lot on my mind lately."

Nicholas reached out a hand, and Takeo passed the wine back reluctantly.

"Well what sort of a general visits his subordinates and drinks their provisions, eh? Don't you have access to better stuff, anyway?"

"You got that from my tent, from the provisions assigned to me."

"And what's your damned point? No one asked you anything."

"Just don't get too drunk," Takeo replied, standing and making his way out.

"Yeah, yeah," Nicholas answered, waving his hand. "And where are you off to?"

"To check on our boy-king. The end draws near, and I'll leave nothing to chance."

Nicholas cocked an eyebrow, but Takeo stalked off without giving an explanation. It wasn't common knowledge among the camp because it was boring knowledge, but Lord Nobu had become a bit of a hermit in the last couple of weeks. The prince had shut himself up in one of his tents and hadn't moved for days. As the prince had predicted, few noticed, and Takeo had only discovered it because Yoshida had mentioned it. Not that it was any of Takeo's concern if Nobu went into hibernation, but with a battle drawing near, paranoia seeped in. Anything out of the ordinary needed to be investigated, including any bouts of depression suffered by the army's supposed leader.

127

So off Takeo went, tracking down the prince's tent and the two oni watch guards ever present outside of it. Not that it could be called a tent, though, because this extravagant structure was reinforced with sturdy timbers and richly adorned. Takeo couldn't see how Nobu was suffering in this small mansion.

Tokhta, stopped Takeo with an outstretched hand.

"What business do you have?" the oni asked.

"Let's not do this," Takeo replied. "I have rank now. I don't need an excuse, especially not for creatures like you."

"Our brother has asked not to disturbed," he said, then added, "by anyone."

Takeo's eyes went wide.

"Wait, he's in that gigantic thing alone? Are you insane?"

"Sentries have been posted all around."

"What about below? Or above? Get out of my way."

"We don't take orders from humans. You should know that."

"What, Nobu isn't human?"

The oni laughed and said, "Not for long."

Takeo darted beneath Tokhta's hand, which was easy considering their height difference. The oni snarled and both of the creatures stood up as Takeo bashed the curtains aside, letting moonlight flood into the entryway. A fight would have started if a young, hollow voice didn't crack out from within, straining from disuse.

"It's fine. It's fine. Let him through."

A cough followed, and Takeo glared at the oni. Tokhta snarled but obeyed, sitting back down on the ground alongside the other one. Takeo let the curtains fall back, shutting all into darkness. Well, partial darkness. There was an opening at the top of the tent for ventilation and light, and some of the moon's rays came through. A few moments passed before Takeo could see enough to stumble over to a brazier, fumble around with the flint and steel, and light the contents.

Fire plumed out, though weak against the vast swath of darkness that filled the giant tent. Takeo surveyed the area with a glance and was surprised to find it mostly empty. That wasn't the Hanu style, or at least not what Lady Zhenzhen had instructed. The place should have been stocked to the brim with art, weapons, and other such signs of wealth. Only a single bed remained, shoved up against a corner, swathed in blankets. A motionless lump lay beneath them.

"My lord?" Takeo called out.

The lump shifted.

"Where are your things, my lord?" Takeo pressed, uncertain how to continue.

The mass of blankets rose, then fell with a sigh, revealing Nobu. His face was pale, hair disheveled, and his eyes sunken and red. A moment's glance was all they exchanged before Nobu slipped beneath the sheets again.

"I had them removed," the prince said, voice muffled. "They aren't my things anyway. They're my mother's."

One would have to be deaf not to hear the contempt in those last words, and Takeo sighed his relief. It sounded like this was even more simple than depression—just typical coming-of-age rebellion. Takeo almost smiled. It was good to see Nobu trying to throw his mother's shackles off.

He contemplated leaving right then and there, but that would look suspicious. Takeo was now bound by his manners to at least make some attempt at conversation.

"I'm not sure I see the difference," Takeo said, folding his arms behind his back and taking a stroll about the tent, checking for anything out of the ordinary. "Those things belong to the Hanu family, and thus are yours as much as your mother's."

"What do you want?"

"I came to inform you of our status," Takeo replied. "The catapults are nearly complete. We have time for one more attempt at the Katsu fortress. I wanted to assure you I'm doing all I can to achieve victory, my lord."

A long pause preceded the reply.

"Couldn't that have been in one of those reports you send me?" Nobu asked.

"If I had, would you have read it?"

Nobu grumbled. Takeo shook his head, anger boiling beneath the surface.

"A lot of men are going to die soon, my lord, all to increase your power," Takeo whispered. "Please, try to be worthy of it."

He turned and headed for the exit but stopped when the lump stirred and Nobu rose to the surface once more. Tears streamed down his sullen face. They shared another fleeting glance before Nobu slipped under again.

"I did what you said," Nobu whimpered. "Before the ladder assault, I went out to talk to the troops. They didn't even recognize me. I don't think half of them had ever seen me before. I just fumbled around, muttering some words, and they just stared at the oni the entire time. Fear, just fear, that's all they had in their eyes, and I knew . . . I thought . . . it doesn't matter. None of it matters."

Deep down, Takeo could see this was a problem. Having the Hanu prince wallowing in self-loathing would not help the coming battle, and they'd need every bit of valor to overcome the fight ahead. Yet Takeo had nothing in the way of encouragement to offer, at least not in the traditional sense. Besides, this situation had an advantage. If Nobu was battling inner demons in here, then he'd be kept from interfering with whatever happened out there.

In the end, Takeo decided to fight one battle at a time.

So, he left, letting Nobu's quiet sobs fall on deaf ears. As Takeo pulled aside the curtains, he was surprised to find the two oni standing again, this time faced off against a second foe as equally determined to pass as Takeo had been.

It was Qing.

"About time you came back," the elf snarled, hand on her hip where she kept her throwing stars. "These two things thought to stop me. Can you believe that? Me, of all people."

"They are stubborn, I'll agree," Takeo said.

Tokhta snorted and then plopped back down. The other oni did the same.

"What in the world is going on in there?" Qing asked. "Why won't Nobu let anyone in?"

Takeo cocked an eyebrow and replied, "You haven't heard? I haven't seen you in some time, but you talk as if you left the camp."

"I did. I move faster on my own. I went back to the Hanu keep."

"What? All that way? On your own? Why?"

"Answer my question first. What is wrong with Lady Zhenzhen's heir?"

130

Takeo glanced at the oni, then decided he didn't care if they overheard. He shrugged.

"Some brooding family drama as far as I can tell. The prince is, for a lack of a better word, sad."

"Perhaps you could be less specific," Qing replied, rolling her eyes.

"He's depressed. I don't know how else to explain it. He feels inept, which in his current predicament isn't far from the truth, and he's struggling with it. He'll either come to terms with it or change course; it's inevitable. What do you want me to do? Rub his back and tell him everything will be okay? I answered your question, now you answer mine. Why did you go all the way back to the keep?"

Qing clicked her tongue against her teeth and looked sideways into the darkness. She glanced at the two oni and then nodded away. She left at a brisk pace. Takeo followed.

"Research," Qing said, once they were some ways away.

"We left Tokhta's side for you to say that? Are you sure it wasn't the warmth of Zhenzhen's bed you sought? Perhaps you could be less specific."

"It was just a hunch I had, one you need not concern yourself with yet. I don't want to worry you over nothing. I'll explain once I speak to your viking. Where is he?"

"That's why you sought me out? To ask for directions? What a supreme waste of my time. You could have found that out by stopping and asking any common soldier on your way here, or if you'd have spent even five minutes in this camp over the past few weeks. He's guarding the catapults. Now be gone."

Qing glared.

"I did ask people, you imbecile, and I did go to the catapults. He wasn't there."

"Well I just saw him not too long ago. He probably went to take a piss. Now stop wasting my time."

The two split off after tossing a scowl at one another. Qing, unsurprisingly, couldn't let Takeo have the last word and flung one more insult.

"Choose a better guard next time. Clearly your friend has poor judgment," she taunted. "Only an idiot leaves their weapon behind on guard duty."

131

Takeo stopped dead in his tracks.

"What did you say?" he called out.

"You heard me. Your standards for guard duty are almost as low as my opinion of you. Your dumb sellsword left his maul lying against his tent."

Takeo turned back and bolted.

Chapter 14

Takeo's pace was maddening, reckless even in the darkness. He risked turning an ankle at the slightest misstep, yet he pushed as hard as his legs and lungs would allow. Even Qing, with her elven abilities, was some time in catching up with him.

"What did I say? What happened?" she stammered.

"Do you not know anything about vikings? Nicholas sleeps with that maul and makes love with it on his back. Something's happened to him."

"There was no sign of a struggle, I swear."

Takeo ignored her and pushed harder, dashing through the camp roads. They reached the catapult site within moments, short of breath and sweat starting to form on their brows. The maul was lying up against Nicholas' tent just as Qing had described, its head in the dirt and handle leaning against one of the stick supports so the whole thing wouldn't collapse. Takeo scoured the area, flipping everything over in the process.

"I already told you there was no struggle," Qing said. "No blood, nothing knocked over. The dirt isn't even disturbed."

Takeo searched about until he found the bottle they'd shared. It was empty.

"Damn, I told him not to drink too much," the ronin said. "But still, it would take more than this to knock him out. It couldn't have been poisoned, or I'd be out, too. Did he go find another bottle? No, not without his maul."

"Quiet," Qing hushed him.

"I'm just thinking out loud."

"I said shut your mouth!" she screeched.

Takeo went still, realizing Qing was concentrating hard, eyes glazed over as she focused her inhuman hearing on the world around her. Several long moments drew out in which Takeo dared not even breathe, despite his pounding heart begging otherwise.

Qing's arm flew up, finger extended northwest, away from the camp.

"There," she commanded.

They took off at once.

"It was faint," Qing said in between gasps for air. "Two voices, a third muffled, maybe. I lost it when the wind changed direction."

"There shouldn't be anyone or anything this way but sentries," Takeo replied. "It's our best bet."

They dashed past the construction and discarded materials, into the tall grass of the surrounding plains. The land here wasn't as beaten down as that of the camp, and Takeo was forced to slow his pace, for he'd surely trip and fall sprinting over this undulating ground. That and he wanted to listen. Between the grass, darkness, and wind, Takeo understood he had little chance of finding anyone trying to hide out here, not unless he stumbled into them or summoned the entire army to scour the area.

Fortunately, Qing was there.

After they'd gone some distance from the camp so that the catapults were specks in the darkness, she stopped and held up a hand. Takeo froze, too, and held his breath. Qing darted due east in a short sprint, then stopped again.

"There," she pointed.

Takeo saw nothing, but he drew his sword and approached. The tall grass licked at his elbows. He moved slowly, looking for the glint of steel in the moonlight. He didn't want to get stabbed again. Behind him, Qing drew two throwing stars.

"You can stop running," he called out. "We've found you."

A muffled cry issued out a few paces away, followed by a solid punch. Takeo rushed over, almost falling over a body lying prone in the darkness. His adjusted eyes honed in to see the bound figure of Nicholas rolling in the grass. Takeo ripped the gag out of the viking's mouth.

"Ha!" Nicholas shouted and nodded south. "You guys are screwed now! That way, they went that way. Two of them."

Takeo flew in that direction, but not before Qing chucked a throwing star. It zipped into the grass, and a scream followed. Takeo ran to it and tackled the figure in the dark. Takeo's blade went to the man's throat, and a spare hand went to the man's hair. Takeo drove the man to his knees, facing outwards. The captive whimpered as his throat bounced against the steel.

"Run," the man yelled out.

"Don't," Takeo countermanded. "Stop, wherever you are. You'll never escape, I promise that. You two made a foolish mistake, perhaps your last. Stand up, or I'll kill him first, then you. Do not test me."

A moment's pause preceded another large man standing up out of the grass, his dark figure silhouetted against the moonlit background.

"I'm only going to say this once," Takeo seethed through a snarl. "The first one to talk gets to live."

The two men were big. They'd have to be to subdue a man like Nicholas and drag him this far into the middle of nowhere. They could have been ninjas, but Takeo wasn't convinced. They looked more like shock troops. It was a testament to Takeo's reputation that the two gulped down dry throats and perspired in the breeze.

"I'm sorry," the standing one said to his captured companion. "I have a family."

"No, don't—" the other shouted before Takeo's blade sliced through his throat, and his next words were drowned in blood.

Takeo shoved the man down into the grass where he flailed briefly, spraying the plains red. Takeo's blade dripped as he pointed it at the man who stood shaking.

"Wise choice," the ronin said. "Now start talking. Who sent you, and what are you doing out here?"

"Takeo," Qing whispered. "Look."

In his rage, Takeo had honed in on the surviving kidnapper. Qing's words brought him out of that rut, and only then did the distant light dawn on him.

In fact, at first, he thought it was dawn. Bright light rose up over the camp, and he instinctively put a hand over his eyes to shield his vision from the sun. Then he realized that couldn't be right. The night was still young, and the source was coming from the wrong direction. A second later, he realized he was looking at a large bonfire, of sorts, one steadily growing in size and breadth.

Something large was on fire, then a second, then a third. The flames were massive and spreading, and Takeo feared the entire camp would go up in flames, until he realized it wasn't so widespread. The bonfires were centralized, and also clearly in view.

It took Takeo a half second to remember which part of the camp he had a direct view of.

His jaw dropped open, and his heart plummeted.

"No," he whispered. "No, please no."

Takeo stood helpless as he watched his field of catapults go up in flames.

* * *

Lord Yoshida, finely dressed and sitting comfortably as always, had been enjoying a well-prepared meal with his most trusted colleagues, Lord Sing and Lady Xie, when Takeo stormed into the tent with blood-covered blade exposed and Qing and Nicholas in tow. Yoshida's guards, who'd failed to stop the ronin, rushed in, too, blades drawn, uncertainty flickering across their faces. Everyone froze but Yoshida, who took another bite of freshly cooked meat and began to saw away at another chunk.

"You seem awfully calm," Takeo said. "Haven't you heard the catapults are burning?"

Yoshida met Takeo's gaze and waved off his guards. They seemed reluctant yet also relieved as they withdrew. Takeo's sword grip tightened.

"There's no need for a show," the lord replied calmly. "I've already been informed, and I've sent orders to rouse the camp. We'll have water buckets distributed to put out the fires as swiftly as possible. With luck, we may minimize the damage and perhaps find out how Lord Botan got behind our lines."

"You bastard," Takeo said, clenching his teeth so hard they threatened to shatter. "This wasn't Lord Botan. You did this."

Lord Yoshida went stiff. He flicked his gaze to Nicholas, taking in his presence for the first time, then looked to Qing. Finally, his attention rested on Takeo's sword, dripping blood on the fine rug that adorned Yoshida's tent.

The old lord sighed.

"You killed them, did you?" he said.

"Why would you do this? How can you even look me in the eye? After all your talk of trust and loyalty."

136

"I'll have you know those two men you killed were good people, and they had strict orders not to harm your viking. It behooves someone in your position to show a bit of mercy every once in a while."

"Answer me, damn it."

Another sigh was the response, which made Takeo squeeze his sword that much harder. Lord Yoshida waved to his two companions and beckoned towards the exit.

"We'll have to talk later," he said. "If you'll please excuse us."

"Are you sure?" Lord Sing asked, eyeing Takeo. "I'm not sure it's wise to leave you alone with this—"

"Animal," Lady Xie finished, glaring.

"Neither of you are helping," Yoshida said. "And yes, I'll be fine. This is just a misunderstanding. Leave, please."

For all the bravery in Lady Xie's insult, she and Lord Sing made sure to leave in the opposite direction of Takeo. When they were gone, Lord Yoshida gestured to the rug before him.

"Please, have a seat," he said. "There's plenty of food. Would you like something to drink?"

"What is this?" Takeo replied, not moving. "You burn my catapults to the ground and expect me to eat with you? Those two were right. You shouldn't be alone with me. I'm two paces from cutting you down and contemplating the idea with every fiber of my being."

"Let's not do this, my friend, these meaningless threats. You're not half the animal the others think you are."

"Is my sword not stained with blood?"

"Yet here we are chatting. That's quite a civilized action coming from someone claiming to be a savage."

"Is that a challenge?"

Lord Yoshida shook his head and went back to sawing away at his meal. He hacked off another chunk of meat and slipped it into his mouth, chewing with lips closed. He gestured again to the rug, but Takeo remained standing.

"My lord, you'd best start talking," Qing cut in. "I don't care whatsoever about the relationship between you and Takeo, but you've just put an end to our shogun's assault on the Katsus. That's treason, and it's apparent you have accomplices. When I tell Lady Zhenzhen about this, she'll have your head."

"Was this all to discredit me?" Takeo said. "That's all I can figure. You made me general just so you could intentionally make me fail. Those ladders were sabotaged, weren't they? All those soldiers dead so you could make a political move against a trusted ally. Meanwhile, your cohorts call me the animal."

Lord Yoshida swallowed his food down and went to cut another piece.

"Let me tell you how this conversation is going to end," he said. "After our discussion, you'll see things from my perspective. You three will leave with no more harm done to anyone. Lady Zhenzhen will never hear of this. In less than a week, this army will pack up and leave, and the Hanu will be all the better for it."

"I doubt that," Takeo said.

"Try me."

Yoshida waved for a third time at the rug. Takeo faltered this time. The argument was not starting out like he'd expected, and the overwhelmingly calm nature of Yoshida doused the flames that had been stoked in Takeo's heart. Feeling that Yoshida wasn't going to speak until Takeo took a seat, the ronin did so reluctantly, setting his bloodied sword down in front of him. The rug soaked it in. Behind him, Nicholas shuffled in place, but neither he nor Qing moved.

Yoshida took a sip of wine from his cup before clapping his hands together.

"First, I'll say that you are right," the lord said. "I did want you to fail this assault, but not for the reasons you think. My guess is that you believe I want you out of the Hanu army, but that is wrong. I may have omitted the truth on occasion, but I've yet to lie to you. I still want to see you succeed, Takeo, to lead this army and bring total victory to our forces. I have no ill wishes towards you. I want to see you happy, in a position of power, sipping tea at my mansion as you watch me grow older. I know you see this sabotage as a betrayal now, but I hope you'll see the bigger picture after I'm through. I know you're an intelligent man, and I trust you'll understand that by losing this battle, you will win the war."

He paused to let his introduction sink in. Takeo did not agree but did not feel moved enough to speak out. Yoshida continued.

138

"Remember that conversation up on the hill? About the daimyo rallying against you? That was closer to the truth than you can imagine. Your rapid rise to power has made many consider outright revolt."

"If they do that, the Hanu are sure to lose," Takeo cut in.

"And what do they care? Hm? Most daimyo are like common villagers in many regards; they don't care which lord or lady they serve so long as they're left to enjoy life for just a little while longer. That's where you come in, Takeo. It's no secret, the zealotry you inspire in the common troops. We daimyo, who have been grooming our samurai for eons to be fervent warriors, forget how such passion can become a double-edged sword. You, a common man—worse, a dishonored ronin—are upsetting the balance of power. The ability to exile any warrior we choose is an important power to the daimyo. How are we to react when an upstart like yourself comes along and threatens that?"

"That's none of my concern," Takeo bit back. "I have no interest in wearing a crown. I've taken no title or land. All I've done is to further the daimyo's power."

"I know, I know," Yoshida replied, holding up a hand. "I see that, but they don't. They are blinded by fear, but this is the reality we live in. We have this situation where the Hanu both desperately need you in order to win but also might fall apart before you achieve that goal. Some have already turned their backs on us, refusing to pledge their samurai to our cause, which we so desperately need. You don't think winning this fight will make the situation better, do you? Follow me here, how are we to remedy this problem? How can we get the Hanu daimyo to come back into the fold willingly?"

Yoshida beckoned for Takeo to reply, but he couldn't. Takeo's mouth dried up, and his clenched fists fell open, palms up.

"We make you lose," the lord whispered. "You're on a precarious edge, that's well known. Because you don't have warriors to pledge, like a true lord, you hold power only by way of bringing victory to Lady Zhenzhen. If you were to lose, just this once, in a battle of no true consequence, you wouldn't seem so terrifying anymore. A skillful diplomat, such as I, could rally our forces together, and you could be put in an advisory position once again. Situation thus mended, we could return twice as strong.

139

"On the other hand, we could win this battle. Sorry, let me rephrase, we could have won this battle, as assuredly there's no doing so now. If that had happened, those daimyo who turned their backs on principle would have fled in fear. They'd have joined the enemy, and then Takeo, you'd be truly pressed. Don't you see how that's a gamble we can't afford to take? Surely you see how my plan will work?"

"I tell you what I see," Takeo replied. "I see a man trying to both protect and further the power he has. Doing this will weaken Lady Zhenzhen due to her trust in me, but you'd rise unscathed as a witless servant. In addition, if I'd never found out about this, I would have been devastated by this loss. While the rest of the daimyo rallied to have me cast out, you'd have stepped in and spoken for me, drawing me to your side where you could profit off the victories I'd bring. You'd shelter me but lash me to you at the same time. I'd become a fat slave, so to speak. And the cusp of the issue here is that the daimyo hierarchy would remain untouched, a hierarchy you all seem to think I threaten, despite all I've done to further it. You know, I haven't really thought about it until now, but perhaps you're right. Perhaps I should bring the entire daimyo reign crashing down on their heads."

Yoshida smirked and sipped his wine.

"Now, a comment like that would scare anyone else," the lord said, "but not me."

"And why's that?"

"Because you don't believe in that, and you don't really want that. I've gotten to know you, Takeo, and I've caught wind of this dream of yours. You don't want to shatter the power structure. You want to strengthen it. That's why you're fighting for Lady Zhenzhen in exchange for nothing. You don't want lands, or title, or legacy for yourself; you just want the chaos of the world brought to heel. What would breaking up the daimyo do for this goal of yours? Nothing. It would make it harder to achieve, actually. You don't particularly care who heads this tyrannical kingdom of the future, so long as someone does. So, I ask you, how does my plan not conform to yours? If you're looking for a ruler to seat upon the world, why does it have to be Lady Zhenzhen or Lord Nobu? I ask you, Takeo, why not serve me?"

140

Lord Yoshida extended a hand, palm open to the ronin. Takeo stared at it for some time before casting his gaze down to his bloodied sword. No matter his passion, Takeo was also a slave to logic, and Yoshida had made one strong appeal to that side of him. He swallowed down his dry throat.

"But what about Gavin?" Takeo asked.

Yoshida sighed.

"Come now. You're a soldier. The man lost a hand and an ear already. You don't really think you can save him, do you?"

"I," Takeo started, pausing as his vision blurred. "I had hoped."

"And here I thought you didn't have time for hope, only reality. If that's true, then consider the situation. What's done is done, my friend. The catapults are burned. We haven't the forces for another ladder assault. Our time is out. This battle is lost. You can blame me. You can be angry and threaten to murder me. After all, I did betray you, as you said. However, only one question remains: are you going to let that stop you?"

How is this possible? Am I an open book to this man? When did I reveal so much of myself to him? If I didn't know any better, I'd say he was a sennin. This is insane. He just sabotaged my entire plan. That was why he fully supported my decision to brutalize the akki, knowing they'd flee when the plan fell apart. The first battle, too! How could I forget? His path of assault left the way open for Botan to escape with ease. I've been played a fool from the beginning, and here I sit, with nothing to show for all my rage.

Because he's right. He made it so.

"But Gavin," Takeo pleaded.

My sword, he thought.

"Let him go," Yoshida whispered. "You can't save him. You never could. You burden yourself too much, Takeo. Maybe we can try to ransom him, I don't know. You can't do it all. You act as if the fate of the world rests on your shoulders. Why do you do this? Tell me, who made you the chosen one?"

Takeo's head felt murky. His skin tingled as if lacking air. He couldn't take anymore and stood up.

"Takeo?" Nicholas asked.

Qing's eyes aimed at her feet.

141

"Come," the ronin replied. "Let's go. I believe Qing had something to talk about anyway."

Chapter 15

Takeo made it several steps out of Lord Yoshida's tent before Nicholas dashed in front of him and put out his hands.

"Wait, wait," the viking pleaded. "We're not really going to let this stand, are we? Krunk's in there, too."

"Don't remind me," Takeo said. "And don't stand in my way."

"Yoshida is right," Qing added, head hung. "He's played a deft hand. There is no version of this where he doesn't come out on top. If we retaliate or let word get out, the Hanu alliance will fracture. That might have been avoided if we could have toppled the Katsu and brought them into the fold, but that can't happen now. If we go along with Yoshida, though, Lady Zhenzhen's status will be hurt but left intact. I know he's had his eye on marrying her, for title, and I think this may drive that point home, but at least she'll still be shogun in a way. There can be no victory here, only varying degrees of defeat."

She didn't need to elaborate. The skies in the distance were red with fire, the air thick with smoke, and the night filled with the shouts of water brigades trying to salvage the catapults. There would be heavy celebrations going on in the Katsu fortress tonight. It churned Takeo's stomach just to think about it.

I failed. No, worse. I have been defeated.

"Some sort of concession, then, to free Krunk and Gavin?" Nicholas continued. "We say we'll leave if Botan hands over his prisoners. We can do that, right? You can do that."

"I'll try," Takeo agreed, "but it's doubtful. Botan will know this siege is over. I have nothing left to bargain."

"Then we sneak in. We break them out, maybe kill that scum while we're at it and get your sword back. Come on, we've got to try."

Takeo shoved past Nicholas, as much to close the conversation as to get away from Yoshida. He didn't want any traces of this conversation getting back to the lord.

"Come now, you don't think Takeo hasn't thought of that already?" Qing answered. "I have no doubt we could get in, but getting out? We'd have to rescue what, four people?"

"Three," Takeo corrected. "Yeira can rot. But Gavin won't leave his child, and his child is with Botan, and Botan has my sword. He'll be expecting just that sort of thing."

"So?" Nicholas said. "It's worth it, and you know it. If you got your sword back, nothing could stop you. And besides, Qing has snuck into a fortress before. There's Emy, too. She could help."

"Emy, sure, of course," Takeo replied. "I'll think on it, but for now, the less you say out loud the better. Do you understand? Let's move on. Qing had something she wanted to talk to you about."

"Me?"

"Yes," Qing said. "It's about Dhyana."

Takeo stopped and darted a look at Qing. The ninja shrank under the scrutiny.

"I knew you'd act this way," she replied, answering his unspoken question. "That's why I didn't say anything earlier."

Takeo changed direction and made straight for his mother's tent. His pace doubled, just shy of jogging. Men streamed by him as they awoke and ran to join the water brigade. The loud snapping of huge timbers crumbling to embers echoed into the night sky. The camp was bright as daylight now, flickering in orange and red.

They weren't long in reaching their destination, and Takeo slipped inside along with the others, as crowded as it was. The tent wasn't sized for an audience.

Mako was still with Dhyana, and they appeared worried at the trio's sudden appearance.

"Son," Dhyana said, then lost the rest of her sentence to a coughing fit.

"What's wrong?" Mako finished. "I heard there's a fire."

Takeo didn't feel like recounting the dire situation. He motioned to Qing instead with a single nod. The ninja grimaced, clearly not wishing to do this with Takeo around. He didn't care.

"May I ask you a question," Qing said to Dhyana, "about your tea session with Lord Botan?"

Dhyana nodded, swallowing hard to try to stem her coughing. Her face was gaunt, and he guessed she hadn't been eating well.

144

"Can you explain exactly what happened? Specifically, did he drink any of it himself."

Dhyana tried to push herself to sit up but had trouble. Mako assisted, and Dhyana leaned on her.

"Well, no," the old woman started. "I didn't think anything of it at the time. He just offered me tea, and I agreed. What else was I to say to my shogun? It couldn't have been poisoned, though, could it? I drank it over a month ago."

Nicholas straightened. Qing nodded to him.

"No," the viking whispered in disbelief, then spoke up. "It couldn't be. Um, ma'am. I don't mean to intrude, but could I see your legs?"

Dhyana hesitated, and even Takeo wanted to intervene, but the situation was clearly beyond the unwritten laws of decency. She nodded, and Nicholas bent down and pulled back the sheet that covered her. Carefully, respectfully, he rolled up her dress past her ankles, revealing what in all respects looked like a normal elderly leg to Takeo. Thinned skin, slightly bruised, with different colored veins running about. Nicholas pressed on some of those veins with his thumb. One of them turned stark white as he did.

"I can't believe it," he said. "I just can't. Honestly, look."

"What?" Dhyana asked, then coughed. "That's how my legs have always looked since I got old. Your skin thins. It's normal for old people to have purple, blue-ish veins showing through. And skin whites when you press on it."

"This white though?" he replied and pressed again.

That's when Takeo saw it. Nicholas pushed but only a little bit, and the whole vein turned white as snow. Dhyana had to lean over with some assistance from Mako to even see them.

"So? What does that mean?" she asked.

Nicholas looked back to Takeo, grimaced, and cast his eyes down. Takeo directed his attention to Qing, who swallowed.

"We've all had plenty of suspicions about Lord Botan's purpose for your mother," Qing started. "Among them was the thought that maybe he just wanted to kill her right in front of you, which we always assumed we could stop. Ping is still guarding the entrance. But when she got sick, I began to wonder if perhaps we were too late. I went back to the Hanu keep to do some research, and that's where your viking comes in."

Takeo's heart skipped.

"Nicholas," he said, then firmer when the viking didn't speak up. "Nicholas!"

"Damn it all," Nicholas whispered, shaking his head. "Dhyana, was the tea white?"

Dhyana hesitated, then nodded. She said, "I take it that wasn't just a heavy dose of milk?"

"By Valhalla, I can't believe he found it," Nicholas said.

"My patience is running thin," Takeo said through clenched teeth.

"Why? You already know what I'm going to say. Are you really going to make me say it?"

"If I knew what you were going to say, I wouldn't be asking."

"Fine! She's going to die."

Takeo's heart stopped, and Mako gasped. Nicholas had been right. Takeo did know what the viking was going to say, but that didn't soften hearing the words.

"How?" Takeo asked.

Nicholas sighed.

"There's this legend, in The North," he started, "about a flower. Just one flower, white with star-shaped petals. Legend has it that only one of them grows in a decade, in the dead of winter, when there's no light to snuff it out. I don't really know the details, or the why, or where. It's just a child's bedtime story really, or a running joke at the dinner table. Anyway, in our legend, to find the flower means one is destined for greatness, and lots of our tales start with the hero finding one as a child. What's important to know is that it's deadly to eat. It doesn't kill you immediately, but instead causes you to wither and die over some time after. In viking lore, eating the flower is akin to denying one's destiny, and doing so means you'll die a tragic death."

"The flower is real and has been documented in the past," Qing jumped in. "It's very impractical, though. Because the flower can't survive in light, that means—assuming one can find it at all—the flower has to be transported in total darkness to wherever it needs to go. On top of this, the flower cannot survive outside The North's

146

frigid winter temperatures for long, nor does it have any sort of noticeable seeds, which means it can't be cultivated. This is all known because once upon a time it was considered an option for assassinations, but the practicality of it all is ridiculous. Assuming one does manage to find the flower and transport it back, the target has to consume it within a week, before the flower dies. And all for what? To kill someone a month later? Who has time or money or patience for that? Knives work just as well, and there are other slow-acting poisons, though none so slow as this one. Assassinations are absurdly difficult to pull off as it is, what with how guarded all royalty are in this part of the world."

"I mean, the amount of effort he went through to get this done," Nicholas said. "It's insane."

The silence in the tent was palpable. Nicholas hadn't let go of Dhyana's leg, instead just rubbing one white-streaked vein as if he still couldn't believe his eyes. Tears flooded down Mako's cheeks, and she wrapped her arms around Dhyana tightly. Takeo and his mother met each other's gaze.

"How long do I have?" she asked.

"Not long, I think," Nicholas replied. "According to legend, the white streaks don't show up until the very end. It's a sign of your blood dying within your veins."

Qing nodded and said, "From what I read, at this point, you'll be lucky to make it to morning."

Takeo's eyes fell to Dhyana's leg. It seemed to him that the white streaks had increased in length since this conversation had started. Nicholas felt the gaze on his back and set the woman's limb down. The viking stood up and walked out of the tent, pausing only to place one hand on Takeo's shoulder.

Takeo barely felt it. His body had gone numb.

"I'll, um," Qing said, stopping and starting. "I'll let Ping know you don't want to be disturbed. I'm sure Kuniko can manage the catapults. Oh, and I'm sorry. I didn't want to tell you until I was sure."

"Just go," Takeo whispered.

She stopped, bowed, then obeyed. Takeo heard her muffled commands to Ping on the other side. Takeo met Dhyana's gaze

147

again. The old woman had her arms up, clutching Mako's arms that were so firmly wrapped around her.

Takeo found his will to stand had left him, so he sank to his knees.

"I'm sorry," he said, throat so thick that the words were difficult to get out. "I'm so sorry. I thought we had time."

"Don't be sorry," Dhyana replied, wiping her eyes. "It's not your fault."

"Of course, it's my fault. This is all my fault. None of this would have happened if not for me."

"You can't blame yourself. This is the best thing that could have happened."

"How can you say that?" Takeo said. "You're about to die? How can this be the best thing?"

"Because I got to see you," Dhyana replied, forcing a smile. "I got to meet you, speak with you. It's all I've ever wanted. I could have lived one-hundred more years and died a sad woman, but because I got to see my son again, I can die happy."

"Don't say that," Takeo cut in. "Please, just don't. If I had known, if only I had known."

"What? What would you have done differently? Tell me."

Takeo looked at his hands. They still had traces of blood on them. His sword still had blood on it, too, though Takeo didn't care. It wasn't truly his sword, just a borrowed tool that could be replaced. In a way, it wasn't much different than the way some royalty looked at peasants, or the way generals thought of their soldiers. It was certainly the way Takeo had treated the akki, and that was okay by him. They weren't human. Not even some humans were worthy of humanity as far as he was concerned, himself included.

But this woman? His mother?

"I," Takeo started, then stopped, a shudder running through his heart. "I shouldn't have been so distant. I kept you at bay because I was scared, and I didn't want to be hurt, again, and I thought we had time. I thought we had all the time in the world, or at least if we didn't, it would be because I died. I didn't think; I, I didn't feel—"

Dhyana wiped a tear from her eye before a coughing fit took over. She buried her face into Mako's chest to cover her mouth, and Mako held fast.

148

"Would you say that you love me?" Dhyana asked once it was done.

"I don't know," Takeo replied.

"But at least, please, tell me you accept my love."

Takeo paused, then nodded.

"Yes," he said. "I do."

Dhyana sighed and lay back in Mako's arms, a wave of relief rushing off her shoulders. Her forced smile turned genuine, reaching her eyes and seeming to embrace the entire tent in warmth. Takeo's chest ached with a pain he hadn't felt in a decade.

"If I'm going to die tonight, can I ask something of you, son?"

"What can I do?"

"I know you're a grown man now, and I'm an old woman," she started, "but you'll always be my baby. Let me hold you one last time."

She opened her arms.

Takeo hesitated. Physical contact of any sort wasn't something he was prone to. He even recoiled a hair on instinct, but fortunately Dhyana didn't appear offended. He looked to her hands, her arms, then to her smile. Mako, tears still streaming from her face, pulled away, letting Dhyana down gently as she did so. Takeo took a deep breath and swallowed his unease.

He wanted to deny her. He knew that doing this would only hurt him more when she passed. Yet he couldn't do it. He couldn't say no.

Against every fiber in his body, Takeo crawled over and slipped into his mother's arms.

It was awkward, at first. The last time Takeo had lain close to anyone without carnal intent had been for one night on a mountaintop to survive freezing temperatures. This was much different, and he wasn't sure how to proceed. His hands drifted about aimlessly, unsure where to rest. Her waist seemed too intimate, her face impractical, and her legs unreasonable. He wasn't even sure which way to lie. Should he face her? Turn away? He cringed a hundred times over.

Fortunately, Dhyana took the lead.

She pulled him close and pressed his head to her chest, just so that his hair nestled under chin. Her arm became a pillow for his head as they laid on their sides, and she wrapped her other arm under his and around his back. Through her skin, he could hear the faint beat of her heart. The warmth of her skin was comforting.

Dhyana drew in a deep breath and shuddered.

"Oh, my baby boy," she whispered.

Takeo swallowed.

"You don't have to say anything," she said. "Just be here with me."

Takeo took a deep breath and wrapped his arms around her. He forced down his pride and unease and fear to say the words he might never get to say again.

"I will," he said. "Mother."

* * *

The morning air was crisp but far from clear as Takeo emerged from the tent. The lingering smoke from the catapults permeated the camp and clouded the sunrise. Outside, he found Ping sitting on the grass, hunched over and leaning on his sword, which was impaled on the ground, trying to ward off sleep. It seemed the man had been awake all night, keeping guard, which Takeo could empathize with. He hadn't slept either.

Ping's fluttering eyes snapped open at his general's appearance. Ping scrambled to his feet and bowed a hair too low, so that he almost toppled over.

"Sir, is she?" he asked.

Takeo didn't reply, and that was answer enough.

"My sincere condolences, my lord. I got to know her. She was a kind woman," Ping said. "Uh, Kuniko sends her regards, too. I think word has spread; you should know. She also wanted you to know she's handling the remains of the catapults. She's getting the army organized and trying to salvage what remains of our siege works. Morale is low, people are talking of defeat, but your true followers remain unshaken. I want you to know we're with you, my lord. We know you have a plan. I can take you to Kuniko if you like or relay any message you need. I await your orders, my lord."

Takeo flexed his wrist, cracking the bones that had lain perfectly still for hours. Ping's words had fallen on deaf ears. The ronin's eyes fell to his hands, still bloodied, yet far too clean for his mood.

150

"You're right," Takeo whispered. "I do have a plan."

He strode off, leaving a bewildered Ping still bowed over.

"My lord?"

"Stay with Mako," Takeo shouted over his shoulder, then whispered to himself. "At least one of us ought to survive."

And he went to face Lord Botan.

Chapter 16

Takeo wasted no time in acquiring a mount and spurring out of the Hanu camp. The fewer people who saw him, the better, he figured, so he set a relentless speed that edged his komainu into bloodlust. Its long tongue lolled out and flung saliva into its self-generated wind, its eyes darting for targets as soldiers dove out of the way. Takeo was free of the camp in mere moments, ripping through the tall grass on a direct course for the Katsu fortress. The sun still lay hidden behind the massive structure, and the artistic combination of stone and wood loomed like a glowing beacon before Takeo's approach.

Once Takeo entered within catapult range of the fortress, the grass began to deaden and fall around him, having been trampled under an armored stampede not too long prior. Some places were still soaked with blood, particularly under the boulders. Takeo didn't doubt that his approach was being watched, and in fact, he hoped for it. As he passed into bow range, he spurred his mount again. The komainu snarled, losing its sanity to the pace of the run, and pushed itself harder.

Takeo yanked on the reins as he came within charging distance of the moat, where the walls were so clear that Takeo could see individual soldiers and hear shouts on the wind. It took a massive effort to get his mount to stop, and it whined and snarled in protest. The beast's blood was up, its heart pumping, and it was too lost to sit still. Forced to halt by its master, the komainu settled for a pacing stride, winding back and forth in a tight circle like a caged animal, whirling Takeo about at the same time and making him an impossible target for a bowman at this range.

"Botan!" Takeo bellowed out to the walls.

The whispers on the wind died out.

"Come and fight me!" Takeo yelled. "You coward! I'm here!"

A few quick shouts echoed out from inside the stone walls. Takeo waited, turning this way and that as his komainu flipped from side to side and paced along flattened grass.

"What's the matter?" Takeo shouted. "You're brave enough to dismember a prisoner and poison an old woman, but you can't stand up to straight fight? I'm right here! What are you waiting for? Show yourself!"

A thunderous clang echoed from the gate, and a shower of dust and dirt broke out along the seal between wood and stone. The drawbridge lowered to the ground, clanking and shuddering all the way. At long last, the fortress was open, and a way across the moat presented itself.

And Lord Botan Katsu road out.

He wore immaculate armor, regal and bright in the intensity of its colors. Varying shades of Katsu blue wrapped him from head to toe, embroidered with gold and silver edges. He had recently shaven, his chin unsullied by even a touch of hair. His mount was no less presentable, wearing an equally impressive suit of armor, such that the two seemed an inseparable unit of metal, fabric, and flesh. The komainu had clearly been starved this morning, as it stalked out along the drawbridge snarling and drooling voraciously.

Yet it was Botan's hip that drew Takeo's attention, for there hung the black blade of the Karaoshi family.

Lord Botan brought his mount to a stop when it touched the grass, leaving some distance between him and Takeo. Then he smiled.

"Wipe that smug look off your face," Takeo shouted. "Or does it bring you that much pleasure to kill an old woman in her sleep?"

"It serves her right," Botan replied, also shouting so that his voice would clear the distance, "breeding a monster like you."

"Me, the monster? You wear hypocrisy like you do your wealth. I knew there was something wrong with you. I sensed it the first time I laid eyes on your holier-than-thou stance. I tried to warn Gavin. Never trust a man who believes his cause is righteous, for he thinks himself incapable of evil."

Botan laughed.

"I have no desire to hear the philosophical ravings of a lunatic. I see your camp had quite the fire last night. How tragic. I assume you blame me for that, and I'll gladly take credit, even if it's undeserved. Is that what this is really about?"

153

Takeo clenched his jaw. He had hoped to inflame Botan's temper, but it seemed the lord saw through his every move. Takeo reeked of desperation, and there was no hiding it.

"I know it's me you're after," Takeo said. "It's all anyone's after. Whether they want to kill me, shackle me, or bed me, this whole damned land can't think beyond me for two damned seconds. So fine, you can have me, but on my terms and on one condition: you let them go."

"Them?"

"Gavin, his daughter, and Krunk," Takeo said, "and Yeira, I suppose. Gavin would want that. And damn it, fine, the rakshasa, too, wherever she is. Give them all safe passage to wherever they want. Just get them out of this war."

Lord Botan raised his right hand, which was covered in a thin glove, and pulled at the fingertips one by one. He stripped the glove off and then wrapped his bare skin about the handle of his sword. Even from this distance, Takeo could see the power flow into Botan's veins, the heat and strength that whirled about his body. Botan drew the sword, and with it, a shimmer of heat wafted off the blade's exposed metal.

Takeo swallowed.

"You have my word," Botan said, "that when I plunge this tip into your icy heart, I will release your companions. Now, are you going to be a good little ronin and march quietly over to receive your coup de grace?"

Takeo drew his own sword and yanked the reins on his komainu, directing it at the lord for a charge.

Botan smirked.

"I thought not," he said. "In a way, I'm glad for it."

"I told you," Takeo replied. "On my terms."

The ronin slammed his heels into his mount, spurring the komainu into a dead sprint. The beast dug its claws into the ground and launched into the air with such tenacity that the reins were almost ripped from Takeo's hand. Botan was less than a heartbeat behind, driving his komainu into an unrelenting charge that ate up the distance between them.

Each a skilled combatant in his own right, they drove their mounts into perfect lines that would run along their right side. Botan held the Karaoshi sword out and high in a flourishing style favored by the daimyo, while Takeo held his blade angled down and slightly behind him, as taught by his brother. Each bounded up and down with his komainu's raw gallop, leaning out over the right side of their saddles, loose strands of hair and embroidery trailing behind them in the self-made wind. At this pace, they'd each have time for a single stroke, which was all the time they would need.

Or at least, all that Botan thought he would need.

At the last second before they closed, the two komainu roared, the lord raised his sword, and Takeo vaulted to the left. The ronin dropped his sword, yanked on the reins and sprung from the saddle, ramming his feet into his mount's head, sending the beast just one-half pace to the right.

They collided at break-neck speed.

Botan's komainu had gone low for the throat, and instead received an elongated tooth to the eye, which ripped free as the two masses of flesh rammed into each other. One or both komainu's necks snapped, rolling into each other and then compressing with their weight. Blood gushed from an eye, a tooth, and then the inevitable collision painted the entire scene red before anything else happened. Their bodies whipped over and around, snapping more bones and rag-dolling the beasts. Lord Botan made a feeble swing with the Karaoshi blade before being flung from his saddle, and then he was struck in the upper half of his body by Takeo's komainu, back flipping him a half dozen times before he slammed violently into the ground. Half of this, Takeo didn't catch at all, as he, too, spiraled into the air, head bouncing off Botan's komainu's backside, while a swinging, clawed foot struck his thigh, catapulting him into dirt and grass harder than a minotaur could punch. Takeo hit the ground so hard his entire world went black for half a second, and everything went silent, all the while he rolled across the ground, limbs flailing, blood in his mouth, dirt in his eyes, and body tweaking in ways it never had before. His left arm hit wrong, and he rolled over it, popping the bone loose, while several ribs cracked as he folded over backwards. When his body came to a rest, his eyes kept spinning, and the world seemed to alter in stages of white and dark. His ears rang, and a stabbing pain echoed through every fiber of his body. If given the chance, he would have lain there for some time, hoping.

But he didn't have time for hope.

"Urm, uhh," Takeo moaned as he pushed himself up.

His left arm gave out, and he hit the ground again.

"Come on," he whimpered.

Takeo dug deep, fighting the aching pain shooting up and down his body to struggle to his hands and knees. The world spun, and he had to hold still, closing his eyes and fighting down a wave of nausea. One of his legs wasn't responding to his commands, but he was too battered to know which one. He looked up to see the two komainu lying on their sides in mangled poses. Neither moved. On the other side, Takeo heard a low moan echo out, followed by retching.

He survived. Damn it.

Takeo pushed off one knee, he assumed his good one, and tried to stand. He chose poorly and almost crumpled again, catching himself on an elbow. His stomach doubled him over, shooting pain through his body, and he almost fell to a wave of convulsions. He steadied himself, pushed with all his willpower, and staggered to his feet. He dipped left, then right, catching himself with a half stumble, and made his way back to the komainu.

Lord Botan's bent and bloodied hand flung up onto one of the komainu corpses. One of the fingers was snapped to the side. Takeo's breath held, and then Botan's other hand sprung into view.

They were empty.

Takeo instantly ignored whatever the lord did next and began searching for his sword. His eyes swept about the low grass for a glimpse of anything long, slim, and black.

"You psychotic bastard," Botan said, lifting his head up over the komainu corpse and spitting a wad of blood and vomit over the side. "I'll murder your friends for that."

But then the lord caught himself. He saw Takeo searching and realized they were both unarmed. His eyes went wide, and he whirled about, looking for the enchanted sword. He also struggled to a stand, pushing on the komainu corpse for support. When Takeo didn't see his sword on the first pass, he briefly considered rushing Botan and strangling him to death, but then Takeo heard shouting in the distance. Soldiers barked orders, yet Takeo was too disoriented to catch what they were saying. He remembered Botan had left the drawbridge down, and those men had seen the collision. The two wouldn't be alone for long, and trying to strangle Botan to death wouldn't make a lick of difference.

Takeo needed his sword.

Then he spotted it, off to Botan's right, a flickering of black between the dancing blades of grass. Takeo's pulse rose as his heart jumped to his throat, and he stumbled forward with all the strength he could muster, teeth clenched from the pain.

Botan saw the movement and tried to follow the gaze, searching Takeo's direct path frantically. He spotted the black, too, and made a dash for it, but a hair too late. Takeo barred the pain from his mind and dashed several steps to strike Botan in the neck. The lord dodged, but not well enough, and Takeo instead made a glancing blow off the man's ear.

But in their current state, it was enough to send them both tumbling to the ground.

Takeo landed on his wounded knee, and the resulting spike in pain killed any attempt to stay up. He crumpled and groaned, clawing into the dirt to push himself up and inch forward. He'd lost sight of the sword in the short fray, so his hands began to whip frantically about, searching every bit of space within arm's reach. His fingers hit something hard, his eyes followed to find the glint of steel looking back at him, and a surge of hope spiraled into him. With the chorus of soldiers shouting in the background, there was no time to waste looking for the handle. Takeo grabbed the raw blade, unconcerned with how the steel cut into his fingers, and yanked it free of the grass.

But the blade that came loose had a brown handle, instead of black, and the touch of it didn't send any fire spreading through Takeo's veins. This wasn't his sword, just some abandoned weapon left behind during the ladder assault. His heart plummeted.

Then he heard laughter.

Takeo turned about on his hands and knees, slowly, sweat collecting on his forehead, blood dripping from his freshly cut fingers. Lord Botan stood just a few paces away, looking much stronger than he had just moments ago, with the Karaoshi blade reunited in his hand.

"I have to give you credit," Botan said, lifting the blade up so that it flickered in the sunlight. "That was a damned good attempt. You truly are a legendary man, Takeo. But all legends have an end."

Takeo tried to whirl to a stand, but Botan closed the distance between them in half the time and kicked the ronin back to the ground. His movements were a flash to Takeo's eyes and the blow struck almost as hard as the collision did. Takeo hit the ground and bounced, another rib cracking as he cried out. He tried to raise his sword, but Botan's foot slammed down on the wrist, killing his strength. The blade fell from Takeo's hand. Sunlight poured into his eyes until Botan's silhouette loomed over him, sword tip raised.

"And this is yours," he said, and thrust down.

There was no time for Takeo to dodge. Before he even realized Botan had moved, the sword tip reached his chest, striking center mass, and . . . stopped completely.

Takeo froze, one hand shielding his neck on instinct, the other pinned under Botan's boot. Botan froze, both hands wrapped about the Karaoshi blade with the tip pressed to Takeo's chest. Even the air seemed to die out for an instant, and all that could be heard was the chorus of soldiers yelling in the distance, growing ever louder.

Botan's arms shook with force, and a vein bulged out of his neck from effort. The lord gritted his teeth as he put all his enchanted strength into driving the sword through Takeo's body, yet it wouldn't so much as pierce the skin. In fact, Takeo didn't even feel the pressure from the force at all.

"How is this possible?" the shogun grunted. "Curse your infernal soul."

Takeo was equally stunned, wracked with disbelief, but all that left him as, through the sword's tip, a familiar fire pulsed and spread throughout his body, filling him with strength unbound.

Damn, that jinni thought of everything.

Takeo's hand flashed up and grabbed his sword by the blade. Botan gasped just before Takeo kicked up with one leg, striking Botan with such force as to drive the shogun away. Takeo tried to hold fast and rip the Karaoshi sword free in the same motion, but Botan had the better grip, and the sword instead slipped through

Takeo's fingers. The blade didn't so much as nick the ronin's skin as it passed through.

Botan stumbled but caught himself from falling. Takeo struggled up to his feet, the enchanted strength having left him and his feeble, impacted body reduced to normalcy.

"Perhaps you're right," Takeo said, a thin, death-cheating smile slipping across his face. "Maybe I am cursed, but I accept that. Give up now, and I'll spare your life."

"Unfortunately for you," Botan replied, flicking the blade to hide it behind his back, "the only thing that's changed is that now you get to die slowly as I beat you to death with my bare hands."

Botan cut his last word short, his gaze focused ahead. Takeo also became distracted as he looked past the shogun to the drawbridge. It seemed the Katsu soldiers had finally gotten their act together and were charging out, blades ready, a small horde of them. It stunned Takeo to see so many. He didn't understand why they were only coming out now, and in such numbers, when Takeo saw that Botan had the same stunned look on his face as he looked over Takeo's shoulder.

Takeo's ears perked as he realized the shouting was coming from all directions. He glanced over his own shoulder to find an equally sized mass of Hanu warriors flying down the grassy plains towards the opened Katsu gates. Nicholas, Ping, and Kuniko led the charge.

Takeo spun back just in time to watch Botan become a blur to the human eye. A split second later, a fist appeared in Takeo's gut, slamming him up off his feet and back several paces. Takeo hurled blood as he flew, tripped as he landed, and rolled across the grass. He stood up only to find Botan at his side again, which he caught a single glimpse of before the lord's hand slammed into the side of his head. The world pitched black as Takeo hit the ground. The ronin's arms flailed before him, hoping to catch just one touch of his enchanted blade. Instead, his blurry vision was filled with a blue boot, armored and raised to strike down onto his neck.

The only thing that saved him was a flash of gray that streaked over Takeo's head and collided with the lord, swiping him from view. Takeo's hearing came back just enough for him to hear the loud thud as Botan hit the ground, followed by a triumphant roar.

"That's two for two, old man!" Nicholas yelled.

Nicholas had struck Botan with a flying hammer, again, and Ping dashed into view, leaping over Takeo and taking a defensive stance. Kuniko was next, a hair behind and shouting orders.

"Protect our lord," she yelled. "Spears! We need spears!"

Takeo tried to push himself up, but he had nothing left. Between the komainu collision and Botan's brutal assault, he teetered on the edge of blacking out. Yet up he went somehow, until he realized it was Nicholas who had hauled him to his feet.

"By Valhalla, how are you still alive?" the viking said.

"I'm cursed," Takeo mumbled.

"I'll say."

"My lord!"

The voice came from a short distance away, and Takeo looked up to see Botan being pulled to his feet by men of his own, the first to reach him, a heavy maul lying in the grass at his feet. Botan could barely stand, seeming only to be conscious after such a blow by holding onto the Karaoshi blade.

"My lord, we must retreat!" one yelled to the shogun. "The gate is open."

"Not without the ronin's head," Botan spat back.

The lord shoved off those holding him up and shambled forward, arms and legs shaking, yet the hand that held the Karaoshi blade was steady. The only thing standing in his way was Ping, and the boy did not move.

"Run!" Takeo commanded, or tried to, as words were difficult to form.

"Take him and go!" Ping shouted over his shoulder, then leveled his blade at Botan. "You'll not touch my lord."

Botan was a flash to the eye, his unease tossed aside for one fatal second before the Karaoshi blade punched through Ping's chest, spilling blood out of his back. Ping stood shocked for all of a half second before Botan ripped the blade free, and then Ping collapsed.

"Damn it, no!" Takeo shouted.

Nicholas took one look at Ping, Botan, and Takeo and swore.

"So much for running," he said. "Sorry, old pal."

Botan stepped over Ping's body, and just as the mad dash of samurai on either side collided, Nicholas hefted Takeo over his head and threw him back into the Hanu ranks.

160

A multitude of hands and arms broke Takeo's fall, looping about his crippled limbs. Takeo swore, demanded someone put a blade in his hands, but he wasn't half as loud as Kuniko, or anyone else for that matter.

"Protect our lord! Fall back! We haven't the numbers for an assault. They're pulling the drawbridge up!"

"Lord Botan, we have to retreat!"

"What are you idiots doing? Loose the arrows! Kill him!"

Takeo heard the whistle of arrows, heard them thud into the armored troops around him, followed by grunts or screams. Soldiers leaned over, shielding him with their bodies, and all Takeo saw was the ground flying by below him as his troops carried him away.

Chapter 17

"I know what you're going to ask," Takeo said, left arm raised as a surgeon wrapped bandages around his waist. "You want to know why I did it. What was I thinking?"

In truth, it was doubtful Mako would ever work up the courage to ask such a question. She sat with her legs pressed together, hands clasped at her waist, and her head hung. She only lifted her eyes enough to meet Takeo's once every few seconds. There was a glint of anger behind those beautiful eyes of hers, resentment that he would do something so foolish and reckless, knowing that it meant leaving her behind. She'd never say it, but he'd answer the unspoken question anyway. He just needed the surgeon to leave.

There was no need to say anything. This surgeon had worked on Takeo before. Her name was Hoa and she knew to be quick and silent about her work. She'd seen him worse off, having saved him from the brink of death not so long ago. Once he'd been made into a general, Takeo had sent for her to be his personal surgeon.

Hoa finished and left, not bothering to make any useless recommendations such that Takeo stay in bed for a few days. She'd worked with shogun before.

"Firstly, I want to say that I'm sorry," he whispered, trying his hardest to sound sincere. "I wasn't thinking about you in that way. I knew you were safe, which is more than I could say for others that are close to me. Hm, I just said that didn't I? Others that are close to me. Plural. But it's true."

"The knight?" she asked.

Takeo nodded. He looked down at his bandages, and then to the warm meal arrayed not too far away. He shook his head. Since when did his actions warrant such extravagance?

"Can I ask where my mother is? What happened to her after I left?" Takeo said.

"Nothing. She's still in the tent. No one is sure what to do, about anything it seems. I heard Kuniko arguing with Ping outside while I waited for you, before they left to get you. They said there's talk of

162

defeat since the catapults burned. Is that why you went out there? To get revenge?"

Takeo nodded again, though he didn't hear Mako so easily as he should have. His senses grew dull as his thoughts slipped into the back of his mind.

"We're defeated," he whispered. "I'm defeated. It took the combined effort of all my enemies to do it, but they've brought me low. Botan sits holed up in a wall of stone, Qadir is knocking at the Hanu doorstep with an army, and Yoshida sabotages me from within. My sword is taken, my friend ripped away, and my heart torn asunder. Even if I could bring Botan down, I'm not sure I could claim a victory at this point, but that's irrelevant. What's done is done.

"I wanted to kill him, Mako. Either that or die trying, that had been my goal. Those are the only two ways I know of rescuing Gavin at this point. I know you don't understand, but he represents something to me, my morality, if you will. He's a good man, one of the few truly good people in this world, and if I can't bring him happiness, then what am I doing this for? Is that not my aim, to bring peace to men like Gavin, so they can put down their swords and pick up their children? Violence, war, greed, the desires of a rakshasa combined with the worst of humanity took from me the only real love I'd known until last night. I can't believe she loved me so much, after all this time. Unconditional, they call it, right? Such love should be allowed to flourish, even if I can't have it. If I can't save Gavin, then how can I hope to save anyone else? I'm lost. I've lost. I've lost so much. I've lost things I didn't even know I had.

"Like Ping."

The name tumbled out of him before he'd thought it. It actually surprised him to say it, yet after doing so, the realization stunned him. He thought of so many more, however, from Emily to his mother, from Gavin to Nicholas, Mako and his brother, all those villagers who'd shown him so much kindness as a child.

It proved too much, and Takeo didn't have the will to fight anymore. Tears threatened to fall, and he let them. He closed his eyes and shuddered. Then a hand touched his face, and he opened his eyes to find Mako had crawled to sit beside him. They shared a gaze, then wordlessly, she pulled him close, shedding tears of her own, and he rested his head in her lap. She ran her fingers through his hair, and he wept into her gown.

"I watched him die, that boy," Takeo said. "No, Ping was a man. He fought with me at that ruined fortress. He believed in me. He gave his life for me. I don't understand. That sort of thing should affect me, shouldn't it? I should have felt at least some sort of kinship with him, at least some sort of remorse at his death, and yet I'm empty. Where there should be pain, I am hollow. I don't understand what's happening to me, Mako, or what has already happened. It's like . . . it's like I can't feel things like I used to, about Gavin, Emily, and sometimes even you. I have this strange sensation where I know the emotions that should run through me and react like I'm supposed to, but the motivations aren't actually there. Like when I watched Gavin get tortured up on those walls, there was no pit of fear or anger that welled within me. I manifested it, based on memories, but it didn't seem to naturally occur. It doesn't make any sense, and I don't know what to do about it. I'm losing something precious, Mako, yet I can't bring myself to care.

"And so, I thought that if I had to fail, if I had to die, at least let me go out saving one person. Please, I begged at Botan's feet, let me not live a life where I'd have to hold one more person as they died in my arms, like my mother, like Emily."

Mako's hand swept through his hair as he cried, his hands clutching her clothes and his body curled up, ignoring how his insides screamed in pain at being so compressed. However, the pain felt good, in a way, because it was so much more preferable to feeling nothing at all.

"You're lost," Mako whispered, sweeping his hair behind his ear.

Takeo nodded.

"I've been lost, too," she said. "I've been lost for a while, and things only seemed to get worse as they went on. First, Okamoto was taken from me, from us, but then I lost you, too. Then my parents and our whole village was destroyed. You remember? You came back only briefly before leaving me again. You've never asked what happened to me, between then and now, all those years you were gone from my life, all those years I was cast adrift. You've never asked, and I've never told."

She paused, one tracing finger having found the scar that ran along his cheek, faded though it was. Her touch did not linger there and instead retreated to the safety of his hairline.

"There's a reason for that, though," she continued. "It's because it's not important, to either of us. What matters to you, to me, is that we're here now, together, and things are going to be better because of it. You don't ask because you don't want to hear, but I don't tell because I don't want to relive it. It's the same reason you never talk about her, and the same reason you were hesitant to talk to Dhyana. When the past is painful, it can be difficult to acknowledge. Sometimes we can only survive by numbing ourselves and looking to the future.

"I don't think you realize this, Takeo, but to many people, you've become that future."

She paused. A conversation started up just outside the tent, including some shouting. Takeo had been too distracted to hear all of it, but it sounded like demands to see him. No doubt there was a fair bit of confusion flowing through the camp, what with the catapults burned and Takeo charging off to face Botan alone. People wanted answers.

Kuniko's voice rang out, and the shouting died down. Mako continued to run her fingers through Takeo's hair.

"I didn't realize it until I overheard Ping demanding to join you on the battlefield," she went on. "For the longest time, I thought it was just me suffering under the greed of the daimyo, as they used everyone beneath them to vie for power. People ask, why is food hard to come by in a land like this? Juatwa is beautiful, plentiful, or at least it should be. Why do we starve but the daimyo are fat? Why are we always in danger, but not them? We don't have half the number of deadly creatures or marauding bands that other places are rumored to have. How is it that death is so common here? It shouldn't be. It doesn't have to be, but few stopped to think about it until you showed up and pledged your life to the cause.

"The past is painful, Takeo. You and I, we're not the only people who've suffered, who've lost, and who've searched for something to latch onto. I can't answer these questions, but I can tell you that you can't give up. You carry more lives than just Gavin's these days, and your shoulders are heavy because you carry the dream of an entire people.

"We're all lost, Takeo, but we're following you. So please, don't give up. Lead us out of this abyss."

He couldn't recall when, but sometime during Mako's speech, Takeo stopped crying.

* * *

Nicholas, although very much attached to weapons in general, was not attached to any specific weapon, per se. For example, he'd wasted not one single breath on the maul that he'd flung into Botan, instead Nicholas took from the armory one of the heavy warhammers one would use to destroy a gashadokuro. He twirled the weapon about in his hands, testing its weight as he walked just behind Takeo and Qing on their way to Nobu's tent.

"You know, I get that you're suffering here, Takeo, and normally I'm not real inquisitive," Nicholas started, "but I have to ask. The next time you get a brilliant idea to go down in a self-righteous blaze of suicidal glory, can you tell me first?"

"What's this about, Takeo?" Qing said, cutting off the viking. "You've summoned us with no explanation. It's clear we're headed to Nobu, judging by the path, but Kuniko seemed to know more than we did. Why isn't she here?"

"She's busy issuing orders and taking care of people who ask too many questions," Takeo said. "We're going to tell Nobu this siege is over. You're here to act as Lady Zhenzhen and Lord Virote's will. Nicholas is here in case the oni try to give us trouble again."

Nicholas sighed and gazed off toward the setting sun. Satisfied with his new weapon's weight, he sheathed it into the straps over his back.

"So, we're really calling it quits, eh?" he asked. "I thought maybe you'd changed your mind, the way you charged out to face Botan, but I suppose there's nothing more to do at this point."

"I'll admit even I am a little surprised," Qing said. "I've witnessed your tenacity. I expected you to break before you bent."

"If it were only me, I suppose I would," Takeo answered. "However, recently, I've had to accept that my actions have further

166

reaching consequences. Yoshida is right. I must aim to win the war, not always the battle. No one is my enemy who helps me reach this goal, not even him."

"And Krunk and Gavin?" Nicholas said.

Takeo came to a stop and hung his head. He remembered Botan's promise to kill them for Takeo's insolence and hoped the shogun had been lying.

"I don't know," the ronin admitted. "We'll think of something."

He marched on. They weren't long in reaching Nobu because, this time around, there was no guessing which tent Nobu was in. Tokhta and Borota were stationed outside the entrance, both seated and dozing in place, unconcerned with the smoke that still lingered in the air or the general unease that permeated the encampment.

As the trio approached, Tokhta cocked one eye open and snorted.

"Our orders remain the same," the oni said. "No one is allowed inside. Don't think to disobey again. We'll not be so forgiving."

"If your orders haven't changed," Takeo countered, "then you'll recall that Nobu said it was fine if I entered. Has he rescinded that decision since I was last here?"

Tokhta opened his other eye and flicked a gaze at Borota. Takeo smiled.

"Well now," the ronin said. "I don't think I've ever seen you indecisive before. How comical."

The oni snarled.

"Only you, then," it said. "The other two wait outside."

Takeo shrugged. "Fine by me. I'll just have Nobu let them in, too. You've done nothing but inconvenience me. Congratulations. You're as powerful as a stick lying in the road."

Veins popped along Tokhta's neck, though their intensity was lessened between the oni's red skin and the fading light. Takeo marched between the immortal guards, slipping into the darkness of the gigantic tent.

It took a second for his eyes to adjust. Nobu had let the fires die out again, leaving the opening at the top as the only source of light. At this time of the day, that meant only a slim ray slipped in and ran along the top fabric, casting everything beneath into shadows. He expected to find the lord in his bed like last time, so it stunned him to see the prince's dark outline standing in the middle of the room.

167

"My lord, sorry," Takeo said in reaction, catching his hand before it fell to his sword, shifting the movement into a bow. "I didn't see you there."

Nobu gave no reply, and Takeo didn't wait for one to rise.

"I have terrible news, though I'm sure you've heard of it by now, if not smelt it in the air," he continued and stepped forward. "I hope you'll understand that I did everything to prevent this but—"

Takeo caught himself. Something was wrong. Lord Nobu was completely covered in darkness due to the lack of light, but Takeo could see that the lord hadn't moved since Takeo had entered, not even to flinch. Then it dawned on Takeo that Nobu's head was cocked at an odd angle, and there was an overturned stool at his feet. Also, the lord seemed taller than he last remembered, until Takeo's eyes dropped to the feet and saw that the prince was floating in the air.

Not floating—hanging.

Takeo gasped and dashed forward, kicking the stool out of the way, and grabbed hold of the prince, hoisting him into the air. The rope that hung about Nobu's neck slacked, yet no strength returned to the lord's body. He fell limply over Takeo's shoulder, his cold skin brushing against Takeo's face. Now that they were close, Nobu's grim, lifeless expression shined through, forever frozen in time.

Takeo swore and released the prince's corpse. It swung freely, the rope creaking as it stretched from side to side.

"What the—" he started, breathless. "He didn't, no. Did someone? Damn. Damn! Damn it all."

Takeo clenched his fists, mind reeling, eyes whirling about for some explanation.

"Oh no, this is terrible. How can this be happening?"

He grabbed Nobu's corpse and checked his wrists.

"No marks, no signs of a struggle, oni haven't heard a thing," he went on. "Son of a—ah!"

A thought struck him. He opened Nobu's clothes to check the boy's stomach. His fingers found a single mark at the navel, a thin prick so shallow that it was red but did not bleed.

Shit. He tried to seppuku like a true warrior, blade against his stomach, but he couldn't do it. He couldn't follow through, so he hung himself.

Takeo stood rooted, lips parted as he watched Nobu's body drift in silence. He didn't know what to think at first. Admittedly, remorse was not within him, but there was plenty of shock, followed by apprehension.

"Hey, are you going to let us in or what?" Qing called out.

"Not another step," Borota warned.

"Piss off, you oversized orc, or I'll send you crawling back up some dead lord's arse," Nicholas replied.

Before Takeo could say anything, the tent's opening was flung wide, and the last vestiges of evening light came pouring in. Three figures of varying size appeared and froze as Nobu's swaying corpse was illuminated.

"By Valhalla," Nicholas sputtered out first. "He's—"

"Shut it, don't say it," Takeo cut in. "Don't say a word. Get inside and close the entrance."

Nicholas obeyed, but Qing was too stunned for movement. She stood with eyes wide and mouth agape, blinking less often than was comfortable.

As for Tokhta, he did nothing more than cock an eyebrow, wrinkling the skin around one of the horns that protruded from his head. He nodded to Borota, who glanced inside, frowned, and then the two shared a look. They shuffled to a stand, swung their kanabos over their shoulders, and started to march off.

"Hey, hey!" Takeo shouted and rushed out of the tent, glancing about to make sure there weren't any onlookers, only to find three servants who quickly made themselves scarce at the sight of Takeo's dark look. "Where do you two think you're going?"

"The deal is broken," Tokhta muttered, neither pausing nor turning back.

"Hey!" Takeo tried again.

But the oni were tall and covered the ground quickly, and Takeo would have had to chase after them at this point, which would draw attention. He swiveled about and marched back into the tent, making sure to draw the opening closed.

Takeo swore.

Qing had gone inside by now and had paced right up to Nobu, looking up at his crooked neck as he turned just a hair at a time with the dying motion set in place by Takeo. She grabbed his hand, cold and lifeless, and held it with both of hers.

"My lady," Qing whispered. "This is going to break her. Why, my little prince? Why would you do this?"

Nicholas swore and swore again.

"What in the world, I mean really?" the viking said. "What is wrong with this place, this night, this day? Takeo loses his mother; Zhenzhen loses her son. This isn't right, I tell you. All these people dead and not a single battle to show for it. This doesn't sit well with me, Takeo. I don't like where this is going."

"It's going to get worse," Takeo said.

Nicholas swore again. Qing glanced over her shoulder. Takeo continued, rubbing his forehead.

"Grief aside, without the oni and akki to bolster the Hanu's depleted ranks, Zhenzhen stands little chance of retaking the Katsu fortress, let alone standing against the Nguyens. She could dispense of me and thus bring many daimyo back into the fold, but that still leaves most of Juatwa divided and easily conquered by a skilled general such as Qadir, and Emily did not die just so another rakshasa could sit on the throne of the world. I don't care how skilled a politician Yoshida is. With Nobu dead, politics won't stop what's coming. This is not a defeat we can afford. We have but one chance, one last resort that I never would have considered while Nobu was still alive."

Qing and Nicholas shared a glance.

"Wait, you're talking like we have a chance at victory, but you also said things were going to get worse," the viking recounted. "You're giving me a bad feeling."

Qing narrowed her eyes.

"Your allegiance lies with Lady Zhenzhen and her alone, right?" Takeo said to her.

She nodded.

"And you trust me to bring victory no matter the cost?"

She paused, then nodded.

Takeo stared at Nobu's swaying body, knowing deep down that he shared some part in whatever had driven the boy to suicide. He should have felt guilt, but instead, all he saw was hope.

No—reality.

"Then let's get to work," he said.

Chapter 18

Lord Yoshida, despite all his talk of trusting Takeo to make a good decision, was not a foolish man. No lord or lady survived long in Juatwa without some insurance against being stabbed in the back by each and every person they knew. So, when Qing appeared at his tent late in the night, saying Takeo needed to speak with him at Nobu's tent immediately, Yoshida made sure not to go alone. He brought the Lady Xie, which was easy to do considering she'd been in his bed, and also sent for his right-hand-man, Lord Sing. They all brought their contingent of honor guards and made their way through the camp with Qing in the lead because, despite the late hour of the night, it would be considered rude and insolent not to answer their general's summons.

After all, Yoshida really did want Takeo on his side.

"I assume this is about retreat?" Yoshida asked of Qing. "I saw the signal arrow shot through the night sky. I can only imagine that's why Takeo is having us meet at Nobu's tent."

"That's not for us to discuss here, my lord," the ninja answered.

"Oh, come now. It's not like the matter isn't being discussed by everyone on all sides of this war. I'll bet even the Nguyens know the situation by now. The need for secrecy has passed."

Qing marched on in that uncanny silence that unnerved Yoshida. It was strange how her footsteps made no noise, almost inhuman. Until this day, he'd always been sure to stay on Lady Zhenzhen's good side, not just because it was good politics, but also because of Qing. He had a feeling that if Lady Zhenzhen ever wanted him gone, she'd send this ninja to do the task, and he wasn't so certain Qing could be stopped.

Takeo was waiting for them atop the low hill where Nobu's command tent had been erected. At the ronin's side stood that towering mass of flesh called Nicholas. Yoshida always thought of vikings as a mistake, an improbable and disgusting crossbreed of a human-orc love affair gone wrong. Nicholas, for his part, did appear somewhat solemn on this occasion, with head bowed and hands clasped. Takeo appeared grimmer than usual.

Yoshida scanned the otherwise empty setting.

"Takeo," the lord said.

"My lord," Takeo replied and bowed.

"Is Nobu not here? Where are the oni?"

"Lord Nobu is inside," Takeo replied softly. "The oni, however, have left us."

Yoshida's gaze drifted to the tent, then slowly back to Takeo, where the two locked eyes.

"Us?" Yoshida asked.

"The Hanu army," Takeo replied, then nodded to the three daimyo. "You'll want to leave your guards outside for this."

A pit welled in Lord Yoshida's stomach. He waved one hand at his guards, telling them to stay at the ready, and then marched inside the tent. Lord Sing and Lady Xie mimicked him.

It was dark inside, as the moon wasn't bright enough to illuminate anything within, and Yoshida worried that he'd made a mistake. A moment's reflection reminded him that there was nothing to gain by his death in this moment, as no daimyo would follow Takeo's orders without his support. He was safe.

A moment later, Qing and Takeo followed them inside, leaving the brute outside with the guards. That made Yoshida feel better, until Takeo struck a light and Nobu's corpse sprung into view.

Lady Xie gasped and clutched Yoshida's arm. Lord Sing covered his mouth and averted his gaze, a small wave of nausea passing over his features. Lord Yoshida stared unblinking while his lips hinged open ever so slightly. It dawned on him that a putrid smell was starting to fester, and not just because the young boy had loosed his bowels upon death.

"I found him like this, alone," Takeo said, leaving the small brazier and taking a stand next to the daimyo. "Qing, Nicholas, and the oni did, too, shortly after. Tokhta and the other oni immediately left, saying the deal is broken."

Outside, the ever-chatty Nicholas started up a conversation with the guards. The man's boisterous voice was an annoyance that broke Yoshida from his trance. He took a step towards Nobu but then stopped again, thinking better. He turned a hesitant look towards Takeo.

"I've checked for marks," the ronin answered unprompted. "Qing scouted the tent. No signs of a struggle. No signs that there was anyone in here but Nobu. There's a tanto on the bed, the ceremonial dagger flecked with just one touch of blood on its tip. We think Nobu tried to seppuku first but couldn't follow through, so he strung himself up, probably sometime this morning."

Lord Yoshida could only stand in horror and shock for so long before the clock-like inner workings of his mind went to work, turning and twisting away as hundreds of possibilities flashed before him. His eyes went wider still, and he took in a quick breath.

"The oni are gone," Yoshida started, whispering.

"My lord, what was that?" Lady Xie asked.

Nicholas was now arguing with the guards outside, something about the army needing to retreat and how vikings would never do such a cowardly thing, followed by some counter from the guards about how Nicholas would run to his ship after raiding a pathetic village.

"Will you shut that man up?" Yoshida demanded. "I can hardly think."

"Nicholas is making noise on my orders," Takeo explained. "You don't want any of the guards, or perhaps anyone else, to overhear our conversation, do you?"

Yoshida paused as his anger slipped away.

"You're right," the lord said. "As tragic as this is, there's no time to waste. The oni are gone, and thus the akki, too. We're in retreat, and our shogun will appear vulnerable. She's likely to lose more status at this point and bleed further allegiances to our enemies. My little ninja friend, you must agree some drastic countermeasure is needed."

"Let me guess," Qing said, arms folded across her chest. "A marriage with you?"

"Precisely," Yoshida replied, nodding. "That's why you've brought me here, isn't it? Between losing her heir and this battle, our lady will struggle to hold the daimyo to her, all but the most loyal. There needs to be a perceived change in leadership, one most desperately needed, even if—"

Yoshida paused and gestured to Takeo.

"Even if," he continued, "the leadership stays mostly unchanged. You'll still lead these armies to victory, Takeo, and no longer will you have to worry about seating either an immature boy or a tyrannical oni on the throne. It can be a capable, knowledgeable individual—me. This way everyone wins. This changes everything."

"It most certainly does," Takeo replied.

In the span of two heartbeats, the ronin dropped his arms, drew his sword, and rammed it into Lord Sing's side. The blade punctured both lungs, judging by how Lord Sing let loose nothing more than a moan before blood gurgled up from his throat. Less than a blink behind, Qing drew a dagger and thrust it point up into Lady Xie's mouth, nailing her jaw shut before a scream could let loose, the sound instead deadening into her enclosed lips.

Yoshida bellowed a low shout for his guards, but his cry was muffled by the sudden violence, the tent's thick fabric, and Nicholas' horrendous shouting just outside. Before Yoshida could scream again, louder this time, Takeo dropped his blade and sprung atop the surviving lord.

Takeo was lightning fast, strong despite his recent injuries, driving one knee into Yoshida's stomach while a fist connected with his temple. Yoshida's lungs expunged their air, his sight darkened, and he fell back on the ground. Before he could suck in a breath, Takeo pinned the lord down and wrapped his fingers about Yoshida's neck. The ronin squeezed.

"I'm sorry, my lord," Takeo said, gritting his teeth as he strangled Yoshida. "We can't get any blood on that outfit of yours, so you'll have to die slowly."

The daimyo fought for air, clawed at Takeo's hands, then tried to push the ronin away. No attempt seemed to have any effect. The ronin outright ignored the struggles and continued to squeeze the life from the old man. Yoshida mouthed any word he could think of, "Stop, no, wait, please, why?"

"Don't make this harder than it has to be," Takeo replied. "You brought this on yourself. I would have gladly served you, or any lord or lady, if only for one stinking moment they would appreciate all I've sacrificed to help them. My love, my friends, now even my family, just once I wished someone would look down and realize all I could mean to them. I thought that could be you, my lord, I really

175

did, but then you had to go and stab me in the back. Say what you will of Lady Zhenzhen, but at least she's never tried to sabotage me. In her own, strange way, she loves me."

Consciousness faded in and out for Yoshida, which at this point seemed a blessing considering the pain that wracked his throat and mind as he was deprived of life-giving oxygen. He couldn't fight Takeo anymore. He hadn't the strength. Takeo's last words were barely comprehensible, as was Nicholas' loathsome shouting growing ever fainter. Lord Yoshida's eyes rolled back, dropping Takeo to the bottom of his vision and bringing into view the tent's roof flickering in orange light.

Then another person came into view as darkness blurred the edges of his vision, an older man with a commanding aura that took but half a second for Yoshida to recognize as himself. While his body went numb, he was struck by a dim curiosity. Was Takeo truly so cruel as to hold a mirror over the lord's head as he died? The thought was never finished, however, as things went dark and the pain faded away.

Takeo kept his grip on Yoshida's neck until he was absolutely sure the lord had passed. During the ordeal, Qing had to pull the two bodies away lest their wounds pool blood on the old daimyo. They needed his clothing as immaculate as when the lord came in. The dirt from the floor could be brushed off. Blood would be too obvious.

In the meantime, Emy stood over Yoshida and concentrated, adjusting her disguise to match the lord in every way. She changed the hair color once, twice, adjusted the follicles, lengthened, then shrunk her nose, and even matched the lips where they had cracked. Takeo thought to tell her that such complexity wouldn't be noticed on this dark night, but then thought better. Nothing could be left to chance.

Once Yoshida was dead, they stripped his corpse, and Emy donned the clothing.

"Any questions?" Takeo asked.

"None," Emy said, mimicking Yoshida's voice with bone-chilling accuracy.

"Get to it, then. By the sounds of it, Nicholas is about to start a fight with the guards."

The arguing outside was indeed growing rambunctious. Nicholas' shouts were barely audible over the others, and Takeo feared the viking had gone too far, rousing suspicion. Emy put an end to that, though, slipping through the tent's exit and demanding an explanation for all the noise. The guards instantly went silent, except for one that dared indicate Nicholas' rude insults, but Emy only replied that she expected better from those who served the Yoshida family. She then rattled off a sharp demand to send messages to all the daimyo in the camp. She needed parchment, ink, and the Yoshida wax seal immediately, as she needed to distribute orders that dared not be defied.

One guard asked where the other daimyo were, and Emy replied simply with, "Did I stutter?"

Silence followed, minus the pounding footsteps of several guards sprinting off.

Takeo smiled.

"Have Nicholas dispose of the bodies," he said to Qing. "He won't like it, but there's no one else. Dig some shallow graves right here in this tent. We need only to keep this a secret for tonight. It won't matter after that. You'll be ready by morning?"

"Of course," Qing said.

"Don't fail me."

Qing looked down at the three dead bodies, each in turn, before turning her cold gaze back on Takeo.

"I can't. There's no other path to victory now," she said. "You've made sure of that."

"We, elf," Takeo corrected. "We made sure."

Chapter 19

The dead space between the Hanu camp and the Katsu keep was the perfect landscape for skulking about, especially at night. The tall grass, despite being trampled under a ladder assault, still provided ample cover. Add to this the boulders and bodies strewn about; it was difficult for Takeo to follow Emy's movements when she was right in front of his face, let alone what the guards atop the high Katsu walls were trying to see. Having served up there more than once in his life, Takeo knew the guards were doing little but acting as a deterrent. The walls were doing most of the work all on their own, while the swift flowing moat took care of the rest. Even with the Hanu camp so close at hand, most everyone knew that attempting to cross into the Katsu keep was a suicide attempt for any normal person.

Hence Lord Botan had taken extra precautions.

"He's added spikes to the lower embankment," Emy explained as she and Takeo crossed from one boulder to the next, edging closer to the moat. "There's nowhere to stand or hide, and the rocks have been cleared away, so there's little to grab, assuming you can fight the current."

"None of that matters," Takeo answered, pausing to wince as one of his fresh wounds stabbed him with pain, protesting the way he crouched in the grass. "Just tell me how you get inside."

"I don't know if you can follow me. It's tough, even for a rakshasa."

Takeo didn't reply. Emy sighed.

"The guards have a permanent posting at the moat's entrance and exit," she explained, "leaving the middle section guarded on a pacing schedule, so there's a small gap if I time it right. I cross at the dead center, near the drawbridge. The wood is easier to climb than the stone, and there is a small chain sticking out in the crack between the wall and the drawbridge about halfway up. I watch the guards for the right moment, dash across the moat, pick through the spikes, scale the drawbridge to the chain, then vault up to the ledge. One time, I got lucky and was fast enough to clear the distance before a guard came. The next time, I had to disguise myself as a drunken woman who'd lost her way. Even then, the guard must have thought I was a ninja, as he went to yell, and I had to snap his neck and toss him over before anyone else arrived. I don't think they found his body, but Botan's paranoia takes no chances. He doubled the guard after that. Time will be impossibly short."

"Lead the way," Takeo replied.

Emy blinked. She knew better than to question him, yet she couldn't stop herself from wanting to. It must have bothered her rakshasa mind to no end that a mere human could baffle her, so she instead refocused her efforts. Takeo could see the way her attention pulled away as she thought for one, two seconds, then twitched her whiskers.

She nodded, indicating she understood.

"It doesn't matter if they see us," she said.

"The gatehouse," Takeo continued. "Get us there. Leave the bodies in our wake if need be."

"Are you strong enough to hold on?"

Takeo scoffed. "I'll choke you if I have to."

Emy smiled, her canines shining white in the low light. They slipped into the darkness and made their way to the moat.

Takeo's stomach churned as they passed the spot where he and Botan had fought. The komainu corpses lay untouched, though now they were marred with the bloat and stench of death. Their carcasses oozed onto the plains, yet also provided excellent cover, so neither Takeo nor Emy hesitated to skirt the edges of those masses of flesh. Takeo briefly caught sight of the area where Botan might have ended him, if not for the diabolical cleverness of one lone jinni.

It occurred to Takeo that immunity to his sword had not been a part of his wish. For a moment, he wondered what that meant. Was that ability part of the curse, perhaps? No, it couldn't be, could it?

But that was all the attention he had to spare. That simple distraction cost him dearly as his foot caught a dried weed in the darkness and crunched it. Doubtful though it was that the sound would carry over the moat and up the walls, Takeo and Emy instinctively dove into the grass, and Takeo cursed himself. As usual in times of error, he thought of his brother and how a mistake like that would have earned Takeo a severe beating.

179

Well, he couldn't really call it severe. Severe implied a beating more violent than normal. To Okamoto, severe was normal.

Emy's tail flicked, indicating her annoyance, but she had sense enough not to look back. Takeo gathered himself, and when she set off again, he followed with all his attention on the task at hand. They reached the edge of the moat soon after.

In one way, this was the most dangerous part of their journey. The ground over here had been pounded flat by the opening and closing of the drawbridge for a lifetime. Plus, the weeds and grass had been cleared away to make a more royal entrance that led into the fortress. Hence there was little cover, yet they had to stay here awhile for Emy to scan the walls above, timing the guards.

"Soon," she whispered.

Takeo climbed onto her back, hooking one arm around her neck and the other about her shoulder. His gaze slipped down to the swift moving moat mere feet from their hiding place, and he began to regulate his breathing so that he was ready to hold his breath in an instant.

There was no need for him to scan the walls. There was nothing he could see that she would not.

Without warning, Emy dove from the grass and into the water. Half of Takeo's prepared air was forced from his lungs as chilly saltwater slammed into his eyes, ears, nose, and wounds, and Emy's hair instantly became matted and slick to his grip. She dove deep, so that they traveled in total darkness while the current pulled at them with unrelenting strength. Takeo's lower body drifted away, which he allowed so as not to interfere with the rakshasa's powerful strokes. His lost air turned out to be of no concern as Emy turned upwards and breached the night air in half the time Takeo had expected.

Not a moment was lost. Before Takeo took a refreshing breath, Emy scampered up the shore and into the pike nest. Takeo wrapped his legs and arms about her body, but even this proved a problem as Emy was now wider than usual. Fresh cuts adorned Takeo's legs as rusted spear tips marred their path, but this too was over quickly. Emy only went half-through before leaping onto the walls.

Her rakshasa claws extended and dug into the ancient wood as the two slammed up against the solid surface. The ronin's head struck one of Emy's shoulder blades. His legs slipped from around her matted fur and clothing, but a dire need and a strong sense of survival kept his arms locked like iron bars. He could feel his forearm digging into Emy's neck, cutting off her air, but not a word was uttered from either of them.

Emy did not wait for Takeo to steady himself before climbing.

Claws dug into timber, and she hauled both herself and Takeo into the night sky. Occasionally they struck an old nail, a rusted hinge, or even a large metal brace, but although things these slowed her progress, she did not stop. Her hind legs added to the ascent, climbing until the ground below was a mass of shadows.

The scene shifted again, and without warning, Emy came away from the wall, causing Takeo's stomach to lurch as they were flung out over the abyss, raining saltwater, and it took a half-second pause for Takeo to realize Emy had reached the chain. When they swung back to the wall, her feet softened their impact, and she began to climb twice as fast, hauling their combined weight with ease. Takeo dangled down, choking Emy further. He used his left arm to yank on her shoulder and swing his lower body up, wrapping his legs about her waist and interlocking his feet. His arm eased off her throat, and Emy took a deep breath of air.

They propelled themselves towards the wall's lip, or so it appeared as the combination of wood, stone, and darkness drifted by them. Takeo scanned the edge, spying a torch's light radiating against the parapet some short distance to their right and lazily approaching. He resisted the urge to grab his sword, instead tightening his grip on the rakshasa for the final vault that would take them into the Katsu fortress.

Emy let loose a tiny growl as she summoned strength, then yanked on the chain and kicked with her feet in a single motion. Takeo was yanked like he was riding atop a komainu that had broken into a sprint, hair streaming through the air while he gritted his teeth, until Emy's claws scraped against the stone edge. They came to a brief stop, heralded by a soldier making an alarmed shout. The second Emy was over the wall, Takeo released her, dropping to the walkway while she dashed with inhuman speed. The soldier didn't have time for a second shout as rakshasa claws tore out his throat. The torch clattered to the ground.

From behind, another voice called out into the darkness, wondering what the first had been about.

"Let's go," Takeo commanded, picking himself up and drawing his blade.

There was no need for a direction. Takeo understood this fortress like the curve of his sword, and Emy had spent a fair bit of time getting acquainted with the place, too. They dashed to the nearest set of stone steps that would take them down to the gatehouse.

And that's when their luck ran out.

Inside the fortress, the place was lit in strategic locations with sconce torchlight, the two nearest being one at the top of the stairs and one at the bottom. As Emy and Takeo reached the open staircase that would take them down to the courtyard, they found themselves bathed in light just as two soldiers were beginning their ascent from the bottom. All four paused only so long as it took to blink before the soldiers pulled their weapons free and began to charge up the stairs, shouting at the intruders so loud their voices echoed about the courtyard like a gong.

Emy readied her claws, but Takeo peered over the side.

Directly beneath them was a row of lean-tos with wooden roofs lying against the stone of the fortress. Takeo knew from experience these would be covering weapons, lying at the ready for use in case the entire garrison was summoned to fight. He flung his gaze to the gatehouse, a small stone room set directly on the farther side of the drawbridge, where heavy chains slunk down into it for use in lowering and raising the gate. The slits where the chains went through the roof were too small for any man to fit through, yet the exposed chains were too thick to break. Anyone attempting to do so would be exposed.

Takeo dove from the stairs to the wooden roofs below, breaking his fall with an acrobatic roll that sent spikes of pain shuddering through his fractured ribs. The roof shook a moment later as Emy landed beside him, grabbed his clothes, and yanked him to his feet. Takeo dashed across the wood, his footsteps a thunderous clacking that mixed all too well with the intensity of the shouting that rose all around them. The roofline shook again as the other two soldiers joined them, albeit far away, while darkened figures darted out of nooks and crannies about the courtyard. The stationary torches began to move as soldiers ripped them from their sconces and hefted them toward the commotion.

Takeo narrowed his gaze on the task at hand.

He reached the last lean-to and leapt off the side without pause, aiming to clear the remaining distance to the gatehouse in a single bound. Four guards already clogged his path, the sum of which Takeo only counted on instinct before his right foot cracked into the face of one of them.

As that one hit the ground, moaning, the other three recovered their shock and drew swords, which was all the time Emy needed to vault onto the scene. She slammed one guard into the ground with her landing and struck a second with her claws. The third squared off with Takeo, making one deft parry before the ronin's second attack punched through the man's lungs.

Blood pooled about the scene, and the torchlight was mere moments from reaching them. Dozens of Hanu were en route, with many more voices echoing off the stones all around.

"The lock, rip it off," Takeo commanded, reversing his blade and executing the injured guards on the ground.

True to Emy's first report, the gatehouse was sealed with a heavy iron door, not so much as a slit defacing its protection. However, for whatever reason, the lock was on the outside and padded like a normal prison door. Emy grabbed the lock with both hands, braced against the stone, and yanked with all her rakshasa might. The locking mechanisms within broke before the iron itself, and Emy pushed the door open, darting inside with Takeo short on her heels.

Takeo slammed the door shut and braced himself against it, digging his heels into the stone cracks and turning himself into a human brace. He could only hope that Emy could deal with whoever was inside alone.

Yet she wasn't moving, or so it seemed in the almost total blackness inside.

"What is it?" Takeo asked.

"There's a second door," Emy replied, panic slipping into her voice. "How did I not hear about this? Damn that paranoid shogun."

Takeo was about to respond when the soldiers on the other side reached their shelter and a hard slam jarred Takeo's entire body. The door was knocked back a hair before Takeo rammed it shut again, and then a second slam rocked him in place. Angry shouts vibrated through the metal.

"What are you waiting for? Rip the lock off," he yelled.

"There isn't one," Emy growled back. "The door's right in front me, and there's nothing, just metal on stone. Everything is on the other side, lock and hinges. It won't open!"

The door rocked again, and Takeo gritted his teeth as he struggled to maintain his position. Only by way of sheer leverage was he holding the door in place, but this wouldn't last long. In fact, it wouldn't even last for more than a few seconds. Takeo might be faster than any man, but he certainly wasn't stronger than any two.

"Break it down," he grunted, legs shaking. "Do something!"

The small hallway rang as Emy rammed against the door with all her strength. It was too dark for Takeo to tell if anything happened, but a second ring pierced his ears a moment later. Again, again, and he heard Emy grunt in pain, then roar. The scraping of claws digging into stone echoed among the shouts and slams, and Emy hit the metal door again with all her might.

The door burst open, sending Emy sailing through atop the thick sheet of metal to crash and slide across the floor. Torchlight poured in, illuminating the flying pieces of bolts and hinges that had shattered under her assault before they rained down on stone like empty gunslinger shells. Just beyond the short hallway was the man-sized drawbridge wheel, wrapped with the heavy chains.

Also illuminated were four guards with swords poised in the air.

The blades rammed down, and Emy screamed as one punctured her calf and another her arm. One she dodged completely by the sheer luck of rolling over, and the last scythed into her collarbone just an inch from her neck. With her one free hand, she lashed out at the one with the blade close to her neck, raking her claws up the man's groin, and his screams turned the room into an echo chamber. The man fell but left the blade, and Emy ripped it free while guards drew back for another strike.

Takeo braced against another shudder, only barely holding the door in place as fingers wrapped around the edges. Then he pushed off the door and darted inside, letting the whole thing loose unexpectedly. The guards on the other side plummeted through, three of them all at once, crashing atop each other and choking the way with their flailing, scrambling bodies.

Takeo sprinted into the chamber. Sword in hand, he rammed one guard straight through, abandoned the blade, and tackled another, sending them both to the ground.

"The door!" Takeo screamed, then cut short as he and the guard fell into a brawl.

Emy leapt to her feet, grabbed the iron door as if it were made of paper, and dashed to the entrance. She reached it just as the mass of guards on the other end recovered, and the opposing forces collided with a sickening thud.

The rakshasa won.

The iron door was rammed back into place, though slightly off center, and Emy braced herself against the stone. The one guard not entangled with Takeo was quick to follow, charging Emy and impaling her unprepared body through the shallow beneath her ribs. She roared, but she was no human. It would take more than that to drop her. She let loose one arm to grab the grinning soldier by the throat, his expression turning to shock just before she yanked his head into the metal door. He crumpled, and she pulled the sword out slowly, gasping and grunting, all the while holding the door against the trio on the other side.

Takeo only caught glimpses of this as he struggled with the last guard. Not a small man by any means, he knew how to throw a punch and had quickly caught on that Takeo didn't take blows to the stomach well. The battle quickly turned one-sided as Takeo was forced into a corner and the guard wailed on him. The fight might have ended there if Takeo's hand hadn't found a broken hinge, which it clenched and then slammed into the guard's temple. The man crumpled, and Takeo climbed on top of him to finish the job, slamming down again and again with the hinge until spurts of blood, bone, and brain coated the scene.

Takeo stood up and whipped his vision clear, sucking air through strained lungs. He saw Emy struggling to remain steady, eyes blinking in long strokes, one hand holding the door, one hand holding her wound.

It was already starting to seal up with her rakshasa abilities, but she'd been stabbed thoroughly four times and had lost a fair bit of blood. Takeo could tell that she was leaning on the door as much as she was bracing herself against it. Only the shouting and the steady slams against her frame kept her conscious.

Takeo darted over and used his sword as a wedge against the door, assisting her defense.

"Can you hold?" he shouted, but she only closed her eyes and did not open them, so he slapped her hard. "I said, can you hold?"

Emy's eyes dilated, her ears flattened, and she bared her canines. A blood-chilling growl issued from her throat.

"Better," Takeo said.

He dashed to the wheel and made a quick inspection. He knew these devices well; they were designed to be difficult to operate by one man, though not impossible. The drawbridge was operated by two torsion bars. Right now, both were in place, but only one was wedged by the weight of the bridge. He'd have to get it free all on his own.

"Hurry," Emy roared as the door rocked against her.

The shouts echoing off the stone walls were maddening, making Takeo's heart race despite the clear path before him. He grabbed one torsion bar, the loose one, and yanked it free of the wheel. He held the bar up in both hands like a weapon and slammed it down on the other, jarring it in place and sending vibrations shuddering up his arms. Takeo took a stance and swung again, the bar ringing so hard in his hands that it hurt. Again, again, again, and it seemed he was timing his blows with the slams against Emy's shaking frame.

Nothing.

He screamed and swung again, aiming not for the lever but for the floor beneath as if he meant to snap the bars in two. They collided, sending the bar spiraling from Takeo's hands, while the other bounced up, freed for just one second, then flew loose as the wheel spun free.

The chain rattled like thunder in the tiny house, picking up speed until the chain was a blur to the human eye. Takeo backed away, and not a moment too soon, as one of the torsion bars rolled under the wheel, caught the chain, and was flung like a chaotic projectile into the wall, carving out a chunk of stone.

Precious moments slipped by as the wheel spun and spun, the heavy chain making rapid, horizontal laps as it unwound at a frightening pace. Takeo held his breath and braced for impact. The entire floor shook like an earthquake as the drawbridge crashed to ground. The wheel spun back once, yanked against its chain, and then came to a rest.

Silence followed. Even the guards on the other side of Emy's barricade had stopped. Takeo's ears were ringing from the noise, but it seemed to him no one was breathing. He looked up at the slits in the gatehouse roof to find thin rays of morning light beating back the blackness of the night sky.

Then faint at first but growing in intensity, he heard the low roar of an army in the distance.

Chapter 20

A violent slam struck the wedged door, rocking Emy in place. The sword Takeo had used as a wedge flung free and slid across the ground. Emy's ears flattened and she bared her teeth as she strained to ram the door back in place. From the other side, voices rang out in a unified shout.

"They brought a battering ram," Emy called out.

The door slammed against her, knocking her back a full hand width before she growled, dug her claws into the stone cracks and thrust back. The metal clanged hard against the walls, yet not so loud as to drown out the steady command from the other side for the men to throw their backs into it.

"Hold, we have to hold," Takeo replied. "We can't let them raise the gate."

He grabbed a torsion bar and sprinted over, digging one end into the ground and ramming the other up against the door. He leaned on it, adding his weight to the leverage.

The next slam jarred Emy's side more than Takeo's, but they weren't flung back like before. The bar vibrated so much that it made Takeo's teeth chatter and turned his insides to mush.

There were only two portals in this entire room: the door and the chain slits overhead. The former was an echo chamber of howling and frantic commands, but the latter was a hole through which the outside world could be glimpsed. Takeo heard the telltale sounds of catapults being cranked into place. Occasionally, he even heard the chorus of a flock of arrows being let loose into the morning air. Commands were being issued to raise the entire garrison, calls for donning armor and grabbing weapons, and for some damned fool to get into the gatehouse.

Another slam against the door rocked Emy and jarred Takeo's senses. He had to clench his jaw to keep from biting his own tongue. A secondary thud vibrated the small room, yet the torsion bar did not shake, and a sinking feeling dropped into Takeo's stomach. He opened his eyes as a third and then forth thud struck the gatehouse, and he was able to identify its source on the adjacent wall, facing the courtyard.

"They're trying to break in," Takeo said.

As if to confirm this, the wall shook loose a layer of dust, and two stone blocks in the dead center cracked inwards. The torch on the ground cast brooding shadows over the scene as another thud echoed out. One of the two blocks gave way, further thinning that line of defense.

"When they break through, you take them," Emy said, straining as another door-breaking ram struck her bruised shoulder. "I can hold this one."

A chunk of stone was flung out from the wall, and the end of a metal hammer blew through covered in chunks of rock and gray dust. It was yanked back through, letting in tiny fragments of light to fight against the orange flicker of the torch.

Takeo waited for one more strike against the door, then dashed to the new opening, scooping up a katana along the way. As the next hammer blow fell against the wall, so did a length of blade stab through, and Takeo felt resistance and heard a scream come from the other end. He quickly pulled his weapon back before anyone could grab it, noting the layer of blood that ran down its length, then dropped the blade and dashed backed to Emy. He flung himself on top of the torsion bar just in time, though he didn't brace himself hard enough, and the impact jarred him so bad that he lost his grip and fell to the floor. But the door held, and several seconds passed before the next hammer struck the wall.

"Damn it, Qing. Where are you?" Takeo growled and stumbled to a stand.

He paced back over to his sword, stopping to shield himself as another chunk of stone was flung free and blew bits of pebbles and dust into his face. He grabbed his sword and, in the process, got a clear view of the rows and rows of armored Katsu blue troops on the other side, two of whom were wielding warhammers. At the sight of Takeo, or his shadow more like, with hair cut to shoulder length, their eyes widened.

"It's him!" one called out. "He's inside!"

"Break it down, boy," came the reply, somewhere to the left. "Hurry, or we're all dead."

189

The hammer blows fell, one after another in rhythmic fashion, bashing chunks of stone with feverish passion. Takeo swore and shielded his eyes again. He wasn't going to get another strike in, not at this distance and not with the hammer blows felling like they were. He ditched the sword and fell back to Emy, bracing the bar again.

Another jolt shook the two in place, but it was clear death came only from one end now.

"Where are they?" Takeo asked in between hammer and ram strikes.

"The fighting has reached the drawbridge," Emy said, ears flicking. "Best I can tell, Botan sent a force out to stop our troops from crossing inside. They're trying to hold the line outside the fortress, probably with the hopes of getting in here and raising the bridge again."

"I should have known," Takeo said.

Just then, a heavy thud struck the roof, and the morning sunlight coming through the chain slit was blotted out. The only thing Takeo could imagine was that some officer up on the walls had gotten desperate and dropped a boulder on them. Not so much as a crack appeared, though, but then something worse happened. A heavy roar echoed down to them, quickly followed by a flurry of hammer blows on the stone.

"Damn," Takeo said, teeth clenched tightly. "Damn it, damn it all."

A full block of stone fell free from the roof and crashed to the ground.

"How can that be?" Emy snarled. "They'll break through the roof faster than the wall."

"The roof is thinner at the top," Takeo explained, more as outlet for his rising fears than anything else. "The stones have to be lighter because of the weight, plus there's already a hole, structurally weak. The walls can hold for another minute, but the roof won't. Not against that kind of assault."

"Well then," Emy said, straining as she dug in her heels. "You better get ready to fight."

"Die," Takeo corrected. "Get ready to die."

He lurched off the door after the next thud rocked them both and dived for his sword. Another hammer blow to the wall spit chunks of stone across him, and he shook his head to clean pebbles from his hair. Takeo kicked the torch on the ground out of his way, then stood a pace from the ever widening hole above them. Sword poised to skewer, he prayed the soldiers above were overzealous enough to jump first and look second. With luck, he'd kill several before they took him down.

The hammer blows from above pounded furiously, faster than those against the wall, and the air became choked in dust as chunks of stone flew in all directions. Whole blocks plummeted and littered the floor. In no time at all, the chain slit was wide enough for a man, and a dark figure plummeted through, blocking the sun and howling like mad. He hit the ground, and Takeo went to thrust, but stopped only because the massive man hadn't dropped his warhammer despite the fall.

Takeo's blade paused just a hair's length from skewering Nicolas' throat.

"By Valhalla!" Nicholas swore, stumbling back and throwing up a hand far too late. "Takeo! You almost killed me."

Takeo blinked, just as stunned as the viking, and dropped his sword tip.

"Nicholas? How did you get in here?"

The viking grinned and pointed up. "Damned Katsus are holding a good line. It was taking too long for my liking, and Qing's. She said you needed help. Thankfully, I brought rope and a grappling hook. As for how I got down here, well, let's just say that gate chain can hold some weight."

"Well, as glad as I am to see you, I think you just doomed us. Soldiers are going to come pouring in here now. We need to hold this room until our troops get inside. We can't let them raise the drawbridge."

Nicholas took one look at the wheel, one look at his hammer, and his grin grew.

"Hold the line," he said mockingly. "What a samurai thing to say. Let me show you how a viking solves his problems."

Nicholas roared and swung his hammer into the wheelhouse, cracking the mechanism and tilting it with the force. He swung his hammer again with the same intensity he had just used to shatter stone, and the bolts gave way. A third strike, and the wheel snapped free, sliding into the nearby wall. The chain went slack, and Nicholas kissed his hammer.

"By Valhalla, am I going to miss this!" he cried out.

A samurai in blue armor plunged through the hole above and both viking and ronin leveled the intruder in a heartbeat. More voices collected above them.

Takeo glanced back at the wall. The hole was almost big enough there, too. Nicholas followed the gaze before the two shared a nod. Takeo dashed to the wall while Nicholas held his ground beneath the roof. The room vibrated with another roar as a second enemy plunged in, only to meet a swift end at the hands of a man with shoulders as broad as an ogre.

Outside, the thunder of screams and battle cries was deafening. Takeo dared hope the growing intensity meant the Hanu army was slowly winning, but his nagging logical mind didn't discount that what he heard could be nothing but echoes.

That was until the hammer blows against the wall stopped, and no one else dropped into the hole above Nicholas. Takeo shielded his eyes and approached the wall, holding his breath and daring to hope.

Through the opening, he saw the sea of blue troops had all but forgotten him. Instead they face off against an unseen opponent to Takeo's left, and the roars that flowed through to his ears did not come from the Katsu soldiers.

"Emy," Takeo shouted. "Pull back the door."

She gave him a questioning look, then checked herself and obeyed. The rakshasa yanked the door away, and a host of unprepared Katsu samurai stood in the entrance, battering ram dropped to their feet. They were looking away, back through the entrance, fighting against a tide of red that cut them off. The wide channel that marked the grand entrance beyond the lowered drawbridge was thick with Hanu samurai howling like mad. Takeo and Emy quickly put an end to the three Katsu lives that stood between them and their allies.

"He's here! He's here!" someone shouted, and through the mass of Hanu troops, Kuniko pushed her way into view, eyes glinting in the morning light.

"My lord!" Kuniko shouted and waved through the entrance, unable to bow in the press of bodies.

Takeo nodded, pride swelling within him, and he looked to Nicholas.

"Lift me up," he commanded.

Nicholas' outstretched hands became footholds, and Takeo climbed out of the hole. He stood tall on the gatehouse roof, alone above the masses, and finally got a clear view of the battlefield. The Hanu had pushed across the drawbridge and were spreading out into the courtyard. Nicholas wasn't the only person to scale the walls, as there were small fights breaking out along the upper levels, and the Katsus were retreating to solidify their numbers. Takeo could see through beyond the fortress gate a great swath of red, roaring and waving their swords, covering the landscape outside. At the sight of Takeo, their general, who had brought down the Katsu gate, the cheers intensified. Understanding the nature of morale, Takeo pointed his sword into the keep and shouted at the top of his lungs.

"Bring me their heads!"

The answering roar was deafening, and the Katsu troops seemed to wilt beneath his command.

Takeo leapt from the gatehouse and into the fray, taking his familiar place among the soldiers. He lost his view of the battlefield, but there was no need for it. He, the soldiers, the daimyo, even the very walls of the fortress knew the outcome now. The invaders were inside, and there was no closing the gate. It was every man for himself.

Screams and shouts echoed about the stone like a chorus of gongs, occasionally broken by a particularly loud noise, such as a door being bashed open or a catapult being rolled off the walls. Those who fought by Takeo were invigorated as they spearheaded an assault into the Katsu ranks, cutting foes down like crops to harvest. Blood flowed, bodies fell, and madness took hold. That was until one voice, calm and collected boomed out over the mayhem.

"Karaoshi!" Botan yelled in that commanding voice of his. "Takeo, stop this at once! Takeo! Stop or they die!"

193

Takeo froze, sparing the life of the next Katsu samurai about to be felled by his blade. His sudden stop made those nearby pause, too, on either side of the conflict, and Takeo scanned the carnage that still raged on around him.

"I know you're out there, Takeo!" Botan yelled out again. "Everyone stop! Stop, I say! Obey your lord!"

The screams and shouts began to be stifled, as did the killing. The growing silence spread, sapping the madness from those who had not heard Botan's voice, until the two armies came to a standstill. A thin yet clear line parted them.

Takeo searched and found what he was looking for, a glint of blond in the sea of red, blue, and black. On one of the middle levels leading into the keep, Gavin had been brought forward and forced to his knees at the top of the stairs. The knight's hands—no, hand—was resting in his lap, while the stubby end of his left arm hung at his side. A large, white patch was wrapped about his head, pressing a bandage to where one of his ears used to be. Gavin blinked as his eyes strained against the morning light. That was until he found Takeo and the two locked eyes.

Takeo couldn't say what he read in Gavin's expression. It was stoic and, at this distance, hard to make out. It wasn't happiness, yet it wasn't anger either, and all Takeo could do was nod. Gavin dropped his head.

What interested Takeo, though, was the blade held to Gavin's throat, and the Katsu samurai who wielded it. Botan was still nowhere to be found.

"I know you're out there, Takeo!" Botan yelled. "Don't try anything! My samurai are on strict orders to kill the knight unless my commands are followed in the absolute. Where are you? Come forward! Alone."

Now that the silence was all encompassing, Botan's voice rung clear. Takeo deciphered the direction, yet he did not move. His mind spun as he stared at Gavin, whirling around as he tried to figure out what to do. He took in the Katsu soldiers surrounding the knight and the distance from them to his nearest ally, but the distance was too great. And the man holding the knife to Gavin's throat had a snarl on his face. There was a fanaticism in that look that Takeo didn't want to test, yet he had to. There was no other choice. He couldn't lose him, not Gavin. It was all for nothing without him, wasn't it? Someone had to live, someone had to be worthy of it all. The prophecy couldn't end with Gavin's death. Takeo wouldn't allow it.

"Clock is ticking, Takeo," Botan shouted again. "Come to me. I have the ogre. It's time we put an end to this."

He'd been about to look away when someone caught Takeo's eye. On second look, he realized whom he was seeing. Emy met his gaze, disguised as a commoner, and she disappeared into the Katsu line. She headed towards Gavin, and hope re-entered Takeo's heart.

This was her plan. She can drift about unnoticed on both sides dressed like that, and she goes to free our friends. Clever girl.

Takeo strode into the Katsu ranks heading for Botan's voice, the lines of blue armor parting as he went. The closest Hanu soldiers made a move to follow, but Takeo stayed them with a wave of his hand. He marched alone into the enemy's lair, the eyes of every soul in the fortress following him.

Out of the masses, Takeo came upon what he feared: Lord Botan Katsu standing behind Krunk. The ogre had been forced to his knees, and the Karaoshi family sword was pressed tightly to his throat. Botan had his other arm around Krunk's head, using one of the tusks for leverage to keep the ogre rooted in place, assisted by the infernal power of the sword's enchantment. Even still, Krunk's strength was immense, and two other Katsu soldiers flanked him, wrestling with the ogre's arms to keep the purple brute pinned.

One might assume that Krunk would cooperate with a blade to his throat, but Takeo saw why so much restraint was necessary.

Krunk's drooling was so intense that he almost frothed at the mouth. His yellow eyes shifted in quick, seemingly random motions, settling on his captors one after another as if shocked to see where he was. He kept trying to stand, with Botan forcing the ogre back to his knees, only for Krunk to forget and attempt the motion again just a few seconds later. At each restriction, the ogre grunted and growled, fighting against those who held him. The blade dug so deeply into the ogre's skin that it bled, yet Krunk appeared oblivious, attempting to stand again and further lodging the edge into his vital flesh.

195

At the sight of Takeo, though, a long look of recognition crept over the ogre's face. Confusion wracked his eyebrows as he squinted and thought, contemplated and pondered, until slowly his yellow eyes widened.

"Krunk know you," the ogre said.

Besides the two others holding down Krunk, there was a very small clearing about Botan, roughly one sword length, which was clearly intended for Takeo to occupy. The Katsu soldiers all around stared intently, yet the only gaze Takeo met was the shogun's.

Even with Krunk at his knees, the ogre was almost as tall as Botan, and there was no mistaking this was purposeful. Botan was completely sheltered behind Krunk's mass, besides his exposed arms and half his face peering out.

"This is it, Takeo," Botan said. "You should have quit while you had the chance. If you had left, you could have lived, but it's over now. Tell your army to retreat, or I kill them both. Do it!"

Krunk gasped, and the enchanted blade pressed further into his throat, hissing and burning. Thankfully, an ogre's neck was not a fragile thing, yet Takeo could only imagine the damage being done. It seemed Krunk was truly poised on the fringes of sanity.

"Takeo," Krunk said. "That your name. We friends?"

"What will it take for you to let them go?" Takeo asked the lord. "I mean right here, right now, completely. All of them."

Botan thought for but a second.

"Kill yourself, after you order your army away."

"Not just going to have your minions do it, eh?"

"And have you become a martyr? Do I look like a fool? Order your army back and take your own life. These foreigners will mean nothing to me, then, and I'll let them go. Everyone wins."

Takeo nodded and drew his blade. Botan tightened his grip on Krunk, making sure only half his face was exposed. Yet Takeo knew it would be useless to strike there. The lord would see an attack coming, and his enchanted strength would protect him from harm.

"No!" Gavin shouted. "Damn it, no!"

The loud yell echoed out across the courtyard and turned every head, including Takeo's. Still on his knees, perched above the crowd, Gavin had come to life and strained against the knife at his throat, tears in his eyes.

196

"Takeo, please! Don't do it! I'm begging you, please," the knight pleaded.

"Gavin, there's no other way," Takeo shouted back.

"No, please no," the knight continued, dropping his head and letting his voice fall to a whimper. "Not Krunk."

Tears fell from Gavin's face, and his shoulders convulsed.

Nearby, Takeo caught sight of Emy again, now just an arm's length away from Gavin.

Takeo turned back to Botan.

The lord had not been idle during this exchange. He'd watched carefully Gavin's tearful plea. Botan saw that Takeo had a shine to his eyes, like tears, but with a mix of determination. He did not see defeat.

"Kill him!" Botan shouted, too late.

Takeo dropped to the right, blade held low and point forward, blocking Botan's sight for a fraction of a second, and then dashed forward and rammed with all his might. Takeo's blade entered Krunk just under the middle ribs, passed through the ogre's lung, scraped along his massive spine, then exited the other side. When the sword's guard struck Krunk's flesh, the tip pierced Botan's chest.

Chapter 21

Lord Botan Katsu gasped as a finger's length of blade stabbed into him, missing his vital organs by a hair. He'd pulled away from Krunk on instinct, saving him from further injury, and the relief that washed over him was his last as Takeo ripped the Karaoshi blade from Botan's weakened grasp and decapitated the shogun a moment later. Botan's head went flying, but before it ever hit the ground, Takeo whirled about and slaughtered the five closest Katsu soldiers in a flash.

Six bodies hit the ground, oozing blood, smoke, and burning flakes of skin set adrift in the wind. The fire that flowed through Takeo was palpable, and he immediately set it to use again to catch Krunk.

A collective gasp broke the silence of the courtyard, and a quiet jolt swept through the crowd. Gavin did not flinch, instead continuing to weep silently on his knees, even as Emy had ripped the blade from the knight's throat a half-second before Takeo's attack. The rakshasa had not dropped her disguise, but her identity was clear now that she stood beside Gavin, mouth agape, dagger in one hand, former Katsu executioner's throat in the other. The man fought against her grip, but his attempts were futile, his legs swinging beneath him. Just as the man lost consciousness, she dropped him over the side and into the crowd but otherwise did not move. The soldiers around her were too stunned, or perhaps terrified, to interfere.

The latter was certainly true of those around Takeo. No one dared step beyond the dead to challenge the ronin, even as he stood preoccupied.

Krunk blinked and looked down, his brows bouncing as he found the source of his pain. He blinked again, a moment's reflection passing over his features.

"Takeo," the ogre said, groaning. "You, you stab Krunk."

"I know," the ronin replied, voice shaking. "I did."

Krunk reached for the sword, but the motion only jostled the blade, spurting blood out and almost dropping the ogre. Takeo held the ogre up by bracing himself against the stone, drawing strength from his enchanted blade, as Krunk leaned into him. The ogre's massive head dropped onto Takeo's shoulder, leaning one drooling tusk onto the man's neck.

"I," Takeo started, pausing, words getting caught in his throat. "I'm so sorry, Krunk. I want you to know that you saved us. You saved us all. I didn't have a choice."

"Gavin?" Krunk mumbled.

Takeo could only nod. He could feel Krunk's warm blood seeping into the cracks in his armor, as well as the increasing weight that the ogre put on him. His stomach hurt, his limbs felt numb, yet what bothered Takeo the most was the complete lack of feeling in his heart. Where he should feel the greatest pain, he felt only the sword's fire, as if his heart was burning away.

In the background, Gavin's quiet sobs filled the air.

"Was, was," Krunk mumbled, saliva rolling down Takeo's back, "was accident?"

Takeo bit his lip. Somewhere, a tear fought up from the darkness and rolled down his cheek.

"Yeah," Takeo pushed out. "Yes, it was an accident."

"Oh," Krunk said. "It okay. Krunk forgive . . . you."

The last of the ogre's strength faded into Takeo's arms, and a long, final breath shuddered out over Takeo's shoulder. Krunk's limp arms scraped across the stone as they fell free, and Takeo slowly lowered the big creature to the ground. The ring of bodies had made a shallow of pool of blood, yet Takeo had no choice but to set Krunk's lifeless body in it. Red pooled about purple skin, and Krunk's yellow eyes stared, glossed over.

Takeo let those eyes bore into him for several seconds before he closed them. He took one steadying breath, and then stood and turned upon the army, his enchanted blade dripping shogun blood, hissing smoke along its blackened edge.

Those closest stepped back.

"This ogre was my friend," Takeo said.

There was no need to shout. The only competing sound was Gavin's sobbing.

"Look at him and imagine what I would do to my enemy," Takeo went on. "Your leader is dead. Your fortress invaded. Your lives rest in my hands. I'll say this only once: surrender. Do so now, and not only will I let you live, but I'll also let your families live. Do not test me."

Takeo let his words sink in, but only for a moment. He was smart enough to know that within every army lay at least one self-righteous dullard who would think this cause worth dying for. The only chance at heading such a zealot off was to make the first move.

He surveyed those soldiers closest to him, singled out the one with the most beads of sweat on his forehead, and took a step toward him.

The man dropped his sword as if it had bit him and fell to his knees. The clanging of the sword was quickly followed by a second as Takeo cast his dark gaze on a second soul, then a third rang out nearby. Takeo knew it was only the cowards that were ditching their weapons so enthusiastically, but herd mentality was a hard thing to resist when coupled with gripping terror, and soon a dozen swords were clattering about the stone courtyard as men and women dropped to their knees in surrender.

That one brave idiot somewhere out there went to shout, but he'd missed his window, and those nearby with more concern for their lives than their honor silenced the fool with a series of punches. More swords hit the ground, followed by knees, and so it went.

The Katsu army kneeled before Takeo, and their collective shuffling of armor rang out loud enough to blot out Gavin's sobs, if only for a moment.

Over the cowed masses, Takeo spied the Hanu army watching. He selected Kuniko and Qing out of the crowd and nodded to them. They each slipped through the courtyard to his side. Kuniko bowed low. Qing hesitated, then offered a shallow version.

"My lord," Kuniko said.

"Take them out, but do not disarm them," Takeo commanded. "They are allies, not prisoners—or at least they will be within the hour. We may need them soon."

"My lord?"

Takeo turned to Qing. The ninja nodded.

"I'm certain the rest of the daimyo have figured out what has happened to Yoshida by now," she said. "They'll want to collect their sworn samurai and execute you for your crimes."

Takeo's only reply was to put his gaze on Kuniko. The girl blinked once, twice, then raised her brows. She bowed low again.

"Understood, my lord," she said. "Your will be done."

Takeo sighed, thankful Kuniko was loyal enough not to need a full explanation. The girl didn't understand what had happened, but she didn't need to. All she understood was that there was a plot to overthrow her idol, and that was enough. As Takeo hung his head, his eyes inadvertently fell on Krunk's lifeless body, and a lump swelled in this throat.

"Was it worth it?" Qing asked.

Takeo ripped his gaze away, intending to respond but instead found Nicholas atop the gatehouse. The viking's maul lay at his feet, the shaft held loosely in one hand, his large mouth hanging open.

"I hope so," Takeo replied.

He broke his gaze with Nicholas and paced off into the crowd. Kuniko began shouting orders, but no one moved for several seconds as Takeo continued to steal the attention. The crowd parted for him like soil before a plow, all the way up until Takeo took the stairs to reach Gavin's side.

And Emy's.

The rakshasa still held her disguise, or rather forgot she was changed at all. As Takeo approached, she drew back only a hair, as opposed to the full step most others took. Her eyes were sharp as she watched him, the dagger held tightly in her grip. Takeo sheathed his enchanted blade, but did not release the handle, letting power continue to course through his veins.

He ignored her and offered a hand to Gavin so that the knight could stand. Gavin looked at it, and only then did Takeo realize his arm was drenched in blood.

Gavin turned away.

"We can deal with this later," Takeo replied. "For now, just do one thing and one thing only."

"What's that?" Gavin asked.

"Collect your family and look after Krunk."

Gavin shook his head, eyes red, cheeks drenched in tears. He sniffed.

"And where are you going?"

Takeo stared up at the Katsu fortress, to the tallest tower.

"To make it worth it," he answered.

* * *

Once Takeo ascertained the location of the Lady Anagarika Katsu, he made a direct path to her. He took Qing as a witness and the next available Katsu commander as an envoy, but otherwise he needed no assistance from them. Takeo knew the way well, and he climbed stairs, passed through halls, and made deft turns in absolute silence.

He paused only at the final hallway, one long and wide that led to a set of closed double doors. The memory of his last visit here was unpleasant and eerily similar to his current situation. Like then, he approached in the wake of an assault, one that resulted in a loss for the defenders. Like then, he approached the shogun under no peaceful terms with full intent to do harm. Like then, he had betrayed those he'd fought with for so many years.

Unlike then, he was not accompanied by someone he loved.

Takeo let the memory pass and strode down the hall. He was expected, it seemed, as there were guards at the doors, and the way was open for him. He did not pause before entering.

A lone woman waited inside, wearing a simple blue kimono and sitting on a large pillow. Takeo surmised she was a little over a decade older than him, but it was difficult to tell because age lines were assaulting her features, and he judged that time would not be kind to her face. Before her was a low table covered in brushes alongside a half-finished painting, all of which were set aside. The woman had her hands clasped before her, unconcerned with the way her paint-covered hands marked her clothes. Takeo thought her stoic at first, the way she sat up straight, but then he realized it wasn't with courage that she held herself high.

Her bottom lip trembled.

"Lady Anagarika Katsu," Takeo said.

She paused, uncertainty in her every move. Normally, Takeo despised such things, but this was different. He drew resolve from her lack thereof.

"Takeo Karaoshi," she finally replied.

Anagarika swallowed down a dry throat. Takeo stepped away from the entrance, following the room's edge. It was a circular room with large windows all around, designed for solitude rather than safety. It offered a commanding view of the ocean, the coast, and the courtyard outside. Takeo stopped to admire the view.

"Your cousin's body lies somewhere down there," Takeo said.

"So I heard," Anagarika whispered. "I've been kept informed by my guards. I knew you'd come for me soon."

Her eyes fell to Takeo's sword and the way his hand rested on the pommel.

"From what I've been told, you and Botan ruled as equals," he said. "I find that hard to believe, considering I've never seen you until now. Botan has always ruled from the front, leading the armies, wearing the crown so to speak. The way I see it, the only way you two could be equals is if, unknown to most, you were in the background pulling all the strings. I'm talking specifically about the most important strings, like getting the lesser daimyo to fall in line."

Takeo stepped away from the window and continued on, circling around the room. His pace slowed as he reached the opposite wall, stopping at one window in particular with no special view. It faced north, over the ocean but not far from the shore. It was the newest window in the bunch, having been replaced some years ago, but there was no sign indicating that. Takeo only knew because he had watched it shatter.

"Am I wrong?" he pressed.

"No," Anagarika finally replied.

She bowed her head over the table, like a prisoner before an execution, one that didn't want the blade to miss and prolong their suffering. The window that Takeo was at put him behind her, but she did not look for him. At the entrance, Qing and the guards watched in complete silence.

That was good. Takeo wanted them to watch. Legends were easier to spread with more witnesses.

"You wouldn't know this, lady, but something happened last night that changed everything," Takeo continued. "I'm not talking about the death of my mother—of which I know you played a part— or the burning of my siege weapons. In a way, those events were but two of the many small steppingstones that have led me here.

"Last night, I murdered three of the most powerful and influential daimyo in the Hanu kingdom. I did so in cold blood and then tricked their armies into doing my bidding. The strange part is that these individuals committed no crime. They did not aim to ruin my plans or dispose of me. In fact, their ultimate plan fell very much in line with my own. Minus my pride, my sword, and my friends, I should have had every reason to follow their orders. They died, you see, not because they made any sort of mistake, but because I did. I made, as the vikings say, the greatest mistake of all: denying my destiny."

Takeo slid his hand down the handle of his sword until his skin touched the guard. His fingers wrapped tightly around his weapon, letting the fire rage within him. He had total control over it, though. He knew he did. It was always that way. He understood now why Botan had failed to kill him with this weapon. The fire Takeo felt was no jinni enchantment at all. It was a piece of his own soul, forged into death.

Takeo left the window and paced around the room to face Anagarika again. Her head remained cowed, but her shoulders shook. She did not whimper, though, and that was more than Takeo could say for some who had kneeled before him. Against his better judgment, this woman earned a level of respect out of him.

"I tried my damnedest to serve the daimyo caste," Takeo said. "I made myself useful, indispensable even, thinking that in doing so they would rise up and fulfill my dream. Unfortunately for me, the only thing they ever saw was a threat to their power. Unfortunately for them, that time has passed. To call me a threat implies that I can be stopped. What I am is a reckoning.

"Look at me."

Anagarika raised her head swiftly, but her eyes hesitated to meet Takeo's dark gaze. She stopped first to view her soldiers, all four of them, standing well within reach of assisting her, yet none seemed poised to move. Their attention remained fixated on Takeo's hand, the one that rested on his sword. It was clear that the secret was out now, and that everyone would soon be telling stories about the power of the Karaoshi blade.

"Listen," Takeo commanded. "I don't want anarchy. Quite the opposite, I want stability and control, not just for Juatwa, but for all the world, and I will stop at nothing to see this through. The daimyo can be instrumental in such a plan, if they choose to be. A new table of power has just opened up, and all the seats are up for grabs. So, I have but one question for you.

"How good are your survival skills?"

Anagarika's shoulders stopped shaking. The gaze that she held with Takeo left behind its reluctance as she tilted her head ever so slightly. She took a steady breath, the first since Takeo had entered the room, and then bowed.

"Impeccable, my lord," she said.

Chapter 22

There was no battle. Takeo exited the Katsu fortress with Botan's head in one hand, his sword in the other, and a second army at his back. No doubt there were some misgivings among the mix of Hanu and Katsu soldiers, as just that morning they'd been fighting to the death, but Takeo didn't need them to be friends. He just needed the image, which proved more than enough. Those Hanu daimyo who had banded together in Takeo's absence, after discovering the bodies of Nobu, Yoshida, and the others, quickly deduced that their chances of success lay in living to fight another day. They took their troops and withdrew.

Or at least those troops that obeyed.

An odd thing occurred that Takeo hadn't thought to try. Kuniko issued orders that the army was to stay together in order to escort Anagarika and Botan's surviving family into Lady Zhenzhen's custody. It would be an admittedly large escort, wholly unnecessary for the task, but it inserted a level of gray into the affair. The Hanu army now had two sets of orders to obey. On one hand, they were told to flee by their daimyo; on the other, they were told to stay by their general.

By Kuniko's report, a good two thirds stayed, and the Hanu daimyo fled all the more quickly because of it. Upon being complimented, Kuniko had but one thing to say to her lord.

"My father was a coward, not an idiot. He understood power, and more specifically how it stemmed from desire. People want to follow you, my lord. They just need an excuse."

And so, Takeo and his army returned to the Hanu fortress proud, victorious, and bearing terrible news.

Takeo had thought that at least one of the fleeing daimyo would reach Lady Zhenzhen first and tell their version of the story. However, whether because of his victory, his sword, Qing's involvement, or something else, that wasn't the case. Lady Zhenzhen learned of everything upon Takeo's return, including her son's death.

206

She locked herself in her throne room for a week. The city suffered worse.

Lady Zhenzhen mandated one hundred days of mourning throughout her newly expanded empire. During this time, no festivities or celebrations could take place. Only songs of her son's greatness could be sung, and everyone was expected to spend the first hour before sunset remembering their prince and thanking him for all he'd done. Attendance to the funeral was mandatory, though unnecessary, as Nobu's corpse was taken on a tour of every street in the city. Anyone caught doing anything other than mourning the poor Nobu and how he had given his life to save the kingdom would be deemed a traitor and sentenced to death.

Throughout the procession, Lady Zhenzhen was brought to tears and made several comments about the number of people that had turned out for the event. They truly must have loved her son.

When Takeo could get away, he spent much of his time with Lord Virote. Now that the entire Hanu power structure had been undermined, the old man became an open book. Problems were laid bare and all solutions discussed.

"Who would have thought a single battle would both cost and gain us so much?" Virote commented one evening, rubbing his eyes as the two of them poured over maps, notes, and family trees. "My nephew's only surviving line, dead. Oh, how I failed him. I warned Nobu's grandfather as much when he made that deal, that signing such a treaty with the oni would only delay his family's death rather than prevent it, but he was at the end of his rope. Now Nobu is dead, and the oni are gone, and you've turned half the daimyo in the land against us."

"I'll bring them back," Takeo had replied.

"You'd better. Juatwa is an even split now. Those once loyal to us have defected to the Nguyens. Sure, you've brought the Katsu lineage to heel, but doing so has merely balanced the power of this land rather than concentrated it."

Takeo had sighed and clenched his teeth in frustration.

"How can any of those daimyo serve a rakshasa? How can I, a human, even if a ronin, be considered a worse master?"

"Qadir plays a better game than you, Takeo. He knows how to appear as a willing instrument, and he's never killed a shogun. I'm

207

sure it helps that you made him a cripple, too. The daimyo defecting to the Nguyens can convince themselves that they serve a shogun as opposed to a rakshasa. With you and Zhenzhen, the reality is easier to see. We must remedy this situation. Since we cannot ban you to the background as Qadir has done with himself, we instead need to legitimize your current position."

Takeo had stared hard at the old man in the flickering candlelight. An understanding passed between them.

"No."

"No? What do you mean, no? You speak as if marriage to Zhenzhen is monstrous as opposed to inevitable. Listen, I won't argue with you, Takeo. You have cunning enough to formulate your own solution, but this method provides the easiest, most direct route to victory. Tell me I'm wrong."

Takeo had not, but that didn't mean he agreed either.

"Tell me, old man, why are you helping me so much? Your family isn't in line for the throne. Nobu is dead. No offense, but I doubt you'll live long enough to see the fruits of your labor. Here we are, night after night working over battle plans, alliances, plots, and I just can't gather why. What benefit do you stand to gain from your toils?"

"We've been over this once. As the sword does not question the warrior, so does the pen not question the author. We tools of greater ideals work until we break or are cast aside."

"And when the sword gains sentience?"

"I'll make you a deal, ronin. I won't question how you choose to die if you don't question how I do."

"Fair enough, but one last thing."

"Hm?"

"Don't call me ronin again."

As for Lady Zhenzhen, she may have locked herself in for a week, but that didn't mean she was alone. Takeo still had orders to obey, especially if he wanted to regain her trust. Her son was dead, some of her most trusted generals executed for a treason that could not be proved, and her immortal oni allies gone to flight. The Katsu armies be damned, Lady Zhenzhen had made it clear how thin the ice was beneath Takeo's feet and also how that ice could be strengthened by the frequent application of body heat.

208

He did as he was told, staying in Zhenzhen's throne room long after she was finished with him. Between her and Lord Virote, Takeo found some difficulty in getting away to see others, including Mako. At least with his newfound position, there was no need for Mako to do any menial labor to earn her spot. She slept soundly in a room befitting a royal guest.

There was only one other room that Takeo needed, and that was the one for Emy. Gavin, his wife, and his daughter had not returned to the Hanu keep with the army. Takeo had sent them, along with Nicholas as an escort, to a more remote location, specifically to Kuniko's lands. She'd readily offered them up; to which, Takeo had agreed. Krunk's and Dhyana's bodies were sent, too, to be buried on the mansion grounds. Emy wanted to go, of course, but she did not say it. She'd stayed by Takeo's side, a silent understanding between them.

It had to be silent because Emy had not spoken to Takeo since Krunk's death, and he had not spoken to her.

"Aren't you worried she'll try to kill you?" Qing had asked one morning. "There's nothing to tie her to you anymore."

"I always assumed she'd try to kill me eventually," Takeo had replied. "It's in her nature. Humans and rakshasas are not friends. They are either rulers or subjects, master or slave, hunter or prey. Why do you think I had her stalk me as she grew up? I've trained myself against her, and she knows it. She's no more a threat to me than any other ninjas in this land."

Qing had scoffed and said, "What ninjas? This fortress has been eerily silent since your return. I thought for sure there would be a host of ninjas coming after you, what with the bounty that's been put on your head by all the fleeing daimyo. Except, you're not the usual mark. Most daimyo who survive a ninja attack consider themselves lucky and think nothing else of it, or if they do try to hunt down the ninjas that tried, they come up empty handed. You though? You murder them, down to the last child. No ninja clan will touch you."

"So, what you're saying is that I brought peace?"

"You mispronounced *enforced*."

"No, I did not."

Takeo did not stay at the Hanu fortress a moment longer than was necessary. He understood that as the acting Hanu general, he had a duty now even greater than the one he had served on the battlefield. It wasn't just troop logistics and battleplans he had to contend with now, but also more administrative things such as ensuring taxes were collected and borders were secured. A whole host of duties were dumped into his lap overnight, including those for the newly acquired Katsu lands. Takeo needed much help in bringing order to the chaos of it all.

Anagarika offered to help. Zhenzhen wanted to deny her. Takeo persuaded her otherwise. Then the shogun made the demand Takeo knew was coming.

"Marry me," Lady Zhenzhen demanded the night before Takeo intended to visit Gavin. "None of those idiotic daimyo would dare oppose you if we legitimize your rule."

"My lady," Takeo replied, "it's already heresy enough to promote me to leader of your armies. A marriage would not restore honor to my name; it would only ruin yours."

"What honor? I'm a childless widow, incapable of bearing another heir. Trust me, you're not the first to try. I'll not marry some stuffy old daimyo who didn't do a damned thing while Nobu and I were imprisoned. Oh, my son. My son! He's dead, he's dead, and you're all I have left now. Marry me, I command you!"

"There is no need," Takeo pressed. "An alliance through marriage is too strategic. Who knows, perhaps we can avoid bloodshed by marrying you to the eldest Nguyen brother?"

Zhenzhen's hand came across Takeo's face with an extra dose of malice. It went beyond stinging, almost to the point of bruising. The blow raised a level of hate within him.

"You will not suggest that again," she said. "I will not marry one of those vile brood. You will conquer them as you conquered the Katsu, and this time, you will show no mercy. Am I understood?"

"Yes, my lady," Takeo replied.

"And you will marry me. You will reign as my husband, indomitable and merciless, the sort of man I always dreamed Nobu would be. I will fill your heart, and you will fill my bed, and all will be right in the world. You will! Say it. SAY IT!"

Madness glinted in her bloodshot eyes, all the more highlighted by her pale skin. As she eluded the sun, so too did sleep elude her, and she bared a snarl at Takeo with teeth perfectly flat, having been gnashed together night after night. Yet, even still, she was beautiful, as beautiful as she was in dire need of someone to care for her. Unfortunately, that person could not be Takeo.

"I will not," he replied. "My heart is spoken for."

He spoke with more than words. This conversation could not be allowed to continue, so he dropped his cowed expression and gave his daimyo a taste of the defiance that lurked behind his black eyes.

You raped me. In ways I didn't understand, you took from me all that you pleased, which I gave away in fear. However, even then, I could live with that. I've been abused in far more damaging ways. It's not you, my lady, that I am rejecting, but everyone. I will never marry. You own my body, but not my soul. You demanded I love you like I loved her, and so I have done, but I will never give you more than I gave her.

I am spoken for.

Zhenzhen gazed back, an understanding passing between them, and her snarl grew. She raised her hand with all the noble savagery her privileged kind was capable of and flung it towards Takeo's face. He caught her wrist a finger's length from striking.

She gaped.

"Let's get one thing straight," Takeo said. "You need me just as much as I need you."

"Unhand me, you wretch!"

Takeo released her, and she snatched her hand away. She glared, pausing for a moment to rub where he'd grabbed, then swung at him again. Takeo did not catch her this time, but instead stepped back and dodged the blow. Zhenzhen screamed and followed, assailing him with clawed nails and wild swings. He avoided her with ease until she tripped over her own gown and sprawled across the rug-adorned floor.

"I'm leaving now," Takeo said, looking down at her. "I'll be back soon, and then we'll conquer this land together, as shogun and commander. I suggest you find someone else worthy of your hand."

"Don't you tell me what to do," she seethed from the ground, heaving from her efforts. "You will obey me! Don't you walk away."

Takeo did not look back.

211

"I own you! You're mine!" Zhenzhen screamed like a banshee. "Don't think you can get away with this, you dirty ronin. You're not half the man my son was. You will kneel before your shogun!"

The doors banged shut behind Takeo, and Lady Zhenzhen's next scream was muffled. He retreated to the courtyard, only stopping to bring his companion along for the ride.

Not that Emy would have referred to herself as such.

Their destination, the mansion of the late Lord Rithisak Zhao, was not far from the Hanu capital. They could have ridden the entire way there in silence and not felt a bit of unease, but there was one thing that bothered Takeo enough to break their silence. He waited several hours before attempting to speak to her.

"I have to ask," he said. "How did you not know what I would do?"

"I've asked myself the same thing every day since you killed him," she replied, swiftly and without pause.

Emy did not disguise herself anymore. She walked around in her rakshasa skin, with brazen orange fur fluffing out of her human-designed clothes like a pet komainu club dressed to entertain. So revealed, she was taller than most, and she stood with a spine so straight it would bring a tear to the eye of an old knight back in Lucifan. It seemed all charades were gone now. Only the ugly truth remained.

"I suppose I thought we had an understanding," she continued, dropping her head, one ear twitching in the wind. "When I went for Gavin, it was my way of saying that I would protect what you cared about, and in return, I assumed you would return the favor."

"You had to know there was no saving Krunk," Takeo said. "Not only did Botan have my sword, but I was surrounded, and Krunk had lost his mind. He couldn't help me, or us. He could barely comprehend where he was."

"What are you saying? That what you did was merciful?"

"No. I'm saying that what I did was inevitable. You should have known that."

"I did!" she growled back, then recollected herself. "I did. But I hoped otherwise. I believed in you."

The silence between them resumed, though it proved to be short-lived, in relative terms. Emy had a question of her own, and she waited until their destination loomed before them to bring it up.

"So, I'm a prisoner again?" she asked.

"Weren't you always?"

"What is your plan? To bring me along when you face Qadir and use me as either bait or leverage? Surely, you must know he'll be too smart to fall for either. He'd rather look for a new female."

"You've never met a male of your kind before," Takeo replied. "Their feral side comes out in the pursuit of a mate. He'll try something, or so I hope. But you can rest easy, Emy. I will not kill you. After this, I'll consider your sentence complete, and you can go free."

"Really?" She scoffed. "You, with your unbridled hatred for rakshasas, would let one such as me go?"

"So long as you serve out your term amicably, I have no issues turning a blind eye to your nature. I owe Krunk far more than that."

Takeo paused, dropping his head and letting out a long sigh.

"Besides, it's not your wrath I fear," he said. "It's his."

Emy glanced up the path. There, barring their way into the mansion grounds with folded arms, stood the silhouetted figure of Sir Gavin Shaw of the Knights' Order.

Chapter 23

Gavin's arms did not fold so easily with his left hand missing. The stubby end kept trying to roll off the opposite forearm, rather than perch as one expected. The good news was that this awkwardness distracted any onlooker from spending too much time examining Gavin's long, gaunt cheeks and the malformed scar along the side of his head. Botan had cut the ear clean off, but the shogun had provided little else beyond a thin gauze for his victim's recovery. The resulting fever had wracked Gavin's body. From his spindly arms to his shrunken chest, Gavin's once imposing figure was reduced to that of a peasant's. Even his yellowed hair seemed thinner.

Yet all this Takeo would have preferred to see, if only to avoid Gavin's eyes. Where once green light warmed him, the ronin instead found only embers, dying a little at a time under the cold cruelty of the world.

"Emy, good to see you," Gavin said as the two approached. "Takeo."

"It's good to see you, too, Uncle," Emy replied, nodding and dismounting. "Where is my father?"

"I buried him in the Zhao family graveyard. I didn't know what else to do, and Kuniko said it would be fine. I figured it was better than anywhere else. He lies alongside Takeo's other victims."

Emy paused to glance at Takeo. He nodded.

"We'll give you time," he said.

She bowed, low and respectfully, and then headed off. Zhao servants arrived, and Takeo dismounted to hand them the reins. When he and the knight were alone again, Takeo sighed.

"My victims, hm?" he said. "You know, there was a time when I knew you were joking. Now, I'm not so sure. Do you really hate me?"

"I mean, that's what they are. Maybe only Krunk died to your sword, but the blood of the others stains your hands. You know it, too. I know you know it."

"You didn't answer my question."

214

Gavin hung his head and unfolded his arms. He went to put his hands on his hips out of reflex, but inevitably only one caught. The stub of his left arm rolled off. The knight sighed this time and strolled off into the nearby gardens. Takeo followed.

"I," Gavin started, pausing, "I should. I have every reason to, but I don't. It's not hate I feel, but I can't describe it either. I've been thinking about it a lot. You were once my enemy, and hate you I did, but that time has passed. We got to know each other, understand each other, and we even shared a loss. I pledged myself to you, in a way, and even helped further your cause. You never tried to wrong me, not directly, but there came a moment when I realized that I couldn't go on with you anymore. You were headed down a path that I could not follow, and I felt powerless to stop you. Even then, when I left to oppose you, my feelings didn't turn to hate. Even now, when all I had has been brought to ruin, I still can't bring myself to say it's hate. I don't know what it is. Pity? Regret? Grief?"

"You talk as if I died."

"To me, maybe you did."

They turned down a path that would take them to the graveyard, though on a scenic route. Gavin meandered from plant to plant in the Zhao family garden, so well-tended by those servants who seemed on edge now that their mistress was home.

"I know why you're here," Gavin said.

"I think everyone does, to visit and collect my viking for the next battle."

Gavin shook his head and replied, "No, that's just the excuse. The real reason echoes back to that first day we truly met. Not in the streets with the vampire, but in the ruins of Lucifan, when you tried to drown me."

"I didn't try to drown you."

"Of course not. You needed me. You needed me to beat you. You wanted to be punished, harshly, for your failure, like your brother used to do to you time and time again. It was all you craved, and you provoked me until I cracked your jaw open with my fist. Redemption through pain, that's what you wanted, and here you are doing it again. You came because you want me to berate you for Krunk's death. You want me insult you, threaten you, tell you just how vile and horrible you really are."

215

"And why would I want that?"

"Because it's more comfortable than what's happening," Gavin replied. "You're being treated like a hero by Kuniko and all the other Hanu troops. As you stand over Krunk's corpse, they cheer, and you can't stand it."

Takeo's stomach twisted into a knot. Surrounding noises dimmed as his focus drew inward. A measure of cold ice washed through his veins.

He shook his head.

"You know me so well," he said. "Better than anyone ever has."

"It haunts me, too."

They reached the graveyard where Emy was on her knees before the wide mound that made up Krunk's grave. His plot was twice as large as all the others, which made it easy to see. The three adjacent were relatively recent, as well. Two were the headless bodies of Kuniko's parents. The last was Dhyana.

Emy had surely heard their approach, but she waited until they neared before standing and retreating. She made for the mansion, to do what, Takeo was not the least bit concerned.

Not with his sword at his side.

"I have to admit, she's taking this entire thing rather well," Gavin said. "I'm afraid to ask. Will you kill her, too?"

"Please, Gavin, give me at least some respect. I'll let her go once the task is done."

"And which task is that? Slaying Qadir? Conquering Juatwa? Savara? The world? Ah, what does it matter? At least her sentence has a term, and she'll one day taste freedom, unlike me."

Takeo cocked an eyebrow and glanced about their surroundings from the fruit-heavy trees to the large mansion upon the hill.

"Some prison you've found yourself in," Takeo mocked. "Your warden must be real scum."

"Can I leave?"

"Gavin, we've been over this. You and your family are a prime target, and this is a culminating moment. Ninja clans may be wary of me, but Qadir is not. I let you go once, and look what happened. You'll never hold a shield again, and I blame myself for that. At least you got out alive, though, with your wife and child. I can't take

216

that risk again. If you want to lament living a life of luxury, that's fine by me, but you'll do so under my protection."

"Right, right," Gavin muttered. "Protection. No wonder I feel so safe."

A scream echoed out from the mansion, and Takeo whirled on instinct, hand flying to his sword. However, Gavin remained motionless, and Takeo paused. Another scream, then another, and Takeo realized it was Gavin's daughter.

"What is that about?" the ronin asked.

"Who knows, bloody tantrums," Gavin replied, sighing. "I swear, I don't know where she gets it from. She's in a fury from dusk to dawn, screaming about anything and everything, running everywhere, kicking, biting—angels know what else."

Gavin buried his face in his hands, just in time to miss Pleiades breaking away from the mansion in a full sprint down the hill. She was easily recognizable with her blond hair and brown skin, such an odd mix in this uniform land of pale skin and black hair. Some Zhao servant went after her, but Pleiades was surprisingly fast. She was among the grounds and out of sight in no time, though her position was revealed by her screams.

"No offense, but I'm glad I never had children," Takeo said.

"I'm telling you, that's not normal," Gavin replied. "I used to frequent an orphanage, remember? I know children, and Pleiades is something special."

"That's one word for it."

"She'll mellow out one day, I know it. All children do, but I swear something happened to her. Every time I bring up Pleiades' attitude, Yeira just shuts down. I don't know. Maybe something in her family tree got into Pleiades. I'm not sure. I'm working on it. I mean, what else can I do?"

"What about Yeira? Why isn't she working on it?"

Gavin went deathly still and gulped. He didn't look at Takeo anymore, not even in fleeting glances. The knight stared at the graves, turning a touch pale.

"Yeira's not the same anymore," Gavin whispered. "After you fought Botan, he lost his temper. He came back to the keep broken and battered, holding that sword with his bare hands, and I knew we were in trouble. Until that point, he'd been fine mutilating me in

217

small, methodical doses to get to you, but not anymore. He wanted to hurt me this time because he thought I had lied to him.

"He locked himself in a room with me and demanded answers. He told no one else that you were immune to your own sword lest morale fall further, but he told me. I tried to explain that I didn't know—that even you didn't know—but he wouldn't listen. He was in a blind rage, so he called out the worst people under his command and brought them up. They chained me to a wall, and I was terrified at first, but not half as terrified as when they brought in Yeira."

Gavin stopped. Tears filled his eyes, and his throat swelled. Takeo didn't press. He knew what vindictive men did to beautiful women, and in fact, so did Yeira. However, this time wouldn't have been like the others when she was a prized concubine of a Savara warlord. This time it would have been savage, and they had made Gavin watch.

"Don't say you're sorry," Gavin said.

"I wasn't going to," Takeo replied.

"Don't say we brought this on ourselves."

"I wasn't going to say that either."

"They shouldn't call you a lord. No human should hold that title. Only angels are worthy of ruling, and this is why: Power corrupts and is abused. You're not a lord, Takeo, not like the angels were—of light, and of good. You hold that sword, knowing it's slowly killing you, and you don't care. You don't care at all. You're not a lord of anything, except, I don't know—darkness. You're soulless."

Tears continued to drip down Gavin's face, and the knight lost the strength to stand. His knees hit the dirt before Krunk's grave, and there the knight stared, as if his old friend might rise to wrap his arms about him and say everything was going to be okay.

Meanwhile, Takeo stood dumbfounded, feeling just as lost as Gavin looked. The ronin's gaze drifted to his mother, buried as he'd ordered in the only place he thought he might remember finding her again. He stared, waiting for that surge of remorse to resurface, the one he'd felt when he'd realized she had died in his arms, but there was nothing. His heart beat cold and steady, and no matter how many times his mind stated that he should feel something, he did not. For a brief moment he wondered what had changed, until his arm brushed his sword handle and a wave of fire burned through him. He remembered then and thought no more of it.

He surveyed all the damage he'd done to all those closest to him and thought that perhaps it had been a mistake to come here at all. There was nothing more to gain. He was no good to these people. He wasn't even good to himself.

"I think we're done here," Takeo said, turning to leave. "I am sorry for the pain I've caused you and your family, Gavin. I hope you find peace, for both our sakes."

Gavin sniffed back a tear, and Takeo got a few paces away. He thought the conversation concluded, until Gavin called out to him.

"Do you want to know how I met Krunk?"

Takeo paused. It occurred to him that Gavin had never shared that story. The fact that he was bringing it up now did not bode well, yet Takeo felt rooted in place. Did he not owe it to Gavin to listen?

"I always assumed you two met at the orphanage," Takeo said.

"Yeah, that's the story we told," Gavin replied. "That's even the story we told Krunk, too, that he was just dropped off there, because it was better than the truth. Innocent child that he was, he never bothered to question it, or what happened to his parents, or how I got this scar."

Gavin traced a finger down the mark along his left cheek. Takeo bore a similar mark, which he'd earned at Jabbar's claws. Takeo didn't know how Gavin had earned his, though.

"It's going to sound cliché, but it was a dark and stormy night," Gavin said. "Harbor rains can be cold and windy even at their calmest, and this storm was bad. Lucifan's streets don't provide as much shelter as one might think, and the water gets into your armor. I was using my shield as cover and patrolling on foot because visibility was too poor to ride a pegasus. On nights like that, crime usually plummets, so the Order sends out its young, inexperienced knights, both as a rite of passage and because it knows they'll be just fine. Needless to say, my squad didn't expect to find much beyond our sour moods and rusting armor. We certainly didn't expect to find a group of ogres trying to rob a closed-up food shop.

"No one really knows this, or cares, but there are female ogres. Due to their perceived ugliness, we humans tend to think of all ogres as males, but even the ogres don't care what we call them. He, she,

219

it—it's all the same to them, and for good reason. Unless they're naked, it's nigh impossible to tell the difference between the sexes. Also, due to their girth, it's also exceptionally hard to tell if one of them is pregnant, especially in the rain, in the dark, and in a fight.

"I chased Krunk's mother down an alleyway, not realizing I was alone until it was too late, and it just so happened she picked a dead end. I only wanted her to surrender, but ogres don't think like that. She was a trapped animal, and she set upon me. Inexperienced as I was, she nearly killed me. I was lucky this scar was all she gave me, and in return, I took her life.

"I might not have noticed that she was pregnant if Krunk hadn't moved. I'd seen enough death rattles at this point to know that the waving and pushing against her hard stomach wasn't normal. I wanted to leave, to run, to know nothing more, but I couldn't. I checked that she was indeed female and then touched her stomach to confirm my suspicion.

"And Krunk pushed back.

"I didn't think about my next move. All I knew was that if I didn't get him out, he would die. I used my sword for the first time in my life to save rather than kill, and I learned a lot of lessons about birth the hard way. As I sat there in that alley, rain pouring down on my blood-soaked armor, I held this little ogre infant, and I froze. I heard my squad calling for me, though, and I realized my job wasn't done yet. I couldn't let them find me, not like this, not with him. He'd get tossed back into the ogre clans, only to be beaten and likely die without any parent around to claim him. I couldn't let that happen. I killed his mother. It was my fault, my responsibility to save him, so I decided to give him the same chance I'd had in life.

"I took him to Madam Sweeny, to my orphanage. It was the best I could do.

"And angels bless that old gnome and her heart of gold. We made up some story of her just finding him, and no one questioned it. She took Krunk in, gave him a name, friends, love—she gave him a chance. A second chance, really, because I had robbed him of the first.

"Poor Krunk. He never knew that his best friend in the whole world had killed his mother. It's a sin I've carried in secret until now, and a sin I can no longer atone for. I tell you this, Takeo, not to

220

punish you. I know you'll see this story as a means to an end, that I did what I had to, but you're missing the point. We were both raised to understand that the world is harsh and cruel, but you were taught to be harsh and cruel in return. If I'd had that mentality, there would have been no Krunk on this journey. I guess I'm trying to make one last plea to you, Takeo. Please, listen to me. You can't fight the darkness of the world with shadows. You must bring forth light."

Takeo dropped his head. He ran a finger along his hairline and sighed.

"That was always your problem, Gavin. You put your faith in philosophy over reality, and it's that same mentality that put Krunk on his knees with a sword at his throat and your family's life in danger. Krunk may be dead, but you're safe now. Don't you see? I don't have to bring light to the world in order to save it. All I need to do is make a world where such light can exist.

"Even if it hates me for it."

Chapter 24

The trip back to the Hanu city felt long. They took the same roads and traveled at the same pace, but now Takeo had two silent companions instead of just one. Not that he expected anything out of Emy without his express permission, but Nicholas' deadpan silence was disconcerting on a number of levels. In a way, Nicholas was the only one of their original group that Takeo expected to support him. After all, hadn't they already had this conversation, that morality was determined by the winner?

"Have I lost you, too?" Takeo said, cutting straight to the point halfway through their journey.

Nicholas sighed, long and drawn out.

"Lost me? Takeo, honestly, you've been lucky to keep me for this long. We free spirits aren't known to settle down in any one place for this length of time."

"That's not what I'm asking," Takeo said. "If you want to have at me for Krunk, I'd prefer you do it now."

"Yeah, I'll bet you would. I only have one thing to say about that, Takeo, and it's nothing to do with right versus wrong, or cost versus reward, not even victory versus defeat. I'm a simpler man than that, as you know, and if you'd stop thinking about yourself for a moment, you could divine my opinion. However, for the sake of time—and also to prevent hurting your poor little brain—I'll tell you. It all boils down to how I measure myself and everyone else, and thus how you fell short.

"Legends don't kill their friends."

A legend? No thank you. I don't want to be remembered, his mind retorted, but he kept quiet. Takeo understood that this wasn't an attack he could defend against. Nicholas' silence said more than words ever could.

"So, when are you leaving me?" Takeo asked.

Another drawn out sigh ensued, irking the ronin.

"Oh, I don't know," Nicholas replied, flicking his mangy hair off his shoulder as they rode. "I was going back and forth about leaving you long before Krunk. My first thought came after that ruined fortress disaster, thinking this would be a good place for my legend to turn. I mean, think about it. How more epic of a beginning could I have than holding off an entire army with fifty men? But I stuck around, and then I got to slay an emperor, and damn did that seem worth it. You know how many viking tales involve slaying a Juatwa shogun? Let's just say the number is so low that even you could count it. So, hey, what's one more battle, I thought? Might be worth it. Then something came up that none of us predicted."

"Dhyana," Takeo replied.

Nicholas nodded, then shook his head, then tisked, then chuckled.

"I still can't believe it," the viking went on. "I mean, I honestly thought the old flames that burned for my family had died with my sister, yet there are embers."

"I shouldn't be surprised," Takeo said. "You've been dropping some heavy hints."

"It also helps that it would be fitting, you know? A hero always takes a break from his adventurous life to return home. Ah, damn it. I just called that place home, didn't I? I never used to do that. The Great Plains hasn't been my home for awhile, yet the word slipped out. Just another sign that fate is calling me. I saw my mother every time I looked at yours, Takeo, and saw in your relationship all the missed opportunities. What if she's dead? I mean, seriously, what if? I can't even recall our last goodbye. That's just not right. Maybe I'm getting old or something, but it doesn't sit well with me anymore. I might have adopted a second father, but I've only ever had one mother. I need to see her again. I owe it to her."

"Honestly, Nicholas, that's something I agree with. I'm not going to lie; I will miss you. Although we were never formally made brothers through marriage, I can't help but feel we share that sort of bond. However, you didn't answer my question. When are you leaving?"

"Oh, I still don't know. I thought I'd stay one more battle, you know? I mean, with any luck, that's all it will take to fulfill this dream of yours. I can't leave you when you're so close to seeing it through. I just hope I don't regret it."

A thin smile etched its way across Takeo's face, a hint of warmth through all the cold he felt when his sword wasn't in his hands. The two didn't share a gaze, as Nicholas aimlessly searched the tree branches overhead, but they didn't need to.

"Thank you," Takeo said.

"Eh, don't do that," Nicholas replied. "You're not the only person I'm staying for."

Takeo didn't inquire further. It wasn't difficult to guess that Nicholas was speaking of either Gavin, Emy, or some combination of them and one of the many cute soldiers he spent his nights with. It was enough to know that Takeo wasn't alone, not yet. He'd lost too many already, and he wasn't sure if he could handle much more.

A degree of optimism struck Takeo after that conversation. It wasn't much, but after spending so much time in quiet misery, any small ray of hope was enough to illuminate his mood. Despite all of his talk about mercy and necessity, Takeo regretted what he had done. Krunk had been a friend in the true sense of the word, with love and trust handed over unconditionally. Childlike was the word, assuming that child grew up in a utopia of care and understanding. To Takeo, Krunk was an example of how all his efforts could be applied. If only the world could be given a chance to breathe, the violence pacified for just a short decade, so many creatures and people that would have turned into agents of horror could instead be given the chance at a wonderful life.

Like the wonderful life his brother had denied him.

I couldn't save him. No one could. But I can save others. I can save all the others. For Her.

This concluding thought ran through Takeo's mind somewhere on the outskirts of the Hanu city, with the walls rising up in the distance. At the same time, the breeze changed direction, and Takeo's komainu sniffed the air once, twice, and then flicked its tail. There was nothing odd in the movement, as these creatures had a powerful sense of smell, yet Takeo didn't hear a thing. The area was totally silent.

Takeo's hand dropped to his sword.

Seconds later, a black, palm-sized whirl of metal darted out from a tree. Flung so fast and so close, Takeo's brain couldn't make the connection between sound, movement, and decision until the projectile was an arm's length from his neck—far too close for any person to react without inhuman aid. He ripped his enchanted blade free and raised it for a deflection in one flash of speed, yet still he had to duck. The ninja star clanged against his sword and cut a strand of hair free from of his head as it soared by. Takeo might have taken the time to admire having escaped such a brush with death, but not a heartbeat later, Qing dove out of the same tree, sword poised to skewer him.

However, the fight was over by then. Takeo was alert, sword drawn, and riding a komainu. He parried the first attack, the second, and the half dozen attempts after that. He never made a move to end her, or even dismount, and Qing stopped her futile attacks shortly.

She was alone, standing with feet planted, teeth gritted, and shoulders tense. Qing's gaze bore into Takeo with a fiery hatred he'd come to expect. Emy and Nicholas watched with mouths agape, but Takeo felt calm. Actually, Qing's attack came as a relief to him, as he'd always anticipated she'd try to kill him one day. Now he knew which day that was. The only question was why she'd waited so long.

Takeo held his enchanted blade before him, demonstrating his power, and asked, "Qing, what are you doing?"

The ninja's teeth were pressed together so tightly they threatened to turn to dust. Then tears formed in her eyes, and she fell to her knees. Her sword clattered to the ground.

"You were supposed to marry her," she screeched. "Virote assured me you would! It made logical sense, the only logical sense. Surely, you'd do it. I knew you would. We all did! Then everything would be right in the world, and she'd be protected. Why did you say no?"

Takeo paused, his sense of relief slipping away.

"Qing, what has she done? What has Lady Zhenzhen done?"

The ninja sucked in a gasp of air and bit her lower lip. Tears began to drip down her cheeks.

"You're going to kill her," she whispered.

Dread welled in Takeo's stomach. His sword grip intensified.

"Tell me," he said, putting authority into his voice. "What did she do?"

Qing hesitated and then let her gaze fall, shaking her head.

Takeo put his heels into his mount and dashed towards the city.

225

* * *

Black soot from the stone ramparts tarnished the pale skin of Mako's bare feet, their former beauty only hinted at by the dainty ankles that lay exposed beneath her red kimono. Her wrists were free of restraints and untarnished, showing she'd come willingly. Her cheeks were stained with the dreary blend of makeup and tears, although the tears had long since dried up. Black hair fluttered in the wind, youthful and vibrant in a way she would never be again. Mako was nothing if not beautiful, even when hung by the throat, her neck snapped and eyes bulging out.

Takeo did not walk so much as stumble up the steps. Nothing and no one barred his way, as the place had been cleared of people and obstacles so that Mako would hang out over the keep's ramparts alone and untouched. The city streets below had drawn a small crowd, but they had cleared out when Takeo was seen dashing inside the keep on his komainu. Now, the only onlookers were those guards posted within sight and those civilians who could gaze in hiding from either the shadows or behind glass. Nicholas, Qing, and Emy were a short way behind, reaching the keep by the time Takeo had already scaled the walls.

He grabbed Mako's kimono and pulled her lifeless body to him, her cold skin stealing warmth from his. He held her with one hand and cut the rope with other, and she collapsed onto him. Her tall, slender body was difficult to manage as he laid her down on the stone and held her head in his hands.

Mako's mouth hung open, framed in a silent scream that would never escape. Her limbs stretched awkwardly along the ground, stiffening in her prolonged death. Her hair blew across her face in the wind, getting into her eyes, yet she did not blink to clear them. Takeo traced his thumb from her forehead down to tuck the strands away.

He tried to say something, whisper a silent *no* or beg a *please*, but his lungs refused to grant him the strength. It was all he could do to keep breathing, and his heart struggled against a chest that sunk inwards in pain. All the world ceased to exist, all but Mako and all the innocence that had been taken with her.

226

The dam holding back Takeo's grief broke, and he pressed his forehead to hers while his vision blurred into tears. Slowly, he rocked her back and forth, holding her tight in a way he'd never had the courage to do when she was alive. Pain wracked him, deep and unyielding. His sobs rang out against the stone.

He was dimly aware that he was being watched, and a shuffle of armor denoted that a new crowd had arrived. He lost track of that, though, as a sob escaped his lips to be muffled by Mako's cold skin. A moment later, soft steps approached up the ramparts, accompanied by the drag of rich silk along stone.

"Why?" Takeo whimpered without looking up, then louder. "Tell me why!"

"She brought this upon herself for standing between us," Lady Zhenzhen replied, not an ounce of sympathy in her voice. "You said your heart was spoken for? Well, I've solved that issue. I told you once before that you belong to me. I hope you understand now."

Bile rose up from Takeo's stomach, and he choked on it while struggling against his inability to breathe.

"You," he started, struggling to find words. "You killed her for that? You, you bitch. I wasn't talking about her."

"Doesn't look that way to me. Now, kneel to your empress."

A raging fire swept through Takeo's veins, and he thought it was anger until he realized that his hand had unconsciously fallen to his sword. The steel there begged to be released, hungry for blood of any kind. Takeo was more than willing to satiate that desire until a moment's reflection washed over him. As the enchanted blade's warmth spread over him, he felt his grief burn away. Emptiness followed, and Mako's cold skin receded from his touch.

Takeo looked from Zhenzhen to Mako, one hand on her corpse and another on his sword, and the dam against his grief reformed with formidable integrity. He had no questions about why this was happening, not a single doubt as to the cause.

He gripped his sword tighter and let Mako go.

A long, dark smile spread across Lady Zhenzhen's face as Takeo turned to her and bowed on his knees until his head touched stone.

"Good," the shogun said. "Now, tell me. Who owns you?"

He shut his eyes and swallowed. The words burned in his throat. He forced them out.

"You do, my lady."

"And if your mistress commands you to marry her?"

"I will obey."

Zhenzhen's hand slipped around Takeo's chin, making his flesh crawl, and lifted his head towards her. She bent down and pressed her lips to his, stealing a long and passionate kiss. When she pulled away, their lips tugged apart.

"That's my good little ronin," she said. "Now, win me my crown, and I might just forgive your insolence. I may even let you share in the glory."

She kissed him again and then left down the stairs. Takeo looked at Mako again and felt nothing but agony.

* * *

Takeo's next target wasn't difficult to find. Lady Ki Hanu liked to refer to herself as a prisoner within her own castle, and in a way, that was true. She was watched intensely and not allowed to leave the keep without a guard of Zhenzhen's choosing. One might think that with Lord Nobu dead, Zhenzhen's interest in her mother-in-law would fade, but it seemed that was not the case. All Takeo had to do was ask the guard captain where the old woman was, and helpful directions were given.

Takeo took Nicholas and headed there directly.

The Lady Ki was in her room at the top of a tall tower with a wide and open balcony. The room was luxurious, enough for a daimyo, but Takeo had no doubts why Zhenzhen had chosen that room. There it would be easy to spy on Ki, and even easier to assassinate her. Also, the lengthy flight of stairs discouraged the old woman from leaving. Perhaps as an added inconvenience, the room's position had been poorly designed, and the hot afternoon sun poured in relentlessly from the balcony. Takeo could see the light beneath the door as he approached and knocked.

"Come in, Takeo. Come in," Ki answered.

He did so, and Nicholas followed, with the latter shutting the door behind them.

A wide and tastefully decorated room greeted Takeo's entrance. The bed and nightstand filled one wall, while a sizable dresser and an even larger vanity covered another. The vanity was strewn with makeup and brushes. As for the woman herself, she was out on the balcony, resting against the stone parapet with a cup of tea in one hand.

She did not look up as Takeo entered, and he realized she'd been expecting him. It took him a moment, but he saw that from where Lady Ki stood, she'd had a perfect view of all that had transpired on the ramparts below.

"How much did you see?" he asked.

"Oh, I haven't missed a thing," she replied, taking a sip. "I had this tea brought up some time ago, along with a chamber pot so that I might never have to leave. I hardly wished to blink when you arrived. I must say, I'm rather shocked you didn't kill her."

Takeo paced into the center of the room—hands balled into fists.

"I," he started, only to pause and swallow down a dry throat. "I can't. I need her. I may have support from the soldiers, but Zhenzhen is the key to a web of daimyo marriages and alliances meticulously set up by her husband and yours. If I kill her, they won't accept me as their leader, and even if I could convince some to follow me, it'd be too few to stand against the Nguyen's. Mako, she—"

Takeo paused again, a wave of grief threatening to topple him. His hand fell to his sword, burning away the feeling. He collected his thoughts.

"She will have died for nothing," Takeo said, "and Krunk, and Emily, and so many others. I can't. I couldn't. Not yet."

"So then, still ever loyal to this personal quest of yours, hm?" Ki continued.

Takeo did not like her tone. It was apathetic to the point of mockery, and he saw nothing comical about this situation.

"May I ask, then," the old lady said, "what brings you here? What, I wonder, could bring the infamous Takeo Karaoshi up to my chambers when he would not come before? Not even to give condolences for my dead grandson, for the death of my line."

She took another sip. Takeo winced.

"You know I had nothing to do with that," he said. "Lord Nobu committed suicide. I tried to lift and save him before I realized it was too late."

"Oh, yes, you're completely blameless. I mean, it's not as if someone warned you to watch the boy, to take him under your wing and save him from his fate."

"It wasn't fate that killed Nobu. It was that deal your husband made and his mother was determined to see it through."

Lady Ki set her tea down into its saucer, making the ceramics clink together.

"So that's what this is about," she said. "You've finally seen the light about my daughter-in-law?"

"Yes, exactly," Takeo replied. "We can take our revenge on her and save the Hanu clan at the same time. Those alliances tied to Zhenzhen are tied to you, as well, albeit loosely. With your command, your guidance, we could stage a coup against her and still maintain enough forces to engage the Nguyens. It won't be easy, no doubt my part in it will be played up by the other side, but it's doable. I can't make a move against Zhenzhen otherwise. I don't have the lineage, and I—I can't take the other route. Marriage is out of the question. Mako, I can't—damn it. Even before, I couldn't do that to *her* memory."

"You truly loved this Emily, didn't you?"

Takeo glared and replied, "Of course I did."

Lady Ki took a deep breath, picked up her teacup, and took another sip. She turned her nose up at it, evidently finding it too cold to enjoy anymore, and tossed the leftovers over the balcony. The empty teacup clinked louder this time as she set it down.

"So that's it, then," she said. "You need me."

"Yes."

"Beg for it."

"What?"

"You heard me," Ki continued, voice smooth as a morning lake. "I watched you grovel before my daughter with little hesitation, just a moment ago, with that sister of yours dead in your arms. I think you can kneel to me easily. Beg me to help you. Beg my forgiveness."

Takeo wasn't long in wondering what Lady Ki referred to. He went down on his knees, once again putting his flesh to stone, and stooped low. His back strained with the effort to bend so thoroughly. He dug deep in his heart for the right words, although emotion

230

eluded him. What he lacked in empathy he attempted to make up for in honesty.

"Please, my lady," he started, "forgive me. I should have predicted Lord Nobu's impeding death. He grew depressed in those later days, but I was too focused on the battle and my own troubles to take notice. I thought him safe behind his layers of luxury and oni guards, but I never imagined he'd work up the strength to end his own life. In a way, that makes your son braver than me, for I haven't been able to do the same—I was commanded otherwise.

"I apologize, too, for the death of your son, Jiro. I did not realize he would put so much faith in my advice and thus place himself in harm's way against Lord Ichiro. I should have warned him that no good could come of that.

"I am sorry, as well, for taking Zhenzhen's side initially. I have suffered for this decision, thoroughly, and I hope you know that. I can't begin to describe how precious Mako was to me. I've little left to lose, and I want you to know that peace is truly my goal, if only you'll help me see through to the other side of this conflict. Hate me all you want, but please, I beg you, see that I can be useful to you one last time. Lady Zhenzhen cannot be allowed to live, to rule, after what she's done. You can take her place, and I will gladly put you there."

Lady Ki folded her arms. Then she smiled.

"No," she said.

"What? What did I say wrong? What do you want me to say?"

"There's nothing you can say, I'm afraid. I will never help you, Takeo, not unless you can do one thing for me."

"Name it."

"Bring my grandson back to life."

Takeo snarled and rose to his feet, hands balling into fists, yet Ki didn't so much as flinch. If anything, her smile grew.

"You old wench," he said. "I'm offering you revenge. You can't just let her crimes go unpunished."

"On the contrary. I've nothing left to lose, either, as you said. I don't even have my youth. I can do whatever I want."

"Then do it for others. Do it for the Nobus still out there, the children that have yet to be born, yet to know hardship. I'm strong

231

enough to see past Mako's murder. You can see past Nobu's suicide. You stand to be a part of something great. Seize it!"

Lady Ki laughed, full bellied and unforced. The strength of it knocked the wind from Takeo's lungs. He balked at her.

"Oh please," she said. "As if you could be a part of anything great. I must admit, this feels far better than I ever could have hoped for, seeing you here, begging and scraping to convince me. You need me so badly, and yet you're powerless. I'm going to enjoy this next part oh so much.

"Did you know you're not the first visitor I've had recently? Some time ago, my daughter-in-law, of all people, came to visit. I mean, she didn't even come when she heard Nobu died. I had to find out by way of a messenger. Her appearance stunned me until she explained her purpose. She told me about the marriage proposal and your reply—I think she had no one else to talk to, really. She was too embarrassed to mention your rejection to anyone else, and she wanted my advice, as a formerly married woman. I saw an opportunity for revenge, but not against her.

"You see, my dear ronin, when you told Lady Zhenzhen that your heart was taken, she didn't misinterpret your words. I put it in her head that you were speaking of Mako."

Lady Ki couldn't help herself. She burst into another bout of maniacal laughter. All the while, Takeo looked on, pale with parted lips. His stomach churned so hard he thought he'd puke if not for the boiling rage working itself up from the pit of his soul. Out of the corner of his eye, he saw Nicholas equally aghast, arms hanging loose and eyes blinking in disbelief.

Lady Ki laughed harder.

"You psychotic hag," Takeo said through clenched teeth. "Do you know what you've done? She was innocent! Mako never harmed a soul. You're not Zhenzhen. You don't have her protections. And if you won't help me, then I'll kill you for what you've done."

Ki went dead silent and glared at Takeo.

"No," she said. "You won't."

And she tipped backwards over the balcony.

Takeo took one half-step out of instinct before stopping. By then, the Lady Ki was already gone from sight, falling faster and faster to the ground below. The silence was ominous, right up until it was

232

broken by the dead slap of her body against the stone. There was a brief echo against the towers all around, but then an onlooker screamed.

Takeo turned towards Nicholas, their eyes meeting. Neither blinked.

"By Valhalla," was all the viking could say. "I can't believe she did that. What is wrong with this place? It's cursed."

A barrage of emotions assaulted Takeo's senses. He'd been wracked by grief when he entered the room, only to be flooded with anger and now drowned in shock. The heavy mix made his legs shake, and his mind was so clouded he could barely remember where he was, let alone what to do next.

Suddenly, everything hit him at once—Mako's death, Ki's betrayal, Zhenzhen's insanity, Krunk's loss, the war, the Nguyen's, the daimyo, Qadir, Aiguo, Emily, Gavin, Dhyana, and on and on— and he sunk to his knees. Tears poured from his eyes, and the whole world bore down on him, crushing him beneath its weight. He tried to breathe but couldn't. His lungs refused to expand.

"What more?" he begged, his voice a shadow of its former self. "How many more?"

What else did he have left to lose? How was he going to go on now? What hope could possibly shine through this much darkness?

Instinctively, like a crutch to a beggar, or more like a keg to a drunk, Takeo drew his hand up to wrap around his sword. The fire spread out, burning away the pain, inch by bloody inch, until nothing remained. When his insides were ablaze, when he felt nothing at all, he took a steady breath and stood.

Nicholas hadn't moved.

"What," the viking stammered, "what do we do now?"

Takeo twisted his neck so that the spine cracked, releasing the tension that had built up there. His hand never left his sword, though. Fire burned his insides to ash, and it was all he could not to let go, but he was too afraid to do that.

"The only thing left to do," he said. "We win."

Epilogue

"Tell me, Cyrus," Ven's voice echoed back to him. "What is your greatest fear?"

Thunder boomed out, interrupting the steady chorus of rain drenching the forest. Cyrus shook his head to clear the water from his hair and eyes, then wiped his face instead. The shaking hadn't done much, as he was still in human form, but he was due to change into a werewolf any moment now, and his body was prepping for the transformation. His mouth salivated, begging him to pant, and his skin was itchy where the fur had started to grow. Over the past half hour, his sense of smell had gradually become more acute, while his vision through the dark forest had improved. The prey he followed became easier to track, moment by moment, and remained completely ignorant of his presence.

"My stepfather," Cyrus had answered Ven, weeks ago.

"No, that's not true," she'd replied. "Think, Cyrus. If he was your greatest fear, then why did you stop him from attacking your mother?"

Katar and Urddusk Phizeiros were difficult targets to track. Katar had fully healed from the blow Cyrus had given him, and the two brothers were now elven rangers in training. They were light of foot with heightened vision and a sense of hearing that surpassed even Cyrus' in his werewolf form.

They were out exploring far later than was allowed, and the brothers beat a hasty retreat through the muddy underbrush, trying to get back to their village before the storm grew worse.

Meanwhile, Cyrus' memory continued to repeat.

"Tell me, why did you pull Ralph's attention away from Belen? You knew what would happen to you."

"I couldn't let him go after her. I knew what he'd do to her if he did."

"So, what was your greatest fear?"

"That," Cyrus had started, pausing, thinking. "That he'd hurt her. That I couldn't protect her."

Cyrus scaled down the tree to the forest floor, a task that grew easier by the minute as his nails turned into claws and cords of muscle sprouted throughout his body. By the time he hit the ground, his tongue had grown too long to fit comfortably in his mouth. It lolled out as he panted, though he did so softly. He couldn't rely on the rain and thunder to mask his approach entirely. In fact, without such a storm, he'd find this task impossible. Elves were just too deft at detection, and he'd waited weeks for the right combination of weather and timing to make this happen.

At the same time, he was dimly aware that somewhere far to the south, his mother and her clan were undergoing a similar, yet savage, transformation. Unlike Cyrus, they couldn't control themselves when they changed, and they'd rampage through the forest in packs, looking for prey.

"You're afraid something will happen to her?" Ven had said.

"Yes," Cyrus had replied, both as confirmation and in realization.

"You fear this more than you fear Ralph."

"Yes!"

"Then why won't you return and challenge him?"

Even now, Ven's words sent a shudder through Cyrus' body. The bruises had long been healed, but he could still feel them sometimes—and the fist blows that had caused them. He could still see Ralph sitting over him, striking over and over, daring Cyrus to stand up to him. Warning him to never come back. The memory alone made him flinch and sweat and his throat to go dry.

His paw caught a stack of leaves that hadn't been completely drenched yet, making one crunch ever so slightly.

Katar froze and drew his bow. His younger brother missed the noise but relied on his brother's instincts, also drawing his weapon. Cyrus grimaced and crouched beneath a bush, hoping a chance lightning strike wouldn't reflect in his eyes.

"I can't challenge him until I conquer my fear," Cyrus had explained. "My anger, my hate, my passion—they make me weak. I need to be like you, like the elves."

"You don't believe that. You're just repeating what Nathok says."

"That doesn't make him wrong."

"Cyrus, would you judge a centaur by its ability to fly? No, of course not. So then, why would you judge a werewolf by its ability to be an elf?"

The Phizeiros brothers pressed back to back, then continued their retreat to the village, though slowly. Cyrus knew what they were thinking—that a single leaf crunch could mean anything from a twig falling to a harpy nestling in for cover. They couldn't afford to stay out in this weather on account of a chance noise, yet caution was an elf's best friend. Any decision made in the same day a problem occurred was considered hasty. They'd trek on for perhaps a couple dozen steps like this before turning and running again.

Cyrus could wait until then. Even if they left his sight, their scent was fresh enough to track.

"What are you saying? I'm not even a true werewolf, Ven. They don't accept me. I've tried to be with them when they change. They're too, I don't know, wild? They sense my hesitation. They know I don't go mad like them, and they resent me for it. I don't belong anywhere."

"And how does that mentality help you save your mother?"

"Why are you asking me? I don't know. You're the one—"

He had stopped, aware of how his rage was boiling over. It had taken every ounce of effort to shut his mouth and eyes, balling his fists, fighting against his own body, which wanted to lash out with more than words. He had bitten his lower lip until it bled, the pain driving a tiny spike into the wall of fury building within him. He hadn't considered trying to subdue it. It had been all he could do to hold it in check.

"You don't seem to realize your potential," Ven had gone on, completely unaffected. "These feelings you have aren't a source of weakness. They are fuel, like excess wood choking the forest. You must build great structures from them, or they will create a fire too strong to control."

"Please," Cyrus had said through clenched teeth, "not now."

"You want to eliminate your fear before you challenge Ralph, but that will never happen, just as a centaur will never grow wings. What you should be doing is accepting that fear, but then conquering it with love, specifically the love for your mother. Stop letting elves and werewolves define whom you are, Cyrus. Forge

236

your own path and strive to be better. Treat every limit as self-imposed, including the limit you've set on what you're allowed to feel."

Cyrus hadn't understood everything Ven had talked about, but he had caught enough to realize two things. Firstly, he was incredibly lucky to have a mentor like Ven. Unlike everyone else, she took a great interest in him, taking Nathok's instructions to teach him to heart. She was unconventional by elven standards—that was for sure—but Cyrus supposed that was part of the reason she'd taken up the task in the first place. He didn't know what he'd done to earn her dedication, but he never forgot it. How could he when there was no one else?

Secondly, it was fear that held him back from saving his mother, and in some way or another, he needed to conquer this fear. Admittedly, he had no idea how he was to do this, but he knew a good place to start. Challenging his stepfather might be too overwhelming, but challenging his former bullies? It was worth a shot.

The Phizeiros brothers scaled a steep yet short hill and disappeared. They were skirting a mountain's edge as they approached their village on the western side. Not too much longer and they'd reach the patrol fringes where riders atop winged hippogriffs would have been soaring through the treetops if not for the storm. As such, Cyrus reckoned he had just a little more time than usual to track the brothers. He didn't want to be spotted, that was certain. Tracking elves in werewolf form was a deadly game, as Cyrus was liable to get an arrow through the eye or neck if he screwed this up. He didn't actually intend to do anything other than follow the brothers, as that was dangerous enough.

But then again, so was challenging his stepfather.

Cyrus slipped from under cover and made his way through the rain, mud, and underbrush, following the elves by a combination of intuition and scent. In the relative safety of being out of eyesight, Cyrus let his mind wander on his last-thought word: stepfather. It was a title Ralph wore proudly, always certain to remind Cyrus that he was an abandoned child, unwanted and unloved. Cyrus had only asked once whom his real father was, only to have Ralph lay down a stream of accusations about Belen's loose past and questionable morals, concluding with how lucky Cyrus was that he had a stepfather who could forgive and shelter a whore and her bastard son.

Belen didn't talk about Cyrus' father. By her expressions, he detected a painful memory. At bare minimum, it seemed that Ralph was right. Cyrus and his mother had been abandoned. There was no evidence to the contrary.

The pain from that thought didn't hurt so much these days. Having no memory of a father and having always lived this way, Cyrus didn't know what it would feel like to have the opposite. He saw other children, both werewolves and elves, with loving and accepting families, yet he was smart enough to recognize families with fathers, or even mothers, not much different from Ralph. As much as Cyrus dreamed of having a family worthy of the term, he couldn't convince himself that one existed for him. As often as he dreamed of having a father who was bold, courageous, and loving, not one of those words could describe a man who would leave his child behind. During times like this, Cyrus felt that no one was looking out for him, and he could rely on no one but himself.

Then his thoughts turned dark, and he had to remember Ven's words.

"Forge your own path and strive to be better."

Cyrus caught a flash of dark green movement—one of the cloaks worn by the elves. His heart skipped, and he refocused his attention on the task at hand. His werewolf form was a wonderous aid in this regard, as his paws ended in pads that softened his steps and his fur was as dark as the night around him. Normal werewolves had the extra boon of having gray eyes, which didn't reflect the moonlight or lightning flashes so much, but Cyrus wasn't so lucky. His two forms blended for some reason, granting him gray eyes in human form and one blue eye and one brown eye as a werewolf. He didn't know why, and no one else either seemed to know or would tell him, though Ralph swore it had something to do with Belen trying to give him away as a baby. Cyrus didn't remember that, and Belen swore it wasn't true. He just chalked it up to Ralph trying to be cruel, as usual.

The memory proved Cyrus' undoing as his paw hit a patch of mud with an air pocket inside. The layer squished under his step, so soft Cyrus barely heard it, despite being right on top of it.

Katar whirled on the noise with his younger brother shadowing the movement, yet glanced about without direction.

"What is it?" Urddusk asked, pressing up against his brother's back.

"We're being followed. I'm sure of it this time," Katar replied.

"All the more reason to press on?"

Katar shook his head, shedding water from his cloak.

"It's keeping pace. Too quiet for a centaur. Could be a kobold or a werewolf."

"Werewolf? This far north? It couldn't be a clan of them. Our scouts would have seen them approaching before the storm."

"Could be just one, then."

Katar said this absentmindedly, as if he knew the words were a joke until they left his mouth. The brothers shared a glance, and Katar touched a hand to his face, right where Cyrus had struck him so long ago. The two drew tighter, nocked arrows, and retreated slowly.

Cyrus swore internally.

Yet before he could think much more on this, a new scent crossed his nostrils. Faint and lost a moment later, it was enough to provoke his instincts. He sniffed as quietly as possible, drawing the damp air down his long snout. He closed his eyes and tasted the smell, letting it draw forth his memories so that he might identify its origin.

His eyes flew open.

Bugbear.

Cyrus' hair stood on end, and a flash of cold sweat rushed over his body. His tail was tucked between his legs, and he had to fight the urge to run. By scent alone, he had no idea where the bugbear was at, but since the air was still, he determined the beast must be close. One look at the Phizeiros brothers revealed that, wherever the creature was, it was motionless, as neither elf showed signs of having heard it.

Indecision wracked Cyrus, as he debated sticking his head out and yelling at them to run, but then he remembered how his vocal cords didn't work so well as a werewolf. The best he could hope to

239

do was howl. They might run if he did that, or they might shoot him. At worst, his howl would only signal the bugbear and doom them all. All the while, the scent neither grew nor faded, and Cyrus dared hope that nothing would come of it.

Then it was Urddusk's turn to make a false step. In his backwards retreat along the hill's ridge, his heel caught the tip of a large boulder sticking up from far below. At least, it looked like a boulder in the dark night, sheltered beneath the ridge, yet the thud was duller than it should have been for solid rock. Urddusk immediately noticed the difference. Katar heard it, too, and both retracted from the boulder.

Then it moved.

Without light and lacking a werewolf's sense of smell, neither brother could know what they had unearthed in that moment. Both elves mistook the shadow for their pursuer and loosed arrows into it, and by then it was too late for Cyrus to do anything. Not even a howl would frighten them away in time as the dark mound unfurled, revealing its true size.

The bugbear was a black mass in the storm. Its short, thick fur was fully drenched and partially covered in mud, while its bulky head and short snout were mounted upon a neck thicker around than most humans. Despite standing a human body's length below its attackers, the bugbear soon towered over the brothers, and its arms stretched wide to either side. Large claws attached to equally large paws glinted in the flashes of lightning. Rage consumed the bugbear, and it let loose a monstrous roar that made Cyrus quiver despite his distance from the scene.

Katar and Urddusk, pale and shaking in the paralysis of terror, recovered and screamed as the bugbear brought up a stubby arm to crush them where they stood. The elves dived apart, and not a moment too soon as the paw slammed down and sent a small tremor through the area. Katar tumbled away clean, but Urddusk stumbled, and the bugbear swept his paw in that brother's direction. A stray claw caught his ankle, flipping Urddusk over and sending him sliding down the short hill.

The bugbear climbed out of the rut where it had been sleeping and let loose another bestial snarl. Its bulge of a head leveled at Urddusk, and it took one harrowing step forward before Katar

240

shouted. Katar hastily drew an arrow and loosed it, the shot hitting just off the mark beneath the bugbear's sunken and beady eyes. The shaft skirted along the cheekbone, drawing blood before disappearing into the storm, but the monster hardly noticed. Katar made one more useless shout as the bugbear raised its paw to crush Urddusk into the ground.

Cyrus hesitated for one heartbeat.

The bugbear's paw came crashing down, missing Urddusk by a fraction of a second as a second mass of wet fur, muscle, and teeth struck the elf and vaulted them both out of harm's way. Cyrus whirled about as he held the younger elf brother close, breaking their fall by landing on his back and sliding through the mud and leaves. Urddusk recovered from his near-death experience, only to scream as he recognized his savior.

Cyrus flung the elf aside, dimly aware of Katar hastily nocking another arrow. The bugbear dashed unperturbed toward its escaping prey, an impressive burst of speed for its size, and reached back for another massive swipe.

He didn't hesitate this time. Cyrus understood what he'd gotten himself into the moment he'd left cover. There would be no running or hiding now or even carrying the brothers to safety, not against this beast of the forest.

Cyrus launched himself at the bugbear before it could swing.

Werewolf jaws clamped onto the creature's throat, surprising the bugbear and causing it to reel back and roar. Wet fur and blood filled Cyrus' mouth while his body was tossed about, his head rattling with the throaty vibrations of the bugbear's roar. He dug his claws into the bugbear's chest and raked, trying to find purchase so he could rip out a chunk of flesh with his teeth, but he wasn't fast enough. The bugbear swung about and caught Cyrus with a paw.

A claw the size of a large dagger rammed into Cyrus' shoulder, making him lose his hold on the bugbear's throat as he howled in pain. The bugbear's swipe, intended to fling Cyrus into the storm, instead only swung him about, the dagger-like claw holding him tight. The other paw caught hold and slammed against Cyrus, snapping a rib and holding him in place. Cyrus yelped, then snapped at the creature, tearing into the corner of one paw, but the bugbear only snarled and bared its fangs. It opened its massive jaws to tear

Cyrus in two, its hot breath filling the air about the werewolf and giving him a glimpse into the bottomless pit that was its stomach. A gut-wrenching terror ripped through Cyrus' body.

Then an arrow shaft split the darkness and burrowed into the bugbear's left eye.

The creature yelped, then howled in pain, dropping Cyrus to the ground. It swiped at the shaft, breaking it and driving the point further into its skull. It screamed, as much as its thick vocal cords would allow, and then whimpered. It hit the mud on all fours and burst off into the darkness. The thunder of its retreat faded into the distance as the rain and thunder continued to pour down undisturbed. Cyrus barely noticed, so weak was his body from loss of blood. He pressed down on his shoulder the best he could, gnashing his teeth against the pain. Breathing grew difficult as two short figures loomed over him.

"Good shot," Urddusk said, "and you were right. A werewolf was following us."

Katar didn't say anything. Cyrus let loose a low, involuntary whine.

"He saved me," Urddusk said, astonished. "I can't believe it. Look at the eyes; it's Cyrus. Do you think he even knows what he did? He's just an animal."

Still, Katar remained silent. Through Cyrus' fading vision, he saw Katar tighten his grip on his bow.

"What do we do?" Urddusk continued. "He looks bad. I don't think he's going to make it. We should really get going. This storm is getting worse. You think, maybe, before we go, we should, you know, put him out of his misery? It'd be the merciful thing to do. Better that than to let him suffer, don't you think?"

Katar looked to his brother, held the gaze, then swiveled back to Cyrus. A tear rolled down the werewolf's cheek, imperceptible as it mixed with the rain.

"We carry him," Katar said.

"What? But—"

"I said we carry him!"

Cyrus closed his eyes as soft elven hands slipped about his blood- and mud-soaked body to bear him aloft.

242

Author's Note

Thank you for reading my books. I hope you found this tale worthy of your time, and know that I enjoyed writing for you. If you received this book for free, please consider showing your support by purchasing a copy, recommending it to a friend, or writing a review online. Your kindness would not go unnoticed, and I would greatly appreciate it.

Sincerely,
Travis Bughi

Made in the USA
Columbia, SC
08 November 2022